FOREIGN ExPOSURE

THE SOCIAL CLIMBER ABROAD

Look for these other Graphia books

FOREIGN EXPOSURE

THE SOCIAL CLIMBER ABROAD

by Lauren Mechling
& Laura Moser

An Imprint of Houghton Mifflin Company
Boston 2007

Copyright © 2007 by Lauren Mechling and Laura Moser

All rights reserved. Published in the United States by Graphia,
an imprint of Houghton Mifflin Company,
Boston, Massachusetts. For information about permission
to reproduce selections from this book, write to Permissions,
Houghton Mifflin Company, 215 Park Avenue South,
New York, New York 10003.

Graphia and the Graphia logo are registered trademarks of Houghton Mifflin Company.

www.houghtonmifflinbooks.com

The text of this book is set in Apollo.

Library of Congress Cataloging-in-Publication Data
is on file.

ISBN-13: 978-0-618-66379-8

Manufactured in the United States of America
MP 10 9 8 7 6 5 4 3 2 1

To our mothers, for giving us the world.

With boundless gratitude to
Eden Edwards and Tim Rostron.

Mimi Schulman,

Even though you're a total weirdo, I am SO glad you came to Baldwin this year. Remember what I told you on the first day, about how the Baldwin scene's needed some social spice forever? Well, it was true, and you sure didn't disappoint! Have an AMAZING summer in Berlin, and if things ever get stressful, just think of me sailing on the Cape. You HAVE to come visit next summer, OK? Lobster and ice cream for breakfast, lunch, and dinner, and no better seashell-collecting on earth.

Hugs and kisses,
Amanda

Dearest Miriam (ha!),

Hope you don't mind I'm claiming the Brazilian Dance Club's page. I've always felt a certain bond with the group. It's a wonder I haven't joined yet — you should see me at home grooving to my new drumming CD. Magical moments. So . . . you're my oldest old-school friend, the girl I knew way back in the day, the chick who used to try to peek through the crack of the bathroom door and watch me pee in kindergarten. Ten years later and things haven't really changed, have they?

OK, you can kick me now. Ouch!

I was getting used to your ass being in Texas and it's been a little weird having you back in New York. Sometimes it feels like we're strangers and other times like we're related to each other. Relax — I'm about to say something nice. We've had our share of good times this year and I've enjoyed my spot on your living room couch. I hope you survive the summer with your mommy dearest and professor stud muffin and that I didn't make a mistake when I decided to go to the summer studies program at Bennington. When you come home from Berlin and I come back from granola camp, I'm hoping things will be back to normal. And you know exactly what I mean.

Your friend,
Sam

Dear Mimi,

You've been a pleasure to have this year in creative writing. I've so enjoyed watching you blossom from a timid transfer student into the class's resident pistol. You've brought so much insight and constructive feedback to the group discussions, and your writing has never failed to dazzle. I've relished everything you've handed in, from your first essay about your cat to the science fiction story you wrote last week — talk about a kinetic voice! Don't forget to bring a notebook with you everywhere you go this summer.

Kim

P.S. I'll be staying at the Jennings Artist Colony upstate from mid-July until the end of August. Feel free to drop a line if you're so inspired.

Yo,

It's been nice being locker neighbors with you this year. Sorry I'm such a slob. When I cleaned my locker out this week I found a hard-boiled egg from October.

Nastily,
Pete Lombini

P.S. Have we ever even talked before?

Whasssssssssssssssssssssssup, Lady?

What am I going to do this summer without our World Civ class? Life isn't worth living if I can't reenact history for my fellow scholars. You have been my everything — my wind, my fire, my beef jerky. I'm going to try to get Ms. Singer to teach The Return of World Civ next year. You in, Ho Chi Minh?

Yours,
Julius Caesar a.k.a. Zoroaster a.k.a. Aristotle a.k.a. Hammurabi a.k.a. the one and only ghettofabulous Arthur Gray

Mimi,

It's been great bumping into you everywhere I go this year (the bakery with my grandmother, art openings, Hot Bagels during assembly, etc.). You sure *you're not following me*?

Stay cool and don't forget to show up for school next year.
Max-a-million

(That weird thing to the left of this is a drawing I made for you. It started out as the Brooklyn Bridge, but I don't know what it is anymore so don't ask.)

Mimi,

You're such a loser for making me write this. How many times have I told you I don't do yearbooks? Since you insist, here goes the formulaic cheesy note:

I'm glad Baldwin's new girl ended up being so cool, not to mention good-looking and rich. Oh wait — that's me. Haha.
Yearbook rules stipulate that I'm supposed to list all my favorite memories here. Too bad I don't do memories. I'll say this much: I'll miss you and the gang over the summer, but I suspect it'll fly by faster than a private jet.

Let's keep in touch like little stalkers, mkay?

Yours in Eurotrash,
Pia xxx

Dear Mimi,

Life at Baldwin is always a little insane, but this year has been by far the craziest one yet. I blame you. I'm so glad you came up to NYC. You're one of the coolest people I've ever met. You're supersmart, you've got killer (if sometimes slightly questionable) style, and best of all you make me smile even when my face is covered in tears. Your Bugle articles always crack me up, and when you nailed Serge Ziff, I realized you were more than just a comic genius. Now the Ziffster is a has-been and you're practically famous. Thank God Zora let you back into school — the student body was running low on celebrities.

Sucks you won't be around this summer, but I promise I'll send you letters to tide you over in Germany.

Love,
Jess

M,

How weird is it when you're writing in somebody's yearbook and they're sitting right next to you, writing in your yearbook? There's literally two inches of the red staircase's carpeting between us and we could just be talking, but you won't look up from whatever you're writing. I hate writing — it's so stressful. What am I supposed to say? Is this all we're going to have left of each other when we're 99 years old? Sorry so morbid— I've been reading the Jim Morrison diaries.

I have three more yearbooks to sign before the bell rings, so here's a list of this year's highlights, in no particular order.

1. Chilling in my apartment, drinking all of Mom's iced green tea and looking at photography books. Apart from your thing for those Edward Weston pepper pictures, which I'll never understand, you have excellent taste.
2. . . . um . . .

Bell just rang. List kind of sucked, but oh well.

Peace. Love. C ya.
V

My little dumpling,*

I'm touched! Merci *for saving the back page for me. Empty except for my parting letter and the senior class photo.** Aww, will you look at the 12th graders? They're so excited to be heading off to the land of free love and 584 keg parties a week. Now it's our turn to be "upperclassmen," whatever that means.*

This year has had its share of ups and downs. The downs: that idiotic journal of yours, my mom's oh-so-ready-for-Lifetime-adaptation breakdown, Jess's boy-related freakouts. But the ups by far outnumbered those low points: working together on the paper and having Ulla Lippman*** to amuse us, dancing to Bulgarian techno in my apartment at three a.m., watching self-help talk shows instead of studying for our "interpretative performance vocabulary review," planting organic cabbage you-know-where, hitting the squash courts with Amanda France and her preppy posse, and calling you whenever I was on the verge of a mental meltdown.

I don't know what I'll do without you this summer. How unfair is it we'll both be in Europe but in different countries? What if I need your love and guidance? You'd better cave in and get a cell phone. I've come to depend on you.****

xoxoxoxoxoxoxoxoxoxooxoxoxoLily

*That is, my supermodel-tall little dumpling.
**Random aside: Is it just me or does Simon Daffow have his eyes scrunched up in every single picture in this book?
***Check her out at the top right. Don't you feel bad that she didn't get her braces off in time for the picture?
****You're the only one who brought me a jumbo bag of peanut butter cups during my mom's nervous breakdown.

Touch the Monkey

Top three people I'd give anything to spend my
summer with:
Boris, the boyfriend I never see
Lily, light of my social life, fire of my lunch hour
Dad

Top three people I'd give anything not to spend
my summer with:
Mom
Mom's boyfriend, Maurice
Mom and Maurice together

I USED TO LOOK FORWARD to the last day of school, back when
summer was all about improving my backstroke and kicking
back with my cat, Simon. But not this year. As the final days of
tenth grade ticked by, I watched with growing envy as my
friends pranced around in flip-flops and oversize sunglasses. I
would've gladly taken summer school, or even one of those
military-academy-cum-fat-camps advertised in the back of the
New York Times Magazine, over the nightmare that awaited me.

Apart from DNA, my mother and I have very little in common. I'm five-eleven and growing; she's well below the national average for women's height and, therefore, has never suffered the humiliation of being called "sir" by inattentive clerks and waiters. Self-consciousness and bewilderment, my specialties, are completely foreign concepts to her. Once, when I asked her if she ever feels insecure or depressed, she chuckled and said she believes in positive thinking. Mom is a psychology professor, and an expert on denial.

Though usually too wrapped up in thinking positively about her own life to notice any developments in mine, she will occasionally descend from her cloud of self-absorption to hurt my feelings — inadvertently, of course. I often remind myself that, deep down, she loves me a lot; she just has a quirky way of expressing it. I let it slide when, after watching me fumble through a duet from *Anything Goes* at my eighth-grade talent show, she mentioned a position paper she'd read on female adolescents' voice changes. When she scrutinized the beautiful gold heels I was wearing to the ninth-grade winter dance and declared that I needed "three extra inches like a hole in the head," I brushed it off. But when, late last spring, she kicked my saintly father out of the house to shack up with Maurice, the roly-poly physics professor she claimed to be her "existential companion," my patience ran out. If she could live without Dad, then she'd have to live without me too.

But in exchange for letting me hightail it to New York to spend this past school year with poor Dad, Mom extracted a promise in return: that I'd spend the summer with her in Houston. Or so I'd naively assumed. As it turned out, Mom had landed a summer fellowship at the Teichen Institute and expected me to tag along while she conducted spatial-memory experiments on rhesus monkeys.

The Teichen Institute, I should point out, is located in Berlin, a huge European metropolis where I'd know exactly two people: Mom and the aforementioned puffball physicist who'd replaced Dad.

With the school year drawing to a close, I began to dread the experience, and moped around the house accordingly. In the weeks before school let out, Quinn, Dad's delightful darkroom assistant and an honorary member of our family, kept trying to cheer me up by describing Berlin as decadent and fabulous — a city where nobody works or gets up before noon. Quinn was unable to be serious about anything for longer than five seconds, and was a world-class expert at pulling Dad or me out of a funk. One night in late May, he even lured me to the couch and removed a red Netflix envelope from his messenger bag, announcing, "If you don't love Germany after this masterpiece, I'm taking you to Bellevue for a mental health checkup!"

And so I was subjected to *Satan's Brew,* an unbelievably pretentious German movie about a deranged anarchist poet named Walter who's obsessed with a prostitute. Later in the film, Walter becomes convinced he's the reincarnation of a gay nineteenth-century poet and loses interest in the streetwalker. It was a preposterous movie that solidified my suspicion of all things German, but I couldn't tell that to Quinn, who was gasping from start to finish. "This was fun," I said gamely after the movie was over.

"Maybe you should come visit this summer. You can show me all the other German things that deserve a chance."

"You'll be fine without me," Quinn promised, inserting the DVD back in its envelope. "I think your dad would decompose if we both left him."

On the last day of school, my friends and I cut second period to hang out in Cadman Plaza Park, but the huge rectangle of dirt in downtown Brooklyn that served as Baldwin's soccer/baseball/Frisbee/Brazilian dance field had been cordoned off for grass planting, so we sat on a bench in the shade. While the girls entertained themselves deciphering the senseless profanities carved into the bench (my favorite: "eat my burrito"), I was anxious — even more so after I looked at my watch and realized that in exactly twenty-four hours I'd be on a plane. A loud sigh sailed out of my mouth.

"Cheer up," Pia said. "It's only a few months. We'll be here when you get back."

"I know, I know," I said. "It's just . . . there are *so* many things I'd rather do with my summer than study German."

"Like what, study Russian?" Lily ventured, an unsubtle reference to Boris Potasnik, my so-called sort-of-not-quite boyfriend.

Her joke only increased my gloominess, for Boris, too, had become a sore subject in recent weeks. In private, he played the part of boyfriend well, laughing at my jokes, complimenting my hideous freckles, and stashing Belgian chocolate bars inside my laptop case. It was how he behaved in public that troubled me. Whenever we hung out with other people, Boris didn't just ignore me, but made a grand show of doing so. He'd avert his eyes and address everyone else in the room except yours truly, even if I was saying something supremely interesting, which, quite often, I was.

The problem was that Boris and I shared more than a love for smoked salmon and fancy chocolate. We also shared a close friend, Sam Geckman, and Sam and I had a highly complicated relationship, mostly thanks to a few brief and regrettable hookup sessions during the fall semester. Claiming that Sam had a crush on me, Boris thought it inappropriate to "flaunt" our relationship and insisted we "maintain a low profile" as a couple. "Just keep it cool," he told me whenever I vented my growing frustration. But Boris was Russian, and his idea of cool was as cold as caviar on ice.

"It's stupid to be depressed," Jess told me. "It's the last day of school, which means no more Zora Blanchard, no more *Bugle* melodramas, no more loopy assignments from Yuri Knutz. Three whole months of liberation are just an hour away! Next summer, we're going to have to fill out college applications and visit campuses, so this is really it for us — the last free ride."

Jess grinned, so moved by her own motivational speech that she suggested we go around in a circle and name the one thing we were most looking forward to that summer. I rolled my eyes, though I did love Jess for her optimism. While less financially blessed than her friends — she lived with her mother in a shabby walkup apartment in Park Slope and never had more than ten dollars in her piggy bank — she had us all beat for good humor.

"Fab. Me first," Pia said, flicking back her chestnut-colored hair. "I can't wait to learn how to drive a motorboat. I'm getting a license this summer." She was headed to Lake Como, in northern Italy, to hang with long-lost cousins and various villa-dwellers, all of whom, she said, dressed exclusively in leopard print and cashmere.

"And I can't wait to be somewhere where nobody cares about my mother," Lily volunteered. Lily — the daughter of Margaret Morton, queen of the *House and Home* empire — was taking drama studies classes at some millennia-old academy in London, well beyond the reach of her mother's fame. Perhaps in rebellion against Margaret Morton's fastidious, perfectionist public image, Lily lived in men's jeans and sweatshirts and wore her hair in a sloppy ponytail.

Viv, our resident rock 'n' roller, took some time to formulate her answer. She had a big summer ahead of her: a mountaineering tour of Oregon and, later, an internship at Immortal Records in Manhattan. "I'm looking forward to not having to see my ex at school every day," she said, and I tried not to wince. That winter she'd dated Sam — the same Sam who, according to Boris, was pining for me — and now, irritatingly, she refused to get over him. Viv's fixation made zero sense to me, given the vast gulf in their attractiveness levels. Viv, who was half-Jewish and half-Filipino, had creamy skin, wide-set brown eyes, and a perfect body. Sam, on the other hand, was, well, Sam. Smart, funny, and charming, yes, but in the eleven years I'd known him, I hadn't once heard him described as "hot." Viv, when prodded by all of us to say something positive, admitted, "I guess I'm looking forward to spending time in the Oregon wilderness. Maybe I'm secretly an outdoorsy type."

"Yeah, right." Jess laughed. "We won't hold our breath. You know what *I'm* the most excited about this summer?"

"Making piles of money?" I guessed. Jess was sticking around the city for a high-paid gig at an investment bank.

"No, wait, I know," said Lily. "How about working side by side with the hottie who interviewed you?"

"Um, I appreciate the insults," said Jess, "but you're both way off. Actually, I'm most looking forward to this weekend fiction class I'm taking at the New School. The teacher is this awesome woman whose last novel was nominated for every prize under the sun. I'm totally making her my mentor."

Lily and I exchanged guilty looks. We too easily forgot that Jess, with her flowing blond hair and résumé of athletic ex-boyfriends, had a serious side as well. She was one of the *Poetry Review*'s most valued members and spent Sunday afternoons combing used bookstores for first-edition hardbacks of J. D. Salinger books.

"Your turn, Texas," Pia said with that authority I'd grown to love. At the moment, though, I wasn't up to the task. Sighing, I kept my eyes on the empty paper bags that were blowing around the ground like props in a spaghetti Western. What did I look forward to this summer? Surviving it, and that was pretty much it. "I know," I said sarcastically, "maybe my mom will let me touch one of her lab monkeys."

"You know what?" Pia said. "You're a total idiot." But Jess and Viv were laughing, and sweet Lily said, not for the first time, "Remember, Mimi, I'll be right across the channel in case of emergency. Just one time zone away if you ever need rescuing."

An hour later, after our final assembly, where the seniors sang a teary rendition of "Leaving on a Jet Plane," my friends and I left the building as tenth-graders for the last time. We lingered outside Baldwin for a few minutes to watch the annual shaving cream fight between the senior and junior classes, then walked down the block to the Court Street subway station. My train was on a different line, but to prolong the journey home, I accompanied my friends into Manhattan. They planned to sunbathe in Washington Square Park all afternoon. I, on the other hand, would be locked in my bedroom, preparing for my three-month prison sentence. My plane was leaving early the next morning, and if I wanted to attend the grad party that night, I needed to get organized.

I was hoping to pack in one last ice cream break with Dad and Quinn, but when I got home, I found them in the living room with some guy I'd never seen before. With his crisp polo, penny loafers, and phony-baloney laugh, the newcomer reminded me of a preppy serial murderer in a direct-to-cable movie.

"I like that," he was saying to Dad when I popped my head into the living room. He paused to jot something down in a notebook, while Dad nervously fiddled with the large-format camera on the coffee table.

"Now," the mystery guest said in a voice that sounded like it had been slicked down with baby oil, "I've noticed your work bears the imprint of Walter Benjamin. Am I right in detecting this?"

I was expecting Dad to respond in his usual fashion: by pressing the shutter release and snickering. But today he nodded seriously and said, "Absolutely — you can't be a working photographer without considering the implications of Benjamin."

"And obviously you're presenting a perception in your pictures. What is your perception of other people's perceptions of your perception?"

I could barely contain my laughter. Quinn, seeing this, stood up and motioned for me to join him in the kitchen. "That's Darrell," he told me. "He's taking a criticism course at Columbia and wanted to interview Roger."

"He picked *Dad?*" I couldn't keep the skepticism from my voice. While Dad's photography career had almost taken off in the 1980s with a big solo show he called Happy People, it had stalled soon afterward — mostly because Dad had such a relaxed and unambitious personality. After several false starts, he spent the better part of a decade teaching photography at Rice University, and while the magazine and catalog assignments that had since become his bread and butter were nicely turned out, he never mistook them for high art.

"I know, I haven't the faintest clue where this kid came from, but he thinks your dad is some sort of underground genius and sounded desperate to meet him. How could I refuse? Besides, I thought Roger would get a kick out of some star treatment, especially after, you know, everything."

Quinn was referring to Dad's breakup a few months earlier with Fenella von Dix, installation artist extraordinaire. Even though he'd been the one to call it off, Dad had subsequently started to act needy and gloomy again, as he had in the months immediately following his separation from my mom.

"That's a great question," Dad was saying as I exited the kitchen and headed for the staircase that led to my room. "I've often wondered that myself. It's Sontag's earlier theories that really changed my perspective. But I found some of her later writings . . . how should I put it? Reductive, I guess."

Teasing Dad about Darrell would have to wait, I thought. I had work to do. In my room downstairs, I put on *Goats Head Soup,* one of my favorite Rolling Stones CDs, and unzipped the suitcase I'd last used on my trip to Bravura Island over Presidents' Day weekend. I'd gone there to report on my *Bugle* profile of Serge Ziff, a Baldwin parent who'd forked over a cool million to the school after catastrophic investments had placed it on the brink of shutdown. The story became slightly more complicated when I'd discovered that Serge Ziff dealt not only in art, but in illegal drugs. After the Baldwin administration had punished me for writing the article, my mentor Harriet Yates had helped me place a longer version of the story in the *New York Tribune,* one of the many papers her boyfriend, Ed Stern, owned. With Serge now awaiting trial, I was in serious debt to Harriet, whom I'd met randomly one afternoon in the bathroom of a Chelsea art gallery. At fifty-seven, she was nine years older, and about five hundred times cooler, than my mother. She had a formidable reputation as both an artist and a critic, but her real talent was with people; I couldn't imagine my spring semester without her.

I overturned my suitcase and shook out the detritus from my

tropical getaway. A grungy balled-up white T-shirt remained stubbornly wedged in the corner, and I decided to let it be, reasoning that I could always wash it in Germany. I had no idea what else to pack, since I wasn't lucky enough to own the thigh-high leather boots and low-rider cotton underpants that the prostitute had donned in *Satan's Brew*.

Suddenly there was a knock on the door, then a female calling, "Yoo-hoo!"

With the Rolling Stones playing so loud, I could barely make out the voice, and figured it was one of the Upstairs Judys dropping by with another container of mushy foodstuffs. Our friendly neighbors in the apartment above ours were killing time between documentary film projects by taking a one-month intensive Ayurvedic cookery course at the Open Center. In the past week alone, Dad and I had been treated to browned quinoa pumpkin stew and chia seed watermelon soup.

At the second, more insistent "Yoo-hoo!" I rushed over to open the door. Having expected a Tupperware container of burnt grains, I was pleasantly surprised to see my four best friends. "Don't I know you guys from somewhere?" I asked.

"Your dreams," Lily said as one by one they entered my room.

"What happened to Washington Square Park?" I asked.

"A total funeral procession of suburban Hacky Sack players and old dudes playing chess," said Viv, turning up the volume on "Star Star."

"Absolutely *no*body was there," Pia added emphatically.

I should point out that, in Pia's world, "nobody" didn't mean an absence of people, but rather an absence of people worthy of her attention. When I first met Pia, she completely intimidated me. I'd taken her for a world-class snob — which, in fact, she is. But I soon came to learn that she was also generous and hilarious and fiercely loyal. Because her jet-setting diplomat parents spent so little time in New York, Pia was something of a latchkey kid, often pressuring her friends into keeping her company while she ate dinner or did homework. Now that she was dating Isaac, the bespectacled math genius from Stuyvesant High School, Pia's neediness had abated some.

"Let's get you packed and then out of here," she said. "Isaac and some of his friends are going to the planetarium and I said we'd meet them. You already got a start." She gestured to my dirty T-shirt. "We can finish this job in five minutes."

"But Pia, I'm not going away for the weekend — I'll be gone for the entire summer!"

"So?" Pia raised a thick eyebrow at me. "Lest you forget, I'm going away for the summer tomorrow morning, too, and I don't even *have* a suitcase. I'll throw some crap in a couple of shopping bags at dawn. Which is what I recommend you do. They do have stores over there, you know."

For someone with her astronomical IQ, Pia could be remarkably obtuse. She needed constant reminding that not all teenagers had a wallet full of platinum cards; most of us scraped by on erratically handed-out twenty-dollar bills.

"I can't just buy a new wardrobe because I wasn't in the mood to pack!" I told her.

"What*ever*," Pia said. "I'm just saying, if you need a few

things when you get over there, like some T-shirts and socks, I'm sure you'll figure it out."

"I guess," I said. "Not that it matters what I wear or anything, since Germany isn't exactly fashion central." Besides, I thought, however conservative or funky my outfit, I always end up looking exactly the same. Maybe it's my hair — brown, chin-length, and perpetually shaggy, no matter how I try to tame it. Or my resemblance to a giraffe: tall, gangly, and covered everywhere with freckles. Whatever the cause, I never quite manage to look half as groomed or pulled together as the Pias of the world.

"Here," Pia chirped. "Allow me to demonstrate my time-tested packing method."

She marched over to my closet and started transferring armloads of clothes to my suitcase. Viv pitched in by emptying the contents of my underwear and T-shirt drawers into the suitcase, Jess by piling my dirty-clothes hamper on top of the underwear heap. "And now," Pia said, "for the encore presentation . . ."

She instructed Lily to plant herself on top of the now-overstuffed suitcase. Lily did so, and with some effort Pia succeeded in zipping it shut. Unbelievable. "Not ideal," she said, "but it'll do. Now, shall we?"

"Do I have a choice?" I said, shaking my head in astonishment as my friends filed out the door and up the stairs. I called goodbye to my dad and his entourage, then shut the door behind us. But once we were in the entry hall, I remembered something important. "Hold on one sec," I said, and went back into the apartment.

In the kitchen, I dialed Boris's cell. "About time," he said, picking up on the first ring.

"Missed me that much?"

"I've just been counting the days until you finished tenth grade," he said. "Thank God I'm *finally* dating an upperclassman — it's so much more dignified."

I giggled. Boris loved joking about my being one year below him in school, though in age I was only seven months younger. Out of respect for the interview still taking place in the next room, I lowered my voice and told him about tonight's plan. I had a complicated evening ahead: first the end-of-year cocktail party organized in my honor by Harriet and Ed; then the notorious Baldwin grad party. Double-billing usually stressed me out, but both of tonight's events were downtown, a quick twenty-minute walk apart.

"Harriet and Ed's sendoff starts at eight, so if we want to have enough time there before the grad party, we should try to show up right on time. Sound good?"

Silence.

Oh, God, I thought, not this again. I tapped my right Converse on the floor and waited.

When Boris spoke again, his voice was less playful. "Why don't I just see you at the grad party?" he suggested. "I don't think I can make it to Harriet's. The thing is, Mimi . . ." Boris paused. "I kind of made pre-plans with Sam . . ."

His voice trailed off, but I could complete his sentence in my sleep. However much he professed to like me, Boris could not stop harping on Sam's alleged "issues." I say "alleged" because I didn't believe they existed, at least not to the extent that Boris did.

Here's more or less what happened: On several occasions last semester, I made the mistake of kissing my oldest friend in the world. Following this mistake, said oldest friend decided he had a crush on me, but he soon enough overcame this delusion and began dating Viv. End of story.

While Boris continually insisted that Sam was "still in love" with me, I knew my childhood friend's psychology better than that. He was simply freezing me out, punishing me for so openly choosing another guy over him — and a close friend of his at that. Now, I constantly asked Boris, if Sam were *really* in love with me, wouldn't he e-mail more than once a week, or return more than a quarter of my calls, or acknowledge my existence at Baldwin parties with more than a polite nod and mumbled pleasantry? But these examples never seemed to help my case. If anything, Boris used them to reinforce his own argument.

"Boris," I said as patiently as I could manage, "in case you forgot, this is our last night together. I'm going away for the entire summer."

"Relax, you cow," he said — short for "cowgirl," by the way, his private nickname for me — "stop being so pessimistic. Why rush when we have all the time in the world?"

"But this party tonight is in *my* honor. Without you there it'll feel . . . unnatural. Incomplete. You understand that, right?"

"I'll be there, I promise." There was a pause. "In spirit. You know I'm your biggest fan, Mimi."

"I heard that somewhere." I put the phone down and counted to ten.

As I went outside to rejoin my friends, I felt the old anger swell up in me. It made no sense. You'd think that the night before I left town, Boris could publicly acknowledge our relationship for once. But no. Never — at least not when Sam Geckman is in the same time zone, which is pretty much all the time.

Bedbugs or Bust

HARRIET HAD ASKED ME to arrive early for my going-away party, presumably so we could catch up before I disappeared behind the iron curtain. When I got there, though, my fairy godmother was completely absorbed in her lover boy. The two of them were snuggling on the couch like a couple of kittens. Harriet had on her signature red lip-gloss, some of which had smudged off on Ed's earlobe. I loved them both, together and apart — Harriet for being a loyal friend and mentor, and Ed for saving me after I'd exposed Serge Ziff's drug-running operation. And, of course, for wearing such hilarious animal ties — tonight's featured kangaroos.

While the hosts were happily cuddling, members of the catering team buzzed about Harriet's apartment, assembling platters of miniature vegetables and shouting orders about "stations" and "head counts." I settled into a squishy chair opposite the lovebirds, admiring the fragrant flower arrangements in every corner of the room. "I had no idea you were going to all this trouble," I said. "I mean, I *am* coming back in three months!"

Harriet laughed and pointed across the room, where a man on top of a ladder was struggling to insert a vase of pale pink peonies in a high-up nook on the bookshelf. "That's Carlos," she told me. "He's the 'floral designer.' His partner, Horatio, is the 'floral consultant.' They come as a package deal. Sibyl Bruno recommended them."

I knew better than to ask Harriet who Sibyl Bruno was; I could never keep track of all her friends.

"What's new and interesting?" Ed asked me, as was the newspaperman's habit.

"Um, I don't know," I said. "Actually, I heard a rumor that Baldwin's looking into starting a Beverly Hills campus."

"That right?" Ed said, his eyebrows raising with curiosity. "I'll tell somebody to explore that."

"Not now, you won't," Harriet told him, and turned to face me. "I made him leave his portable e-mail thingie at home tonight."

"I'm going to have to make what they call conversation," Ed said.

"What an injustice," I said.

"Now, squirt," Ed said, "Harriet and I were trying to figure this out before you got here. Where exactly in Berlin are you going to be living?"

I sank deeper into the cushion. "With Mom and Maurice. Mom has arranged for a sublet from some imaginary colleague she's never met."

"Where does this imaginary colleague live?" Ed wanted to know.

"Beats me," I said. "Probably some gingerbread house overflowing with mountains of musty German books and military paraphernalia."

"Do you know the name of the neighborhood?" Harriet asked. "Schoneberg? Mitte? Tiergarten? Any of these ring a bell?"

"Afraid not," I said. "I just know that it's near the Teichen Institute. So wherever the academic part of town is, I guess?"

"What part of Berlin *isn't* academic?" Ed asked, and Harriet obligingly guffawed.

I shrugged, feeling left out of the joke and, perhaps, also slightly ashamed of my total ignorance of Berlin. I hadn't opened the *Culture Shock! Germany* book that the Judys had given me, not even once.

"Don't worry," Ed said, reading my anxious expression. "You'll be an expert on German geography in two weeks, tops."

"God, I hope not," I said. "I was sort of planning on sleeping through the whole experience."

I got up to go to the bathroom and returned to find Ed and Harriet standing together by the bar, sipping glasses of white wine and exchanging goofy glances. When Ed noticed me, he pulled a CD out of his breast pocket. "I made this for the party," he said proudly. "I paid some kid a fortune to transfer my music to the computer and make me some mixes. This is the first of many."

"Let me guess what artists you've included," Harriet said over the ringing doorbell. "Frank Sinatra, Frank Sinatra, and Frank Sinatra?"

"I object!" Ed said. "There's some Harry Belafonte, too."

As the owner of a small newspaper empire, Ed dutifully expressed curiosity about what he called "new and noteworthy trends," but his personal tastes were stubbornly old fashioned:

29

steak dinners, hand tennis at the New York Athletic Club, and the Rat Pack.

The doorbell rang again. Neither Ed nor Harriet moved to answer it, so I did. I opened the door to my Barrow Street family bearing a bouquet of purple tulips.

"Sorry to be so unfashionably early," Quinn said as he stepped past me, "but we had to shake that Darrell kid. He wouldn't take a hint."

Dad blushed. "It was fun for a while, but then it got a little strange," he said, accepting a beer from Harriet. "I started to think he'd confused me with another more, ah, prominent photographer. But he knew all these obscure biographical details about me, like my springtime allergies and what part of the Jersey Shore I used to —"

"Wow. Your place looks great," Quinn broke in. "If I'd known you'd gone all out like this, I wouldn't have bothered bringing these wilted tulips from the Korean deli downstairs."

"Don't be ridiculous," Harriet said. She made a show of asking Carlos the 'floral designer' to put the tulips on the bar, "where everybody will be sure to see them."

For the next half-hour, Dad took pictures of the guests filing into Harriet's loft. I found it a little odd that Harriet had invited so many people I'd never even heard of to my going-away party, but then, cross-pollination figured big in Harriet's life philosophy.

When the room was sufficiently full, Ed put on his CD, the first track of which was, sure enough, Old Blue Eyes' rendition of "New York, New York." I gave a whoop and immediately started dancing with Quinn and a few of what Harriet called her "gallery friends," who tended to be slightly kookier than her "museum friends," though less fun than her "studio friends." Harriet has probably met upwards of a million people in her life, and she keeps in touch with all of them. Even if she wanted to lose touch, people wouldn't let her. She's *that* charismatic. I was among the chosen few Harriet saw regularly, and over the past few months, we'd met for tea or a movie almost every week.

It's funny how I've become so much more comfortable hanging out with adults since moving to New York. This wasn't always the case — far from it. In middle school, I'd come home to find Mom and her friends Eileen and Wanda in the den, sipping Crystal Light raspberry lemonade and discussing inappropriate topics like varicose veins and the appeal of men with curly blond chest hair. With my fingers plugged in my ears, I'd scuttle away, and Mom would tease me for being "Little Miss Sensitivity." But on Barrow Street, Dad and Quinn, and now Ed and Harriet, have always treated me as an equal. And compared to my peers, grownups are total softies, a much easier to please audience.

At Harriet's that night, I hardly noticed that most guests were a good two decades older than I, including Dad, Quinn, the *Baldwin Bugle* faculty adviser, Ms. Singer, the Upstairs Judys, a handful of Ed's employees from the *Tribune,* and quite a few total strangers, among them a frizzy-haired woman who showed up with a greyhound as big as a horse.

Lily was there on behalf of my other Baldwin friends, who'd all gone to the runway fashion show also known as Baldwin's graduation ceremony. According to Viv, the senior guys decked out in three-piece suits, accessorized with monocles and jewel-encrusted walking sticks, while the girls wore outrageous nineteenth-century ball gowns. The spectacle was so phenomenal that several dozen hopefuls had shown up with counterfeit tickets.

"You didn't have to come, but I'm so, so, so glad you did!" I told Lily when I greeted her at the door. She was looking especially pretty in a baby blue tank top that revealed more skin than her usual hoodie sweatshirts, and though she'd pulled her long brown hair back in the usual ponytail, she was, for the first time since I'd known her, also wearing mascara and dangly earrings.

"Please," she said coolly. "I'll have enough time to look at the graduation costumes in the fall. The *Bugle*'s doing a back-to-school issue with a graduation fashion spread. And guess who's writing captions?"

"Would that be my favorite editor?"

"No, but it might be her favorite dedicated reporter." Lily wiggled her index finger at me. "You'll have fun with it! Hey," she said suddenly, looking around the room, "where's Boris?"

"Off pretending to live in a spy movie," I said bitterly. "He doesn't want to be 'too visible' in case Sam shows up — can you believe that?"

"I love that guy," Lily said, shaking her head sympathetically, "but he *is* crazy, isn't he? I'll bet he writes you love letters this summer in invisible ink."

"Or secret messages written with lemonade and a Q-tip."

"Or he'll go the ESP route," she said. "You'll wake up in the middle of the night and just *know* he's communicating something."

"What's this about *Mimi* waking up in the middle of the night to talk with a *man*?" This interruption came from Quinn, obviously — who else?

"Actually," I said, turning to him, "we were talking about my paranoid wannabe telepathic boyfriend, Boris."

"I once dated a man who claimed to be able to read the minds of pigeons," Quinn told us. "It was intense."

Behind us, Harriet switched off Ed's music, replacing it with an album she described as "absolutely essential." The composition had no beat, no music, just loud gurgling sounds punctuated by the occasional siren. "Sounds like a ferret getting arrested while giving birth," Quinn observed approvingly.

The studio friends were enthusiastic, the museum friends and gallery friends somewhat less so. I wished Boris could've witnessed these dead serious responses; he would've cracked up. Reporting the highlights later just wouldn't produce the same effect.

While I could've stayed at the party all night — and wanted to, if only to spite Boris — Lily was ready to move on to our next engagement after about an hour. "I hate to bail on my own party," I said to Ed and Harriet, "but like I told you before, we have to get to the grad party soon. They have some weird door policy."

"Oh, no, you don't," Harriet said. "You're not going anywhere until Ed and I make our announcement."

"Your announcement?" I felt the color rise to my cheeks. Hadn't they made enough of a fuss over me already? I was only going away for the summer to take language classes, as millions of overachieving American adolescents had done before me. "Really, there's no need," I insisted.

"Kid, just sit tight," Ed said as he ceremoniously tapped a cheese knife against one of the flower vases. "Can I have everybody's attention?"

Next to him, Harriet was wriggling impatiently. I blushed and glanced at my pontoon feet. Maybe I should cobble together an impromptu thank-you speech? Always start with a joke, my dad had once advised. But which joke would be appropriate for the occasion? I soon became so preoccupied with finding the perfect witticism that I missed the lead-up into Ed's bombshell: ". . . which is why we've decided to get married."

I jerked my head up. So *this* was why so many unfamiliar people had shown up. The guests had erupted into gasps and exclamations and applause. Even Lily was clapping and pounding her Treetorns on Harriet's finished concrete floors. Was I the only one who was shocked and unsettled by this news?

Not that I had anything against marriage, but Harriet had always struck me as too independent to be interested in such a conventional institution. Never in a million years did I expect to see her waving her left wrist like Elizabeth Taylor, flaunting the massive diamond ring that Ed had just presented to her. It looked out of place on Harriet's hand, mere inches from the chipped red fingernails and pink plastic bangles.

But she looked so happy, and soon my disbelief gave way to genuine delight. On my way out, after hugging my dad and Quinn goodbye, I pulled Harriet aside to congratulate her. "That was a nice little trick you played on me," I told her. "Thank God you made your announcement *before* I'd given my thank-you speech!"

She laughed. "You had a speech? In that case, I wished we'd waited!"

"But seriously, Harriet," I said, "you're going to be the best newlyweds ever."

Harriet beamed her appreciation as I babbled on, offering my services as their surrogate New York daughter if they ever found themselves wishing for one. "Way too late for that," Harriet said, "but we still want you around as much as you can stand. Now have yourself an extraordinary summer, and we expect to see you out at Ed's place in the Hamptons before school starts!"

"All I can conclude," Lily said afterward as we walked south on Broadway, "is that either Harriet did an awfully good job covering up her girlie side, or that *everyone* deep down wants to get married. Maybe it's just that most people don't see any need to conceal it."

"So by that logic," I said, "that means *you* want to get married, too?" Lily is less boy-obsessed than most of my friends, so I spoke with some disappointment. Apart from a short-lived crush on Harry Feder, the notorious Lothario of Baldwin whose exploits had earned him the unfortunate nickname Blowjob Harry, she seemed pretty immune to the smellier sex.

"Married?" Lily shook her head. "Nah. But I could stand a little boy-girl action." She paused before asking, "Do you know who Dimitri Zarillo is?"

"Well, yeah — who doesn't?"

Dimitri Zarillo was a junior with a shaved head and wild,

wide-spaced black eyes. We'd only interacted once, when he handed me a flier for *Burn Dinosaur,* a play he'd written that was being staged in Prospect Park. I was sorry to have missed it; the *Bugle* review described actors in bathing suits, wielding water guns filled with ketchup and pancake batter.

"Well, I happen to think he's cute," Lily said defensively. "I mean, I'm not sure why, and the worst part about it is that he's the last person I would want to like. He seems so . . ."

"Self-involved?"

"Exactly!"

"I hate to break it to you, Lils, but I think he is." Still, I was glad to hear that Lily had gotten over Harry.

We were now walking down the Bowery, past a row of lighting and jewelry stores. Though most were closed, their lights were blazing through the windows, so it felt earlier than it was. After passing a knot of panhandlers outside the Manhattan Jewelry Association, we arrived at the address on the invite: an off-putting black door that was bolted shut. Lily, as confused as I was, was reaching for her cell phone when the grating of an adjoining lighting store rose and a short, spiky-haired guy popped out to hustle us underneath it. He led us through a display room of chandeliers and reading lamps, then up a carpeted staircase that opened onto a massive loft with high windows overlooking the Bowery.

"Wow," I said. It was a beautiful space, even when crowded with hundreds of intoxicated high-schoolers. "What is this, anyway? It sure doesn't look like a club."

"It's not," Lily told me. "It's some guy's loft — he lives here. He advertised it on Craigslist. You won't believe how much the organizers are paying him — six thousand dollars for one night. Isn't that smart of him?"

As I gazed around the room, I couldn't help but think that the Baldwin student body was getting its money's worth. Students were everywhere, sprawled over windowsills, crushed against the kitchen island, spread all over the floor. Samuel Richter had fashioned a floor cushion out of a full garbage bag and was napping on it, his face tucked into the knot at the top. Nathan Milliken was sitting in the kitchen sink with a bag of ice on his lap. A circle of freshmen girls hovered by the door, clutching enormous Starbucks cups for protection.

I followed Lily's eyes to Dimitri Zarillo, who was leaning against a column and conducting a one-sided conversation with a girl in sunglasses and a trench coat. We edged over to him just as the girl in sunglasses decided to flee. "See you in a little bit," Lily whispered, deftly replacing Dimitri's conversational partner. He continued speaking, and it was doubtful he had noticed he was talking to somebody new.

Once I was alone, I scanned the room for Boris — never a difficult task, given his towering height and powder white hair. Right away I spotted him in the kitchen area, holding a longneck and chatting with Sam and Ivan Grimalsky. I was on my way over when Pia inserted herself in my path. "Where *were* you?" she demanded.

"Yeah, what took you so long?" Jess asked. "We were beginning to think you'd bailed on us for the senior citizens cruise."

My account of Ed's proposal didn't measure up to their extravagant descriptions of the Baldwin graduation ceremony — or not until I described the ginormous ring Harriet had been given. "You should have *seen* the rock," I said. "We're talking king of bling."

"I prefer queen of obscene," my favorite Russian prince said from behind me. Hurrah! I turned to see Boris looking adorable in his just-woken-up way, with his white-blond hair shooting up like wild grass. I stretched out my arms and wrapped them around his burly torso, but before I could pull him toward me, he twisted out of my grasp and I tripped forward.

The girls all exchanged uncomfortable glances. This was not the first time Boris had disowned my affection in their presence.

"Hi, Boris," Viv said, then coughed uneasily.

He acknowledged her with a slight wave, then shuffled back a few steps. I felt Pia's eyes drilling into me; she hated my tolerance for Boris's less-than-reverential treatment.

"I am *dying* of thirst," Jess said quickly. "Anyone feel like joining me at the bar?"

Pia and Viv hopped to the task, leaving me to glare at Boris.

"What?" he asked, all wide-eyed innocence. "Forgive me for forgetting how uncoordinated you are. Mimi," he added quietly, "you *know* we've got to keep a low profile."

"Can you remind me why again?" I shot back.

Boris tilted his head toward the kitchen, where Sam was leaning against the counter.

"I'm sorry if Sam's your friend," I said, "but in case you forgot, I'm *supposed* to be your girlfriend, and starting in ten hours,

I'm going to be the long-distance girlfriend you don't see for three months."

"Mimi, relax — I'm visiting you in Berlin in a couple of weeks!"

"You're not visiting *me*," I corrected him. "You're meeting me at the airport for three hours while you have a layover. You'll be jet-lagged and your dad will be there and —"

I was about to really lay into him when an older man in a business suit tore into the room and flipped on all the overhead lights. "OK, kids! Party's over, and I mean ASAP! I'm a working man, and it's Bedtime for Bonzo!"

He charged over to the bed and shooed away a couple that had been making out on top of his duvet. This accomplished, he loosened his tie, removed his jacket, and started to climb in. "I'm opening my eyes in five minutes!" he shouted through the covers. "That should be long enough for you to remember where the door is located."

"You can't do this. You rented us the space for the night!" Jasmine Lowenstein, a member of the organizing committee, yelled. "We paid you six grand, and the party just started!"

The man turned over and nosed his head under the pillow.

Harry Feder, Lily's ex-crush, walked up to the bed and tossed his Visa card on the guy's bedside table. "Sir," Harry oozed, "why don't you go to the Waldorf tonight? My treat. Just go easy on the minibar, will you?"

A pillow hit Harry smack on the forehead.

"Let's just get out of here," I said to Boris. "We can go to a diner or something."

But Pia prevented any such getaway, edging between us to announce, "Listen, there are at least two other parties tonight, and my sources say no psychotic bedbugs." She gestured at the owner of the loft, who'd risen from bed and was powering through the room with an industrial-size broom.

I squeezed Boris's wrist. "You go ahead," he said, shaking free of my hand. I instantly saw why: Sam had lumbered over.

Acknowledging me with a cursory nod, Sam went on to tell Boris they could still make the screening of 3-D shorts at Anthology Archives. "It's at twelve-thirty. If we cab it, we'll be fine."

"Really? Cool," Boris said. Sensing my frustration, he looked at me pleadingly, as if *I* were the one behaving unreasonably. "You don't want to join us, do you?"

"Not really, no."

"Cool," Sam said, staring over one of my shoulders. "Well, then, hasta la vista."

"Yeah, hasta la vista," I echoed mockingly.

"OK," Boris said. "See ya." He then crumpled his face to express — what? Regret? Heartbreak? Mild nausea? I had no way of knowing, and at this point I didn't really care. In fact, at that moment I didn't really care if I never saw Boris Potasnik ever again. "Right," I murmured quietly. "See ya."

And that was it for our grand goodbye.

Willkommen in Berlin!

We took a cab uptown to the Lindhurst grad party, which was being held in a townhouse in the West Seventies. The apartment was filled with smoke and jazz and shy boys wearing loosely knotted ties. Framed *New Yorker* covers hung on the walls, just like in the bathroom of my dentist's office.

The Lindhurst School was a tiny all-boys school near Columbia University. Likewise, its graduation party was tiny and, with a few unthreatening exceptions, all boys. When the five of us waltzed into the room, quite a few of the guys just gawked, while the bolder ones swarmed us and offered to get us drinks.

"All-boy parties rule!" Jess cried gleefully. "I feel like a supermodel!"

"Enjoy it while you can," Pia advised her. "The Orbach School girls will be coming any minute."

Viv took that cue to accost a horse-faced boy at the bar. Since the whole Sam debacle, her already-substantial insecurities had multiplied bigtime. She'd gone from barely eating anything to barely eating even less, and as her appetite for food diminished, her appetite for male attention increased. She was becoming needier than Jess — standing creepily close to men on the subway and throwing herself at any male with a pulse. A few weeks ago, when

Pia brought us to an exhibition of Milanese dishware at the Italian embassy, I'd overheard Viv telling a married potter from a population-six-hundred Sicilian village that she found clay "intensely sensual." Good thing the guy didn't understand a syllable of English.

While she and the rest of the girls reveled in the glow of male attention, I shut myself in the bathroom to fret over the Boris situation and all the smoother ways I might've handled myself at the grad party. Maybe if I'd followed Harriet's advice and "laid down the law" months ago, Boris would be worshiping me by now. I stood up and looked in the mirror, examining the face that he could take or leave: the small nose, the freckles, the wide cheeks. Dad says my brown eyes are "sparkling and intelligent," but I'd happily trade up for some baby blues. My delicate collarbone was definitely my best feature; no others sprang immediately to mind.

I stepped back and tried to see myself as if for the first time. No, I wasn't drop-dead gorgeous, but I wasn't ugly, either. I was certainly prettier than Sam, whose company, for some reason, Boris preferred to mine.

"Get over it, mopey," Lily commanded when I dragged back into the living room. "There will be plenty more Borises in Berlin."

How, I wondered, did Lily always read my mind so exactly?

"But you don't understand," I whimpered, "when we're alone, he's so diff —"

Lily wasn't interested. She hooked her arm under mine and took me out to the provisional dance floor on the terrace. As it turned out, the Orbach girls never showed up, and we remained the party's only supermodels. So many guys asked me to dance that, over the next three hours, I nearly forgot about my romantic misery.

I got home around four and — because I was already packed — managed to sleep almost two hours before Dad gently shook me awake. "Three hours till takeoff," he said somberly.

As usual before prolonged separations, we didn't speak much on the early-morning cab ride to JFK. I knew Dad was upset, but I was in no position to console him — at least *he* wasn't spending the next three months in the world capital of anal retentiveness with only Mom and Maurice for company.

When the taxi pulled up in front of terminal four, I slipped my hand into Dad's. After helping me unload my luggage, he hugged me tight and then got back into the cab. As it was speeding off, Dad rolled down the window and made me promise to drink plenty of water on the flight and to call him as soon as I'd landed. "Miss you already," I shouted back in response.

The next twelve hours were a total blur. I remember nothing of JFK except the greasy egg rolls I ordered in the food court, and I remember even less of the flight across the Atlantic. Within minutes of strapping myself into the cramped seat, I passed out. When I woke up somewhere over Ireland with drool dried on my chin, I noticed for the first time that the German man in the seat next to me was wearing head-to-toe black waffle-knit long underwear. On his lap was the *Oxford Encyclopedia of Animal Anatomy*. I closed my eyes again.

By the time I regained consciousness, we were on the ground, and everyone around me was checking voice mail while waiting to be let off the plane. For once, I was grateful not to have a cell phone. Mom was picking me up, and she wouldn't have been able to hold back from leaving me a dozen psychotic messages.

I inhaled deeply as I disembarked the plane, bracing myself for the reunion. I could just picture Mom, in her sweatsuit and red sunglasses, anxiously scanning the crowd for me. "Well, *there* you are," she'd say when I walked right up and tapped her on the shoulder. "I was so worried we'd miss each other; I've been having this spellbinding dream series where I'm in the supermarket and I keep pushing my shopping cart past the milk aisle even though that's what I came for. . ."

The passport hall had about thirty glass booths, all with long lines of frazzled passengers. I took my place in one for foreigners and busied myself with filling out my landing card. When I was done, I idly flipped through my passport and admired the stamps adorning several pages. Like most Texans, I'd been to Mexico several times. I'd also gone to an island off the coast of Belize for a family "diving trip," which soon turned into a family reading-novels-on-splintery-docks trip, since we showed up five days after a woman on her honeymoon had been almost bitten by a shark and Mom developed "safety concerns" about my planned diving lessons. When I was in third grade, we went to Paris, and then Rome when I was in middle school. But on all family trips, my older sister, Ariel, and I pretty much hid behind our parents and their guidebooks. It was only last September, when I moved back to New York, that I really learned to navigate a new place on my own. And I took my first parent-free trip over winter break, when my friends and I went to a gardening commune in the Dominican Republic.

After finally getting my passport stamped and collecting my black suitcase from baggage claim, I passed through the "Nothing to Declare" line and out into the main concourse of the terminal, where drivers held up signs for their passengers and anxious Berliners waited for their loved ones. My own anxious Berliner, however, was nowhere evident. I stood there, right in the middle of the passageway, gazing in both directions as fellow travelers jostled me over and over. Mom was probably locked inside a bathroom stall, gathering "emergency" toilet paper for her purse.

When at last I heard the name "MIRIAM!" crowed over the crush of people, I spun around in confusion. I knew that voice, but it wasn't Mom's. It belonged to Maurice Lancaster, everyone's least favorite hypochondriac stepdad-to-be. That afternoon he had on high-waisted jeans, a Disneyland T-shirt, and a conspicuous blue bandage wrapped around his right elbow. He trundled a few steps toward me, flailing his arms with no regard for the people around him. *"Guten Tag!"* he shouted. *"Willkommen in Berlin,* Miriam!"

I smiled thinly at him but didn't say anything. Though I wanted to ask him what "boundary-shattering" psychology position paper had kept his darling girlfriend from picking me up herself, I held my tongue and simply nudged my seven-hundred-pound suitcase at him. But Maurice, who looked even puffier in the company of so many sleek Europeans, didn't take the hint.

"I hope you don't mind if I decline to transport your *Reisegepäck,* Miriam," he said jovially. "I threw out my elbow on the flight over, and for all the famous efficiency of this country, I'm still searching for that perfect Berlin orthopedist."

"I've never heard of anyone throwing out an elbow before," I murmured.

"I know — aren't my ailments unique?"

I made no reply. When Maurice got started on his failing health, he zoned the rest of the world out completely. We began walking, me heaving my huge LeSportsac duffel bag on one arm and dragging my rolling mega-Samsonite with the other; Maurice carrying nothing but an empty coffee cup and a wadded-up German newspaper. At one point, he even had the audacity to complain about the weight of this periodical. "You wouldn't believe how they load up these *Zeitungs* with classifieds and supplements!" he said. "It's a real commitment, hauling one of these babies around."

Yet again: no response necessary. I remained silent even after Maurice showed me to his ridiculous little midlife-crisis sportscar and took us down the Autobahn toward our new home — or, as Maurice repeatedly called it, our *Zuhause*. When I rolled down the passenger-side window, Maurice reminded me of his extreme sensitivity to air pollution.

Way to pick a place to move. So far, what I'd seen of Berlin made smoggy Houston look like a pristine paradise. The city was gray and overcast, with construction cranes hanging over most intersections.

From the car floor I picked up the Evian bottle that had been banging into my foot and asked if I could have a sip. "Have the whole thing," Maurice too readily offered. "Planes are real germ incubators, and I can't afford to contract anything."

I was too tired to reply, too tired to do anything but sip the water and lean my head against the windowpane. I must've dozed off at some point, because when I next opened my eyes, the car had stopped in front of a miniaturized redbrick house that looked almost edible.

I heard my mother's voice through the window: "Up and at 'em, Miriam — your welcome wagon has arrived!"

She was standing on the curb, decked out as unfashionably as ever in tan leggings and a bright orange ASK ME ABOUT MY LOBOTOMY T-shirt. She was also as exuberant as ever, yanking me out of the car and hugging me and blabbing a mile a minute. "Go on, Dagmar," she said to the lanky guy lurking behind her. His hair was dark except for a long, heavily sculpted blond clump at the center of his forehead that made him look like a unicorn. "You can take everything up to the kids' room, that'd be great, *danke, danke, danke* very much!"

Dagmar did as told, and before he was out of earshot, Mom cried, "Isn't he just the most *fabulous* thing you've ever laid eyes on? He's my lab assistant and muse!"

I thought of Quinn with a pang while Mom continued talking. "He grew up in East Berlin, on the other side of the wall, and oh, Bubble Bath, you wouldn't believe how troubled he is! He doesn't talk much yet, but when he does, he uses the most compelling expressions. Just yesterday, he said, oh, now what was it?" She brought her hand to her forehead; I shielded my eyes from her fluorescent T-shirt. "Oh, yes! He told me that meteors aren't the same thing as seltzer water — isn't that absolutely phenomenal? Not that I have any idea what it means, har! You two will get along great, I'm sure. You both have such highly developed verbal skills."

Through heavy lids I watched the tall unicorn boy hump my luggage up the front steps of the house. He was wearing a black leather jacket with about a million zippers and — even better — white jeans with orange stitching. His profile revealed multiple earrings in his left ear, plus a bull nose ring at the center of his face. For another sad instant, Quinn's image floated into my head. If only, if only. Life was completely unfair.

I turned to Mom, who seemed to have changed very little since I'd last seen her three months ago. As always after long absences, I tried to determine if the woman whose womb had once housed me was attractive; her ridiculously frumpy clothes made it difficult to tell. She was five-four, with disproportionately short and stumpy legs but an otherwise narrow frame. She had brown eyes, a ski-jump nose, and thin, perpetually un-made-up lips that never stopped moving. And for as long as I could remember, she'd worn her sandy brown hair in a monkish bowl cut that fell just below her ears.

She was still yammering on when she brought me inside and offered to make me dinner. Not having eaten on the plane, I nodded gratefully and collapsed at the kitchen table. "We're so happy to have you in our little household," Mom said, her back turned as she rummaged through the refrigerator. Maybe, just maybe, she was planning to make me an apple and cheese sandwich — my favorite as a kid. Occasionally, Mom emerged from her manic self-absorption long enough to make such meaningful little gestures.

"Interesting décor you got here," I said, indicating a wall that displayed approximately fifty digital clocks. On the windowsill above the sink were clown figurines and a jar of dirty water with half-dried roses poking out. A few petals had fallen and dispersed around the bottom of the container.

"Mmm-hmm." Mom nodded absently, chopping something on the speckled linoleum counter. She switched on a German learning tape as she cooked. *"Ich möchte gerne ein Elektriker sein,"* she repeated several times, followed by the English translation, "I would like to be an electrician."

Lulled by her repetitive practice, I rested my face on the table and was beginning to relax when a digital version of Bob Marley's "Redemption Song" came booming out of a speaker on the clock wall. I jerked up to see Mom switching off her tape and grinning at me.

"I *knew* you'd get a kick out of this," she said. "They have an internal clock wired up to a sound system so that every hour, on the hour, there'll be a different musical treat."

"So, Miriam, what do you think?" Maurice asked as he bounded into the kitchen. "Your mom told you yet about her plans to sell you into the slave trade?"

At first I thought Maurice was making some weird Bob Marley reference, but then Mom spun around and shot her boyfriend a threatening look. "Not now, Maurice," she said. "We'll discuss it after her nap."

"Discuss what?" I asked, now fully awake.

"Oh, nothing," Mom answered breezily. "Don't pay the joker any attention. This summer is going to be *so* much fun. Tell me what you think," she said, placing a bowl before me. "Just a little something I threw together."

My eyes bulged at the mishmash of unidentifiable white foam, black seeds, cubed tomatoes, and chunks of hard-boiled egg.

"Hold that bite!" Maurice shrieked, though I'd made no move toward the messy concoction. He opened the refrigerator and removed a yellow notepad from the butter shelf. "The eggs were purchased last Saturday, boiled three days ago," he read. Without asking, he stuck his head over my bowl and took a good, long sniff. "All right, then," he said, seemingly satisfied. "These should be safe."

Maurice applauded the results of this risk-free meal, but my appetite was long gone. I took a few tiny bites, thanked Mom, and trudged upstairs to the room that Ariel and I would be sharing when she got back from Spain. Or perhaps I should say *if* she got back from Spain — my nineteen-year-old sister kept postponing her return, and after fifteen minutes in Berlin, I could easily understand why. Ariel's white rapper boyfriend, Decibel, had been paid so much money to DJ a family friend's wedding in Ibiza over Memorial Day that he'd rented a room in a *pensione* for the rest of the month. After three days in Berlin, Ariel had joined her boyfriend on the party island, justifying her defection to my mother as a "totally necessary added-value business move." This past spring, she and Decibel had founded an independent record company in the garage apartment of his parents' Austin home, whereupon Ariel promptly shifted her collegiate obsession from sororities to upstart rap acts.

Our room was furnished sparsely, with two bureaus and unmade twin-size beds. Ariel had marked her territory with a University of Texas pillowcase and Leafy, the green teddy bear she's had since she was a baby. Ariel's silver Nike visor sat on the bureau, perched atop a neat stack of the hot pink terry-cloth sweatsuits she wore everywhere. On the wall, taped at knee height, were two ripped-out pages detailing an "Abs of Granite" crunch program, and on the bedside table an unopened bag of fat-free gummy bears. For as long as I could remember, Ariel had been obsessed with having a perfect body.

I threw my bags down, sat at the edge of the mattress, and kicked off my shoes. Then I settled back to stare up at the ceiling and let the events of the last two hours replay in my head. But I was still too tired, and my thoughts too jumbled.

The latch on my suitcase was jammed, and I couldn't unclasp it until my fourth attempt. The contents sprayed up in the air and poured out onto the floor. So this is what happens when you let Pia pack your bags for you. As I rummaged through the heap, my hand came upon an unfamiliar object. Its surface felt cool and round, like a Magic 8-Ball. I pulled it out from under a tank top to see that it was a snow globe with a piece of folded-up paper taped across it. I peeled off the note, which was in a jagged cavemanlike handwriting I recognized all too well.

M,

I came to say goodbye, but you're still out partying. I want you to know how sorry I am that our last night had to be this way. Sam will chill out soon and everything can be normal again. In the meantime, I hope you know this: every time I see you, I want to jump up and down.

B

P.S. If you don't believe me, shake the stupid thingie. Go on.

I shook the snow globe and saw that the white snowflakes weren't the only objects floating. There was also a little black-and-white drawing encased in clear waterproof coating. It showed Boris with his arms outstretched and a red heart scribbled on his chest. I squinted and brought the snow globe up to my face. It almost looked like he was waving at me. This was one of the nicest things anybody had done for me, ever. Why did he insist on being so hard to hate?

Once in my pajamas, I turned out the lights and lay down on the naked mattress. Then I took the snow globe from the shelf and held on to it, shaking it in the dark. Maybe I was too wound up to trust my own judgment. Maybe, I thought, everything would be just fine. As I put the souvenir aside and started to drift off to sleep, the opening of "Africa Unite" jingled from a speaker overhead, and Maurice's machine-gun laughter rang out from the kitchen.

May Contain Nuts

I ACCEPT FULL RESPONSIBILITY FOR not having spoken much to Mom in the weeks preceding my arrival in Berlin. Whenever she called to discuss summer plans, I'd keep the conversation short with an excuse about homework or a *Bugle* obligation. "I guess we're playing it 'cool teen'?" Mom would tut-tut, pronouncing the last two words with unmistakable air quotes. Then she'd tell me for the thousandth time that when she was my age, she spent summers helping out at her father's dry-cleaning-supply office. "What I would have given to go abroad," she'd rasp. "Back then, we weren't nearly so jaded."

I never bothered denying these allegations, but I didn't feel jaded in the least when I thought about Berlin. No, what I felt was terrified. I knew nothing about Berlin, and I was getting sick of adapting to new places all the time. I'd just survived being the new girl at Baldwin — wasn't that enough adaptation for a year?

And as much as Mom tried to talk up Germany, she tended to avoid specifics. Instead she'd rave about its liberal immigration policies, or its cutting-edge social programs, like the national "Get Happy" billboard campaign geared at energizing Germany's increasingly depressed population.

"How inspiring is *that?*" Mom had asked from Houston, during one of our pre-summer phone calls. She'd learned about the campaign in a recent issue of the *Economist*. "Around here, the only billboards we have are for malls and shooting ranges."

I felt anything but happy when Mom brutally woke me up exactly one hour into my postflight nap. She flipped on the light and announced it was time to discuss my summer plans.

"I'm sleeping," I moaned. "My brain is still stuck somewhere over Greenland. Can it wait until I'm awake?"

"You sound perfectly awake to me," Mom said. "Why don't you get dressed and come downstairs? Maurice has made a *fabulous* German ale soup!"

Maurice's ale soup tasted just as disgusting as it sounds. The alcohol hadn't yet evaporated and the orange peels bobbing up and down in the broth were tough and jagged. At least I'd already given up on the meal when Mom sprang the news on me; otherwise, I might've choked.

She'd evidently taken the liberty of offering my services to one of her colleagues. As a babysitter. "They're adorable, and so bright, too!" Mom said. "Eight-year-old twins."

"What?!" I'd only babysat twice in my entire life, both times for the Friedmans, two of my mom's colleagues at Rice. The first time was an unqualified success: I spent the evening trying on Mrs. Friedman's makeup and gossiping on the phone to my friend Rachel. On the second evening, however, the Friedmans came home early from their departmental dinner to find me passed out on their sofa while the television roared and twenty-month-old Erika waddled around the kitchen holding a blender part.

"I'm serious," I continued, reminding Mom of this baleful incident. "I don't even *like* children. And what happened to my German classes? I thought I was going to be learning an important foreign language. What happened to that?"

"Oh, that." Mom shrugged. "I think it was a misjudgment. Maurice and I decided if you're really gung ho about studying a foreign language, it should be something useful, like Chinese."

"Emerging markets," Maurice said helpfully.

"If it's so useless," I asked, "then why are *you* studying it — can you tell me that?"

"Besides," Mom went on, ignoring my extremely pertinent question, "this'll be a great opportunity. It's so much more *interactive* than sitting around in a sweaty classroom conjugating irregular verbs all summer!"

"And just think," Maurice piped in, "you'll be earning money!"

"Exactly!" Mom cried. "You can save up for some treat you've always wanted, like one of those carcinogenic cellular phones."

"Or a plane ticket to New York," I mumbled.

The next morning, Mom shook me awake for the second time in twelve hours. "Should I start getting used to this?" I asked, casting an appraising glance at today's T-shirt of choice: a heather gray job with the words YOU ARE NOW LEAVING THE AMERICAN SECTOR. God, genetics were such an awful mystery.

"Yep, start living on local time straight off the bat," she said. "It's the only way to beat jet lag."

In the kitchen downstairs, I was pleasantly surprised to find a Maurice-free table that had been set with a pitcher of orange juice and a basket of powdered-sugar-dusted rolls. The pastries were delicious, each with a different filling. As I ate I watched our next-door neighbors through the window, all dressed for the day and seated around their kitchen table as if at a fancy restaurant. Mom made me take my fourth roll (apple and cinnamon) upstairs while I got ready for my first visit to the Teichen Institute. In the car on the way over, I ate my fifth roll (sweet cheese) and marveled at the suburban sinkhole I now called home. Quinn had assured me that Berlin set the standard for all things cutting edge, but he'd surely eat his words if he saw Dahlem, the characterless suburb thirty miles from the city center where Mom and Maurice had chosen to settle.

The Teichen Institute was a forbidding concrete monolith in the Neukolln neighborhood of Berlin, on a street called Karl-Marx-Strasse. When I commented on the institute's resemblance to a high-security prison, Mom only sighed and said, "Oh, Peanut Butter, you have *so* much to learn about Bauhaus."

She'd arranged for me to meet my new charges the morning after my arrival, without giving me a single day to acclimate. Even worse, Mom was too busy with her incomprehensible academic responsibilities to bother sticking around to introduce me to Nathaniel and Joshua Meyerson-Cullen; she left those honors to her assistant, Dagmar. After parking on the mezzanine level of the Teichen Institute's administrative headquarters, she flitted off to do some of her monkey research. The walls in this abandoned waiting area were painted a pukey orange, compounding the feeling of queasiness I'd had since breakfast.

Making small talk with Dagmar was no easy task. I asked him soon after we sat down, "So, do you study monkeys, too?"

"No, I am learning *from* them," he replied cryptically.

Right then, I heard a loud, unmistakably American voice down the hallway. "If I've said it once, I've said it a thousand times," a woman was saying at maximum volume, "it's extremely difficult *and* expensive to obtain Lactaid out here, so BE CAREFUL — especially you, Joshua! If I find you've been sneaking cheese toast behind my back . . . Well, I'd better *not* find out!"

I looked in the direction of the sound to see a middle-aged woman with long Fraggle Rock hair and a loose-fitting beige tunic, holding the hands of two young boys.

The woman recognized me immediately, and as she stomped toward our tiny table, the sick feeling in my stomach moved a few inches up in my throat. I threw Dagmar a desperate glance, which he registered by whispering, inexplicably, "Tomorrow's breakfast is today's scrap metal."

Seeing no alternative, I came shakily to my feet.

"Mimi, right?" the woman boomed, thrusting out her hand at me. "A pleasure to make your acquaintance. I'm Debbie Meyerson-Cullen, Joshua and Nathaniel's mother." She gestured at the boys standing obediently at her sides. They were fraternal twins, each with his own brand of unattractiveness: one pudgy, with his mother's wild hippie hair; the other slight and stooped over, with a thin stream of mucus dripping from nose to lip.

"I've heard all about you, so I know what we're getting. And I take it your mother has filled you in on the job?"

"Actually," I said hesitantly, "she didn't go into much detail."

I paused to smile down at her sons, only to be met with a double blank stare. Glancing back at their mother, I continued, "If you could give me an overview of everything, that'd be —"

"We're here from Newton, Mass," Debbie said, not waiting for me to finish. "My husband, Alan, teaches at Boston University. Right now he's working on a project on technology and violence here at the institute, which is how we met that wonderful mom of yours. I'm a philosophy professor at Northeastern, but this year I'm here purely in the capacity of hausfrau."

At this, Debbie snorted through her nose, overcome by her own hilarity. The woman strongly reminded me of somebody, but I couldn't quite put my finger on who. "No, really. I'm researching Wittgenstein's picture theory — Berlin has invaluable resources on the subject, you wouldn't believe it. Not even Cambridge can come close!" She snorted again, and to avoid the spittle, I took a polite step backward.

How could it not have struck me instantly — she was my mother's long-lost twin. I'd barely said a word, but Debbie Meyerson-Cullen just kept right on talking. One of the boys removed a small box from her bag and proceeded to work on a jigsaw puzzle on the lounge carpet. "You can probably fill in the remainder of the narrative yourself," Debbie told me. "While Alan's in the lab and I'm in the library, we need a responsible party to look out for our boys. Now, they're extremely precocious and the most adept eight-year-old conversationalists I've ever had the pleasure of raising, but there are a few rules and regs I'll need to brief you on nevertheless."

From her gigantic canvas tote bag Debbie whipped out a clear plastic clipboard and took a stapled-together stack of papers off the top, which she passed over to me. AVOIDANCES AND ALLERGIES, the paper read, and was divided into two columns, one headed "Joshua" and the other "Nathaniel." Page two of the handout was a German glossary for words like "pistachio," "garlic," "gluten," and "triglycerides."

In her frenzy, Debbie still hadn't pointed out which child was which, but no doubt I'd learn the difference soon enough. "It all boils down to a few simple rules," she was saying. "Both boys are highly lacto-sensitive, and Nathaniel is allergic to dust, felines, wax, apples, processed sugar, laundry detergent, and a variety of beans — lentils and cannellini in particular, but pintos will go down just fine. Joshua's the one you *really* need to keep an eye on, because he has a severe nut allergy. Sure, you say, sounds pretty straightforward — you're thinking, 'Just say no to nuts'! But let me tell you, you'd be *flabbergasted* by the number of foods that contain nut traces these days. Even a bag of potato chips can be lethal if it's been manufactured in the wrong factory! Not that the boys are allowed to eat chips. What's the point, when the world contains so many foods with nutritional . . ."

By this stage in the monologue, Debbie had abandoned all pretense of actually speaking to me. I veered backward again, toward the chair, as jet lag washed over me, along with maybe even some residual hangover from the grad party two nights before. Suddenly, the room took on a spinning, hallucinogenic quality, and all the while Debbie kept on talking. Like a self-help guru filling airtime on daytime television, I offered myself encouragement and advice. This could be a character-building experience, perhaps a starred item on my college application. At the very least, I'd have some unbeatable e-mail material.

"You'll see I keep a vocabulary list on the refrigerator," Debbie was saying as she dug through her shoulder bag. "That's where I jot down the boys' notable words. Joshua said 'gadfly' the other day. I don't know where in Berlin he picked that one up, but that kid's like a sponge — a bona fide wordsmith dynamo." I assured her I was impressed.

"Oh! Here you go," she said, extracting an ancient cell phone from the sleeve of a sweatshirt. I took the proffered phone, which had buttons with German commands on them. "I'm programmed as Felix," Debbie said. "It's secondhand and I can't figure out how to change the dang names in the directory, so if anything comes up, just call Felix and I'll come a-runnin'."

Debbie then handed me a bag with keys to the Meyerson-Cullen home, a notebook with recommended meal plans, an *Urban-Kinder: Berlin* guidebook, and a safety fanny pack with a compass, a whistle, and a flashlight. I asked her what she was thinking in terms of hours. "Well, something like nine to five," she replied. "But it being the summer and all, let's take things loosey-goosey, OK? That's not interfering with any plans, is it?"

Before I could think better of it, I admitted that, having just arrived in Berlin, I didn't have much of a life here yet.

"Super!" Debbie exclaimed. "We don't like our babysitters to have lives." She cackled kookily, then promptly resumed issuing instructions and commands and safety warnings. A chill passed over me as I realized I'd be working for a madwoman. Why oh why would my mother do this to me?

"And now I'm off to do some reading at the library," she said. "I trust you can see my little wizards safely to the house? It's right down the street, and they have the route memorized!"

Gritting my teeth, I waved goodbye to Debbie and allowed Joshua and Nathaniel to march me outside the institute. They each gripped one of my hands and tugged me along like an unruly Doberman. "How long have you guys lived here?" I asked. Not the most brilliant question, I'll admit, but I needed a conversation-starter.

"A year," one said in a colorless voice.

"A month," intoned the other.

"Ten years."

"Ten billion years."

"Infinity years."

"Google-cubed decades!"

Oh, brother. If I'd had a free arm, I surely would've gripped my forehead right about now. The Meyerson-Cullen twins were as bad as their mother — worse, if possible. "You guys should go on *Saturday Night Live*," I told them, not altogether kindly.

"I like Tuesday Night Live better!"

"No, I like Wednesday Afternoon Live!"

"What about Sunday Morning Live?"

They kept up this hilarious routine until we reached the drab apartment block where they lived. I was inserting the key in the lock when a voice behind me bellowed: "Surprise! You're on *Candid Camera!*"

"What's that?" I asked the boys, then turned to see Debbie Meyerson-Cullen a few yards behind us, crouched beside a bushy tree. "Just wanted to see if you'd find your way," she said happily. "You've done an A-plus job. I knew I could have faith. This is going to be a top-notch summer!"

"Mom! You're back — hip-hip, hooray!" The frizzy-haired twin released his sweaty palm from my grip and loped toward her.

Still at my side, the runny-nosed one observed, "Mother, you're behaving kind of stalkerishly right now."

"Stalkerishly." Debbie shook her head in wonderment. "Magnificent word choice! See how lucky you are, Mimi? Please don't forget to add that one to the vocab list on the fridge."

With those final instructions, Debbie waved and skipped off down the street.

From: "Vrock2000"
To: "Mimicita86"
Date: June 16, 4:32 p.m.
Subject: Miss u already

Hey babes, greetings from the sweaty big apple. Just wanted to reach out and let u know we miss you. The left behind girls (lily, jess & i) went bathing suit shopping at Century 21 and guess who we ran into? That's right, Yuri Knutz, everyone's favorite Russian Dissident Fiction/ Indigenous Crafts teacher. He was there looking at padded bikinis — by himself! He must have an exciting summer ahead of him. Oh, yeah, and I'm attaching a pic of us modeling our new swimwear on Long Beach. See the lifeguard in the background? Fast asleep the whole time. But kind of a hottie, no?

Vivian

To: "HWYates"
From: "Mimicita86"
Date: June 19, 10:08 p.m.
Subject: none

Hi, Harriet,

I just wanted to send you a very jet-lagged thank-you for having me at your engagement (!) party. Not to repeat myself, but I'm REALLY happy for you and Ed. It's inspiring that you've waited so long for Mr. Right. Maybe there's hope for me after all! I've been in Germany for a little under a week, and all I can say is: so far, so bad. I got roped into babysitting for these eight-year-old robot kids from Massachusetts. Don't want to say anything too mean, but I'm hoping their personalities are still in the development stage. Their mom is insanely demanding and gives me very little time to myself. Mom's manic as usual, and her boyfriend, Maurice, is driving me crazy with his imagined health problems. He's spent the last few days convinced he's suffering from early-onset Alzheimer's, but every time I ask him for an example of something he can't remember, he says he forgets and starts freaking out again. Anyway, fingers crossed the fun quotient increases soon . . . Hope you didn't have too big a mess to clean up, and write when you can.

XXOX Mimi

Wyomophobia

ONLY A WEEK INTO MY POST CHEZ Meyerson-Cullen, and I was already fantasizing about getting into a freak accident. Nothing deadly, obviously, just something tragic enough to keep me strapped to a hospital bed until school started. I'd already tried about eight hundred times to tell Mom how dire my situation was, but she was usually too busy repeating, "*Habt Ihr ein Schwimmbad?* Is there a swimming pool?" to heed my complaints.

One morning at breakfast, I caught her before she'd switched on her E-Z German tape. "Oh, Mimi," she said, "if you don't watch it, you're going to end up like your sister — completely checked out from reality. Next you'll tell me you'd rather be disco-dancing in Ibiza!"

"Yes," I cried, "as a matter of fact, I *would!* I'd give my firstborn child to science if I could be doing *anything* in Ibiza! My job is beyond horrible, Mom. I really hate it."

"Oh, don't be silly," Mom said, reaching for her *501 German Verbs* book. "If you want horrible, try reading that *Woman in Berlin* book I gave you. What a time they had when the Russians took over! Maybe that'll put some of your misery in perspective."

"I don't want perspective, I want salvation!"

"Care Bear, you're a sixteen-year-old babysitter. Forgive me if I'm having trouble feeling sorry for you, but you're not the first, and I'm pretty sure you won't be the last."

Point taken; my life could be worse. Some people have to be coal miners or spend their lives watching chicken nuggets come down a factory conveyor belt. But that didn't make babysitting the hyperallergic twins anything approximating a dream job. The boys were not only obnoxious, but completely unappeasable as well. If I suggested a trip to the zoo, one would frown and remind me of his allergy to polar bear fur. If I suggested a walk in the park, the other would bring up his pollen allergy. I offered to take the twins to museums, puppet theaters, and the Dahlem City Farm, but they shot down every idea. They were sensitive to fluorescent lighting, felt, and hay. Of course — how could I have forgotten?

One day, Joshua surprised me by proposing a trip to the nearby St. Annen-Kirche. "Puleeeeze?" he said. "Our parents take us there all the time." Now, I'm no great church buff, but I agreed readily, even enthusiastically. When we got there, the twins made me wait outside while they went to the men's room. They reappeared ten minutes later, red-faced and sniveling, and told me, through tears, that the stalls had been filthy. "We have to go home," Nathaniel crowed. I offered to buy them ice cream, but with a cry of lactose intolerance they insisted on leaving at once.

We spent most days in the family room of the Meyerson-Cullens' dank little faculty apartment. Joshua and Nathaniel weren't even normal enough to watch TV or play video games. Instead they amused themselves with Boggle and a game called

Mouse that involved crawling under the couch and making high-pitched squeaking sounds. Both boys could study fractions for hours, contentedly ignoring me until I dared pick up a book or pull out my journal. If I demonstrated interest in anything other than the brothers, they'd brutally reproach me.

"Don't be a deadbeat babysitter," one would say.

"Yeah, this is supposed to be an educational social environment," the other would put in. "How can we learn if you're neglecting our blossoming intellects?"

Mostly I just stared out the window, fixing my gaze on the radio tower in the distance and daydreaming about flinging myself off it. Twice Mom urged me to accompany her and Maurice to extremely unfun-sounding cultural events — a choral concert and a Bach organ recital — being held inside a bombed-out church on the Kurfürstendamm, the world-famous shopping street that I, of course, had yet to visit. I declined both invitations, anxious only to get back to the gingerbread house and lose myself in e-mail. From Maurice's prehistoric laptop, I read about Jess's internship, the beginning of Viv's hiking expedition, and Pia's and Lily's far more satisfying European adventures. Boris wrote annoyingly impersonal and short messages about the new restaurants and cheeses he had discovered. Sam, more comfortable on e-mail than he'd been in person over the past year, even sent me a few messages.

But no one wrote often enough, and in my loneliness, I turned to the spam messages a deposed Ugandan prince was sending me; anything to distract me from the eight-year-old terrors of Dahlem. "At least you're earning stone cold euros," Jess had written in one message. I didn't tell her that not only had I not been paid; after two weeks, I still didn't even know what my wages were.

"Mom, I hate to sound like a broken record, but this babysitting gig isn't really working out," I said over our sauerkraut-accented dinner a few days after our last fruitless conversation on the subject. "Lily's mom knows somebody at the Berlin bureau of CNN. I might talk to them about volunteering or something."

"Oh, Seashell, relax — you don't want to be stuck at some desk all summer. You couldn't possibly be bored — what about that wonderful book I lent you about Frederick the Great? You should spend the day outside in a garden just reading and relaxing — the weather's absolutely stunning."

I tried to explain that I had no time to loiter in public gardens with Joshua and Nathaniel in tow, but Mom only said, "That's exactly what you should do! What better way to learn the city than running around with a couple of natives?"

"Mom," I groaned, "they're not natives. They're from Newton, Massachusetts! And besides, they're convinced the sun, moon, stars, and clouds are going to harm them, so we *never* go outside. I'm completely losing my —"

"It'll get better," Mom said placidly, then switched on one of her E-Z German tapes.

"You always tell me you want me to be more communicative, Mom," I went on desperately. "How much more communicative can I be? Here's what I'm trying to say: I'm having the worst summer of my life. I haven't met a single person, or gone *any*where except under the Meyerson-Cullens' couch, where I'm supposed to pretend to be a squeaky rodent on the loose."

"Mimi, I hear what you're saying, and I can *identify* with your frustrations. But a little change of routine will be good for you after New York, I promise . . ."

As she spoke, the man on the E-Z German tape said, *"Es ist viertel nach zwei.* It's a quarter past two." Mom, raising her index fingers to her temples and shutting her eyes, repeated the sentence: *"Es ist viertel nach zwei.* It's a quarter past two."

"Can you not shut your eyes when we're in the middle of a conversation?"

"Sorry," Mom said, her eyes still closed. "I read that it aids memory retention."

"Good God," I said as my forehead sank onto my map of Europe placemat.

Mom repeated a few more time expressions before pausing the tape. "So are we done with the Joan of Arc act?" she asked. "Because I've been meaning to tell you — Dagmar asked if you were available tomorrow night."

"Why?" I lifted my head off the placemat. "Does he need a white slave, too?"

"Can it, Mimi. His friend has a gallery opening, and you're invited."

I was immediately suspicious. "Really? Why didn't he ask me himself, then?"

"Well, if you're going to get technical, I was the one who suggested it. But he didn't object."

"He *didn't object?* What kind of invitation is that?"

Mom dropped a slip of paper with Dagmar's number onto the table, and I swiped it away. But when her back was turned, I stuck it in my pocket. For the rest of the day, I found myself wondering about Dagmar's life away from the rhesus monkeys, and in bed that night, I pictured the two of us dancing on top of a white baby grand at a cabaret lounge while *le tout* Berlin clapped admiringly. I decided to accept the invitation, and by the next morning, I was off-the-charts excited and showed up for work already in party costume — a jean miniskirt, blue fishnets, and a rainbow-striped tube top. I'd thrown one of Decibel's huge sweatshirts over it to avoid provoking Debbie's disapproval.

Of course, she barely looked at me. Even if I'd been wearing nothing but a bicycle chain, she probably wouldn't have noticed anything irregular. Even more typically, when I started to explain that I had plans that evening and needed to leave by seven-thirty, Debbie talked over my request — the first I'd made in two weeks. Luckily, her husband, Alan, was also in the room at the time, and Alan had taken an inexplicable liking to me. I liked him, too, mainly because I felt sorry for him, with his huge frameless eyeglasses and insanely controlling wife.

"I put a box of gentle Ziploc baggies on the kitchen table," Debbie announced on her way to the door. "Use only those for Nathaniel, because he's sensitive to the regular ones. For Joshua, the regular ones are fine. The special ones cost an arm and a leg, so don't waste 'em!"

"Can you be back by seven-thirty?" I asked again.

While Debbie conveniently ignored me, Alan went out of his way to reassure me. "Don't you worry, Mimi," he said. "We'll get you out of here in no time."

Now, I don't think Alan was intentionally lying, but he

should've known he was in no position to be making promises like that. He had about as much sway over his wife as King Arthur had over Lady Bird Johnson.

They didn't come home at seven-thirty. Or eight-thirty. Or even nine-thirty. No, they came home at ten. Though by this point I was frantic and seething, Debbie *still* made me follow her into the kitchen and estimate how many ounces of chicken salad each of the boys had eaten for dinner. Too ashamed to make eye contact, Alan sat down and pretended to read *Everything Pasta Macrobiotic!*

Luckily, when I called Dagmar for the tenth time that night, he was still at home gelling up his unicorn horn and told me, "We are never partying before crack of midnight." We arranged to meet at the local McDonald's and walk to the Dahlem-Dorf U-Bahn station together. Strange as it sounds, after two weeks in Berlin, I'd yet to ride the subway.

When I showed up at McDonald's, Dagmar was already there, dipping the last of his fries in an unfamiliar yellow sauce. He stood up, brushed the crumbs off his all-black ensemble, and kissed me on both cheeks. I complimented him on his spunky pink rubber backpack. He told me I looked "equally jubilating."

Our U-Bahn journey from the southwest to the eastern extreme of the city took over an hour, but the time passed quickly with Dagmar, who turned out to be an extremely engaging companion. I felt loose, and ended up telling him about my plan to meet Boris at the airport the following day. "You say he visits you tomorrow?" He raised his eyebrows curiously. "This seems to me most excellent."

"Not visiting, exactly. I'm seeing him for his layover. He's going to Moscow to stay at his grandparents' dacha, where all they do is plant vegetables and drink vodka."

"Ah, wodka!" Dagmar said. "Wodka is very harmful for the monogamy."

I asked Dagmar about the neighborhood where we were heading. Friedrichshain, he told me, was formerly part of East Germany and now was the city's hottest clubbing area. "The new spot changes always," he said. "The parties commence in abandoned warehouses and disappear one month later. The most excellent are the *de Zegunde* parties. They are thrown by the two most major DJs from Hamburg, who play the music of beautiful violins."

"Violins, really?" I hadn't figured Dagmar for a classical music lover.

"No, no, *violence*." He karate-chopped the air until I understood. "Beautiful violence."

The train finally pulled into our station, and we stepped out into Ostbahnhof, a succession of brightly lit streets thrumming with elegant couples and teenage girls in short, expensive-looking dresses. On every street corner, men stood behind little carts, peddling aromatic pretzels. Though Mom and the Meyerson-Cullens were still in the same city, or at least one of its unprepossessing suburbs, right then I felt very far away from them, delightfully so.

The scenery grew dingier as we neared Friedrichshain, where nineteenth-century limestone buildings gave way to tan apartment complexes and shabby minimarkets. We passed a few places that seemed cool, including the Lee Harvey Oswald Bar, which was painted red and white and filled with monitors playing a loop of Kennedy's assassination. "That's where all the Americans conspire," Dagmar said with a note of disgust.

A few blocks later, I flipped for the Astro-Bar, a little hole in the wall with ancient computers hanging from the ceiling. "Look!" I said, peering inside. "This is so geeky — I love it! Can we go in?"

"No way," Dagmar said. "If we miss Fred's show, he will make fritters of us."

Minutes later, we came to a large warehouse marked only by a tiny red light over the door. For an underground art party in Berlin's most avant-garde district, the atmosphere inside was surprisingly friendly. I'd expected pale skin and sullen expressions, but everyone was smiling or laughing, or everyone except Dagmar's close friend Werner.

"Hallo, Mimi," Werner said flatly when we were introduced. His huge yellow teeth and black leather newsboy cap called to mind an extra in a George Michael video — not, as he soon revealed, a pediatric orthodontist who spoke decent English. "How do you know Fred?" he asked me. "He is my very proximate friend."

"Fred's the painter, right?" I said. "I've never met him, actually — I came here with Dagmar."

"Oh, *ja*? And how do you know the Dag?" Werner pursued.

"Through my mother."

"Your *mother* introduced you to the Dag?" At Werner's shocked expression, I quickly explained that Dagmar was my mother's assistant. "Oh, *ja*," Werner said excitedly, "she is the lady studying monkeys? I hear some funny mentions of this woman."

By this point, Dagmar had detached from us, leaving Werner and me to stroll around the space and look at the paintings, a striking series of landscapes in thick oils.

"These are great," I told Werner, and asked if he'd introduce me to Fred. "I want to congratulate him."

"No, this is hardly possible," Werner snapped. "Fred wishes not to discuss his art. It reduces him into the pothole of low emotions."

While most pictures, he went on to explain, were of the Black Forest, a few were imaginative renderings of Wyoming, complete with jagged mountains and emerald bushes. "It is very devastating," Werner said. "All Fred has ever wanted is to travel to the state of Wyoming, but he is unable because of his hang-up."

"What hang-up?" I asked.

"Me, I am not a psychiatrist, I do not know the name. But Fred has bought tickets to Wyoming three times and yet he never has gone there."

"So he's afraid of flying?"

"No, no, not of flying. His girlfriend lives in Turkey and he is making two visits to her every month. He is afraid, I am thinking, of Wyoming."

As Werner spoke, Dagmar came up with his arm around a woman who had a skunk dye job similar to his own. Before Dagmar could introduce us, the girl said something in German and, within seconds, we were all heading out to the street and piling into a tiny green car. Werner hooked up his iPod to the car's stereo, and put on a song for us at brain-piercing volume. The music sounded like your standard techno melody, but fringed with drilling dentistry noises. "Do you like?" Werner shouted into my eardrum.

"It's interesting!" I shouted back.

My enthusiastic response pleased Werner, who settled back into his seat and resumed head-dancing.

Ships at Night

My NIGHT OUT WITH ĐAGMAR belongs on some all-time top-five list. After the art opening, we went to a club, where I danced until I nearly collapsed, and then I kept dancing until I did collapse. As the sun started to rise, I rested on a barstool, chatting with Werner, while Dagmar and the two-tone woman continued to grind on the dance floor.

When I got out of the cab and entered the house, around six the next morning, Mom and Maurice were fast asleep. Once upstairs, I crawled into bed and fondly reviewed memories of my night on the town. Though still no Quinn, Dagmar *was* pretty cool in his insane Germanic way. I couldn't wait until Ariel and Decibel returned to party with us.

I'd just fallen asleep when the phone rang. It rang and rang and rang and when at last it stopped ringing my mom began knocking on my bedroom door: "Mimi! Phone!" she cried, crashing into the room and catapulting herself onto my bed. "That was Debbie. She's frantic. It's nine-fifteen — why aren't you over there already?"

"What do mean — why aren't I where?" I asked, still barely conscious. "I'm not working today. It's Saturday. I'm meeting Boris at the airport, remember?"

Mom pursed her lips primly. "Well, I'm afraid Debbie is under quite another impression. She says you were supposed to be there at nine and was *very* confused when you didn't show! But don't worry, they're on their way over right now, to save time."

"But Mom, I told her a million times that I was busy today. She almost ruined my plans with Dagmar last night — I refuse to let her ruin today, too! Boris will only be here for three hours, and I won't see him again all summer!" I was whining, but I didn't care.

My mom had never met Boris before, but she displayed no interest in the implication that I had a boyfriend. Instead, she just said, "Mimi, I'm glad you've made new friends so fast, but maybe it's time you refocused on personal responsibility."

"But Mom, it's the weekend! And since when was looking after two of the creepiest boys ever to walk the earth an act of personal responsibility? Don't I owe it to myself to be happy?"

"Mimi, I understand it might be hard when all your charmed New York friends have such fancy summer plans, but I'm afraid this is what life's like for ninety-nine-point-nine percent of the population."

I regarded my mother with pure loathing, the depths of which I'd never really experienced before, even in the months after she left my dad. So this was it, then — she really was the pettiest tyrant of them all. Her whole out-of-it, professorial, head-in-the-clouds routine was that and only that: a routine. Deep down, Mom was a power-obsessed control freak who wouldn't rest until she dominated me every second of every day for the rest of my life.

At the time, the night before had seemed like a much-needed reprieve from the unpleasantness of my summer, but now, in the aftermath, I felt more cooped up than ever. This couldn't go on. I had to figure out a way to get out of here, and fast. I threw on a comfortable tank dress that Boris had once complimented me on and went downstairs to eat my regular breakfast of orange juice and birdseed muesli.

I must have blocked out the sound of the phone ringing, because while I was rinsing out my dish, Mom hollered down to let me know that Alan had called to say they'd be five minutes late. "I love you, Alan," I mumbled, and lunged toward Maurice's huge laptop, waiting out the slow Internet connection in a last-ditch effort to contact Boris before his plane took off. It was late, but he might still get my desperate message in time.

> My magical Russian prince,
> SOS!
> Am trapped in castle with reggae-playing cuckoo clocks
> and wickedest of witches. Please rescue ASAP. Will see
> you in Terminal 3 at 3. I'll be the cowgirl in arrivals.
> Moo & Xox
> Mimi

I realized, obviously, that Boris couldn't possibly rescue me. He was off to spend a summer in a dacha outside of Saint Petersburg with his high-living, non-English-speaking grandparents. Boris had his own all-Slavic social scene there, and his father was a certifiable psychopath. Still, it did sound absurdly romantic, a summer on the wide-open steppes of Russia with my towering towheaded boyfriend.

After writing Boris, I quickly scrolled through my new messages. My friends' reports were pretty much the same. Pia was still living it up in Lake Como, playing tennis by day and hanging out in overpriced restaurants with the spawn of internationally known socialites by night. Jess was falling out of love with banking (and Trevor, her coworker) but not with her writing course; Viv was cruising around Oregon in a five-star tour bus.

Mom entered the kitchen and suggested I wait for the Meyerson-Cullens outside, but I just nodded vaguely and didn't move. I was reading a fascinating note from Lily, and nothing could pry me away from it. She was fully established in the "ridiculously huge and disorganized mansion" of her mother's old friends in London. She'd written,

> By the way, the Foxes love to have young people
> around, and they've extended an open invitation to ANY
> of my friends who want to shack up here with me this
> summer. After hearing about your Serge Z. exploits,
> Phillipa (the mom — a.k..a. Miss Hot Shit Social
> Connection) said what a shame you weren't here — she
> could land you an internship at her friend's magazine
> (this woman knows everyone — the prime minister
> included!). The magazine's called the *Muckraker* and it's
> like the *Bugle* — if the *Bugle* were about old politicians

who keep getting caught with their pants down. You'd
love it! Think it over, seriously.

Before I could consider this most seductive of offers, a succession of honks sounded from outside and my mom brayed my name. "MIMI! The Meyerson-Cullens are outside. Picking you up was way out of their way, so hop to it!"

When I got into the Meyerson-Cullens' minivan — the clunkiest vehicle in all of Europe — I was pleased to see Alan behind the wheel and no sign of Debbie. Alan was much nicer than his wife; perhaps he'd understand the urgency of my situation this afternoon, particularly after letting me down the night before. After listening to him detail Debbie's plans to load up on junipers at a discount garden-supply store in the suburbs, I explained that I had to be at the airport at three o'clock sharp.

Instead of shaking his head, or admitting his complete powerlessness, Alan actually volunteered to drive me out there. "I'll swing by for you at two-fifteen," he said. "That should give us plenty of time."

My eyes teared up in gratitude to poor Alan, who hadn't exactly lucked out in the wife-and-children department. "Thank you," I said. Then, under my breath, "You're a good man."

But by two-forty-five that afternoon, I was feeling less charitable toward him. The Meyerson-Cullens still hadn't returned from the plant nursery. How dare they prioritize a plant-buying expedition over the most important event of my entire summer? Joshua and Nathaniel were sprawled on the living room floor, one doing a prism worksheet and the other an acrostic. I lay between them, too tired to do anything with the logic games book they'd given me except drool all over it. It was like hell, only worse.

I tried to reach my mother, but she and Maurice were evidently out enjoying the unseasonably cool afternoon, and it went straight to voice mail. Then I called the Meyerson-Cullens' cell phones, but neither of them picked up either. When Debbie and Alan finally strolled back into the house, it was almost three-thirty. The twins leaped off the floor and ambushed their mother with hugs.

"All right, kiddo," Alan said to me. "I know we're a little pressed for time, but hold up for a sec. I gotta take some Rolaids."

As he stepped into the bathroom, I couldn't stop myself from crying out, "It's three-thirty already and you *promised* you'd be on time!"

But Alan had turned on the bathroom fan and was humming to himself as I raged and fumed on the other side of the door. I guess total obliviousness really was the only way to survive his marriage.

I was already buckled up into the passenger seat when Alan sauntered casually out of the house, in no apparent hurry. As I sat there inhaling and exhaling, looking again and again at my watch, Alan took his sweet time transporting batch after batch of miniature pots of greens from the back seat of the car to the open garage. When he finally got behind the wheel, he regarded me with surprise. "Don't you worry, Mimi. Berlin has such efficient highways, you'd need to bring your own Krazy Glue to get stuck in traffic." He revved up the engine and pulled out of the driveway, still without having apologized for his tardiness. "You look a little beat," Alan said lightly. "What say we stop somewhere and grab a coffee?"

I just barely refrained from screaming, What is *wrong* with you? Shut up and drive, you selfish lunatic! Instead, I pointedly glanced at my watch and said through gritted teeth, "Thanks, but I think we should just get going."

"You're not *catching* a plane. There's this place right down the —"

"I'm *fine*," I snapped. "I'll get something at the airport. Can we just hurry?"

"Okaaaaaay." Alan sounded hurt, but in the emotionally dense tradition of his family, he soon got over it. "Say," he said pleasantly, "I was thinking maybe, if Debbie can spare you, you could swing by the institute tomorrow morning. I'm running a panel on the intersection of technology and personal lives, with a focus on text messaging and trauma and all that jazz. I'm expecting a lot of students, maybe some . . ." He took a short, thirsty breath. "There might be people closer to your age. You could drop by."

"Sounds really great," I said, unable to contain my sarcasm. "I hear cell phones are the wave of the future." I was trying very hard not to let on the degree of my stress, or observe too closely the car's grindingly slow progress along the clogged feeder road. Outside the window, the scenery alternated between the same discount supermarket and the same blackened industrial plant.

My time with Boris was shrinking and shrinking, and there wasn't a thing I could do about it. It wasn't until we passed a sign with a picture of an airplane that I eased back into my seat and stretched out my legs, the better to view the coarse brown hairs scattered across my shins. If nothing else, I certainly was adapting to local fashion.

"No fretting allowed," Alan said after missing the lane for terminal three a second time. "The customs officials here are thorough to a fault. Last time I waited in line, I read an entire issue of *Popular Science* and reprogrammed my PDA. Scout's honor — your friend won't be out in arrivals until five."

"You really think so?"

"At the earliest — I guarantee it. Oh, and before you run away, here." Alan reached into his pocket and pulled out a fifty-euro bill. "For snacks," he said.

I gaped, unable to decide if I was furious or overjoyed. Was this all the Meyerson-Cullens planned on paying me for the last two weeks? Or was this just an under-the-table tip?

When I looked at Alan, he answered my unspoken questions with a wink. "Promise you won't tell Debs," he said.

I thanked him profusely, failing to conceal my all-out astonishment.

At four-fifteen, when I stepped into the glowing white womb of terminal three and found no spiky-haired Russian giant awaiting me, I began breathing normally again, soothed by the certainty that I'd beaten him there. I ordered a cheese strudel stick and settled into the closest café. And I waited. At five, I bought a copy of the *International Herald Tribune* and occupied myself until five-thirty. By six, when Boris still hadn't appeared, I felt my chest constrict about four hundred times. The arrivals monitor indicated that his plane had landed on time, the departures monitor that his flight to Saint Petersburg was still scheduled for a seven-forty departure. Where else could he be?

I combed the concourse, but it was too crowded; I could barely see three inches ahead of me. As I elbowed my way through the mob, I bumped into women in turbans, vendors on their cigarette breaks, waxy-haired businessmen. And then, just as I was about to give up, I saw a promising sign over the sea of heads. My heart gave a little leap. It wasn't Boris, but a man in black holding a placard that said "Potassnick."

"Potasnik! Potasnik!" I cried, pushing toward the cab driver.

The mustached man smiled at me, then thrust a carbon-copy receipt into my hands. All the words were in German, but I could read the two that mattered: "Agatha Potassnick." Unless Boris and his father were traveling with a long-lost third cousin, there was no Agatha in their party. I closed my eyes, but the room kept on spinning; the background noise rose and fell in my ear like the slide of a trombone. Somehow, I lowered myself into a chair and, hunching forward, pulled my legs tight against my chest. Now that Boris wouldn't be seeing them, who cared how furry they were?

How to Go from Crazy to Craziest in Sixty Minutes

Too DRAINED TO NAVIGATE BERLIN'S BYZANTINE public transportation system, I did the spoiled-brat thing and took a taxi all the way back to Dahlem. Alan's gift just covered the fare back to Mom and Maurice's ridiculous gingerbread house. But instead of retreating upstairs to my room, I simply crumpled on the living room couch and began crying. The anticipation of Boris's brief visit had sustained me since landing in the Fatherland, and now — poof! — I had nothing. I brought a cushion to my mouth and chomped on its corner to muffle my sobs.

Not five minutes after I got back, the front door opened and in walked Mom and Maurice, who were too busy arguing about a German-language movie they'd just seen to notice the bawling teenager on the couch. Evidently, the film hadn't had any subtitles, and neither of them could figure out the plot.

"I'm sorry, Dr. Doodles," Mom said, employing yet another new nickname for her paramour, "but there is no way in Hades they were brother and sister. How would the bicycle scene have worked out? They were *obviously* strangers."

"OK, whatever you say," Maurice grumbled condescendingly. "They weren't brother and sister and it wasn't a sci-fi movie." He let off a chuckle and padded into the kitchen. Mom followed close on his heels, still defending her theory.

"Maurice, I hate to break it to you, but you dozed through the pivotal plot point."

"It was just for one minute, and I did not *doze!* I was resting my eyes. Besides, even if I *was* dozing — which I most certainly was not — who could blame me? These mattresses here are made of pebbles — they're *killing* my lower back."

"I know, our bed *is* a bit Soviet," I heard Mom say, then: "Have you tried Ariel's? It's practically Posturepedic. Maybe you should give it a whirl tonight."

My eyes bugged out. Did Mom really just suggest that Maurice give Ariel's bed, the bed five inches away from mine, a *whirl?* I nearly projectile-vomited my cheese strudel stick across the room.

When, a few dazed minutes later, the phone rang, I jumped. I knew it was Boris, calling to explain the mix-up. Maybe he'd missed the flight; maybe we could still meet up tomorrow. But when Mom exclaimed, "Well, *guten Nacht,* Debbie!" I felt nauseated again. The few glimmers of hope I still had made a beeline for the exit door. "How are — what is it? What happened? She didn't . . . Oh my. Hold on a minute, Debbie. Let's see if I can locate her."

I looked up to see my mom marching toward me. She was nodding, flinching, and murmuring, "Uh-huh, mm-hmm" all the while. "I'm very sorry about this, Debbie, but I think it'd be better if you resolved the issue directly with her. She's right here — hang tight."

And then, though I was vigorously shaking my head, mouthing "NO! NO!" my mom handed me the phone and trotted right back into the kitchen.

"Hell —" I said, and before I got to the "o," Debbie unleashed the torrent.

"Have you not listened to a single thing I've told you?" was her opening salvo, followed by a tirade of insults and accusations about my "inexcusable behavior" that the boys had only just brought to her attention. My crime: Beating the boys? *Nein.* Starving them and making them massage my feet all day long? Double *nein.* Taking the boys for a ten-minute stroll to the St. Annen-Kirche? Bingo.

"B-but," I broke in weakly, "Joshua said you took them there all the time!"

My feeble self-defense only ignited Debbie's fury. "I understand you're not a parent, Mimi, but what I don't understand is why you'd do something this disrespectful and potentially destructive. We're just trying to protect our only children," she added somberly. "It may sound trivial to you, but *very* unsalubrious characters loiter around that church — I simply cannot believe you would permit our boys to roam there unsupervised!"

Then, with no warning, Debbie started to moan, a low, plaintive sound that a dying cow might make.

"Debbie, listen, please, I had no idea. I *never* would've done something I thought you —"

"I'm sure you wouldn't," she said harshly. "You've made it clear from day one that your heart isn't in this." She then proceeded to charge me with various crimes of personality. I was too passive. I wasn't playful. I wasn't creative. And then came the real deal breaker: I wasn't kind.

By this point in the conversation, tears were streaming down my face. I'd never doubted Debbie's insanity, but I'd underestimated her capacity for cruelty.

She was still berating me when the clock struck eight and the strains of Peter Tosh's "Legalize It" echoed through the house. Rather than provide welcome comic relief, the digitalized reggae anthem only underscored how intolerable my situation had become. If I stayed in Dahlem, I'd very likely lose my mind. My family would have to lock me up in a state institution, and I'd spend the rest of my life shuffling around in terry-cloth slippers and playing solitaire on wicker lawn furniture.

The second I managed to get a word in, I told Debbie we should talk later, when she was less emotional, and then hung up the phone without waiting for her response. Once I'd stopped crying, I teetered up the stairs and tapped on the door of the master bedroom, where Mom and Maurice had retreated. They were lying over the covers, watching a German home improvement show.

"Mom," I said, all cool and in control, "do you have a second to talk?"

The phone started to ring. "Will you grab that, Mimi?" she asked me without looking up.

Reluctantly, I picked up the receiver and stood still as Debbie Meyerson-Cullen lobbed insults at me. When I could no longer take it, I pretended that somebody had dialed a wrong number and hung up, and I knew with great certainty that I would never see the Meyerson-Cullens again. I felt a little bad about leaving poor Alan in the lurch, but not *that* bad. If I stuck around any longer, Amnesty International might need to get involved.

"Mom, please come downstairs with me," I said. "We need to have this conversation in private, just the two of us."

"I don't think now is a good time. It's crystal clear what's going on here, Mimi. You're upset with Debbie and you're taking it out on me. Ever hear of transference?"

"MOM, if you don't come downstairs RIGHT NOW, I swear to God you'll never see me again!"

"If you're going to address me like that, I think I'll pass, thanks."

Was she serious? Was anyone *that* dense? At my limit, I hurled the phone across the room. It grazed the top of Maurice's bureau and sent several of his pill bottles flying. One of the vials opened midflight, and blue tablets sprayed all over the rug.

Mom raised her left eyebrow and said, in a kindergarten teacher voice, "Now, you know I've never discouraged self-expression, but aren't there more positive ways of pursuing it?"

"You're right," I replied, and charged downstairs to execute my escape plan.

Part one went without a hitch: I picked up the phone and called Lily, who answered on the first ring. "Mimi!" she cried. "How funny — I was just telling Pippa here about you and the hyperallergenic boys. How's the pollen?"

"Lily," I said, gnawing down on my lip. "I need to get out of here. You have to help me."

Lily promised to work on it. "I think I can manage something," she said. "I'll get back to you right away."

I assumed "right away" meant tomorrow if I was lucky, but Lily wasn't the only daughter of a self-made home-decorating tycoon for nothing. Ten minutes later, she called back to inform me that I had a job interview Tuesday morning, and a bedroom for as long as I needed it. "I've never seen the Foxes this psyched," she said. "They seem to think they're saving you from child slavery, and I guess they want to brag about it to their friends. Everything's ready and waiting for you — bed, food, employment. All you need is a ticket. You can book a flight online. Some of the sketchier airlines charge, like, ten dollars."

"But wait," I said, "What about money for everything else? I think I have twelve dollars to my name."

"Oh, don't even think about it. I'll lend you whatever you need to tide you over before your first paycheck."

"Paycheck?"

"Trust me, when you're a friend of the Foxes, the world is good to you. At least London is."

As promised, U-GoJet's flights were affordable in the extreme. It cost over a hundred dollars to fly to London's Heathrow Airport, but flights to the smaller, more out-of-the-way Stansted Airport were dirt-cheap — about the price of a medium latte. I grabbed Maurice's wallet from the kitchen counter and took out his Visa. He'd undoubtedly notice the charge, but by then it'd be too late: I'd be long gone. The contents of my stomach swirled as I clicked on an itinerary and checked my e-mail while the program searched for an available seat. That was when I read this disturbing message:

From: "Apotasnik"
To: "Mimicita86"
Date: June 30, 2:06 p.m.
Subject: Attn Cowgirl!

Mimi, I'm writing from my dad's BlackBerry. We're in the cab going to JFK and I just realized how royally I've screwed up. Our stopover is not in Berlin, but in Frankfurt!!! I know zilcho of German geography, but any chance you can make it out to the city of hot dogs? Will keep eyes peeled . . .
Missing you . . . Boris
P.S. don't write back to this address unless you have something to tell my pops

This message was sent by my BlackBerry.

An hour ago — even five minutes ago — this message might have sent me over a cliff. But that was before I'd successfully purchased a one-way ticket out of here. Without even replying, I jotted down my confirmation number and logged off, then tiptoed out of the kitchen as if it were a crime scene.

Part two — getting out of Berlin without parental interception — was a little trickier. I called Dagmar from the phone in the den and wheedled him into picking me up at five-thirty sharp the next morning. "I'll explain on the ride over," I said in a panicked tone. "I'd *never* ask unless it was a total emergency."

Dagmar, it seemed, was a remarkably uncurious person. "Sure, sure," he said in his deep voice. "You are highly lucky, because I have obtained my brother Gerhardt's car for this evening. I club tonight and tomorrow morning I am coming outside tooting for you."

The next morning, he arrived right on schedule. As the sky was blurring from black to gray, I grabbed my bags and padded down the stairs so quietly I could hear the blood pumping to my ears. Please, I prayed, please don't let Mom wake up. I moved in silence until the second-to-last stair, when an enormous creak sounded. I stood there breathless with panic and terror. I waited, counting down from one hundred, but still no one stirred in the master bedroom at the top of the stairs. In the end, I made the two last steps, placed my goodbye letter on the hallway table, and slipped outside.

When Dagmar saw me with my luggage, he merely stretched over the seat to open the back door of his sedan. "You missed one extremely excellent party," he told me.

Outside the car window, gloomy suburban Berlin was slowly churning to life. Kitchen lights were coming on inside the identical houses, and I wondered if I'd ever come back here again. God, I hoped not. It was with no small tremor that I revealed my destination to Dagmar, who once again assented without a single question. Though he swore to say nothing to Mom — "What have I to say when I am knowing nothing?" — I didn't totally trust him. Later that morning, they'd be working side by side in the lab. What if Dagmar slipped and revealed my whereabouts? Would she have time to show up at the airport and drag me back to Dahlem?

Call me paranoid, but I made sure to go through security immediately and wait where Mom couldn't find me, in the back corner of a grubby café near my gate. I only left it once, to buy a phone card and call Lily with my arrival information. She said she had rehearsal that morning and couldn't pick me up, but she gave me detailed directions to the house.

After a tense two-hour wait, I boarded the U-GoJet plane. It was the weirdest of all airplanes, with 1970s disco music, mismatched vinyl seats, and silver glittery overhead compartments. My seat was near the front, and the only flight attendant — who was about my age and wearing a silver lamé minidress — started serving drinks in the rear. "Can I get you anything?" she asked in a high trill right as the pilot announced our descent into London. I never got a chance to order, which was fine since even orange juice cost four euros.

Stansted was small and uncrowded, and the customs officer waved me through without a single question. Within a quarter-hour of touching down, I'd boarded a black cab. I was hugely relieved. Mom hadn't apprehended me and now here I was, riding on the wrong side of the road through London. Well, not London exactly — more like a big rural field — but close enough. To keep my mind off the meter, I started daydreaming about the *Muckraker,* the saucy political journal that Lily had mentioned.

About an hour later, we finally entered central London. It was a totally different genre of city than New York, and nothing like the grimy construction zone of Berlin. It was more like, I don't know, a storybook town, with its boxy red phone booths and grand Victorian houses and pigeons and flowers and stately buildings and trees. We followed a red bus several miles before veering off onto a wide street divided by a little waterway with bright houseboats docked on it. Regent's Canal: the major landmark Lily had mentioned in our phone conversation.

We turned onto Blomfield Road, a leafy street of cream-colored Victorian mansions, all overhung with immense willow trees and balconies off the top-story windows. The cab pulled to a stop before the most gorgeous house on the block, number fifty-four. Lily's house, or, I guess from now on, *my* house. A little bronze plaque at the entry gate read BRIDGE HOUSE. "Whoa," I said out loud.

My trance was broken when a wave of static blared through an overhead speaker from the front of the cab. "Here we are, miss," the driver was saying. "That'll be a hundred and ten quid for you there."

"Huh?"

The driver slid the divider open and turned to face me. "That's a hundred and ten quid," he repeated, this time slower. "As in, *pounds*."

I stared at the meter, then back at him. One hundred and ten pounds? As in, roughly twenty-two times the cost of my plane ride? How had I failed to notice the fare climbing to such horrific heights, right before my eyes? Of course, I realized, some catastrophe was bound to befall me. My journey until now had been too smooth. "Uh, give me a minute?" I said, and leaving my bags in the cab for collateral, I ran up the walkway to the house and rang the bell. Thank God it was Lily who opened the door. Before we'd even hugged, I breathlessly explained my predicament.

"Lily, I'm *so* sorry to hit you up after all you've done, but I don't have enough —"

"It's nothing," she said, totally unfazed as she pulled wads of twenty-pound notes out of her wallet. "Of course you didn't know what a financial Hoover this city is."

"A who what?" I looked at her in bewilderment.

"A vacuum cleaner," she explained on our way back to the cab. "Don't worry, you'll pick it up fast." I collected my luggage while Lily settled the outrageous bill with the driver, who hadn't budged from behind the steering wheel.

"This is insane! You just handed him a hundred and twenty pounds!" I raged once we'd shut the front door of 54 Blomfield Road behind us. "You could stay in a five-star hotel for that kind of money!"

"Not in this town, you couldn't," Lily said, and softly patted my cheek. "Oh, Mimi. We have quite an adventure ahead of us."

Emotional Ear Wax

My room was next to lily's on the top floor. I dropped my bags next to my bed, which had not only clean sheets but a Baci chocolate on my pillow. "Is this from you?" I asked, popping the hazelnut treat into my mouth.

"I remembered how much you love them," Lily said, then, "I still can't believe you're actually here."

After checking out the room, I gave my friend a good looking-over. Lily was uncharacteristically chic that afternoon in a black skirt over jeans and an expensive-looking silky button-down in a swirling kaleidoscope of pastels. I wasn't sure if I liked the outfit, but it was definitely different.

"OK, Texas, time for the grand tour," she said suddenly, made uncomfortable by my scrutiny. "The Foxes are all out, so I'll do the honors."

We began winding our way down through the rambling nineteenth-century mansion's four stories. Whenever we stepped into a room, I would declare it my absolute, all-time favorite, only to change my mind upon entering the next room. I loved the Foxes' house down to the minutest detail, from the elaborate plasterwork on the ceilings to the battered rugs arranged haphazardly over the floors. White walls were apparently banned in Bridge

House; all surfaces were painted an exuberant burgundy or char-treuse or magenta or lavender, and all the rooms in the back of the house had broad bay windows overlooking a lush garden.

The house's occasional signs of dilapidation made it all the more welcoming. Here and there, I noticed peeling paint, moth-eaten curtains, broken furniture. It smelled weird, too, almost musty in places. At first glance, the second-floor library was the room of my dreams, with floor-to-ceiling bookshelves connected by a series of rolling ladders, but near the mammoth globe I started sneezing uncontrollably as dust particles detached from Australia and floated, Tinkerbell-like, into my nostrils.

In the garden-level kitchen, Lily served me tea in a beauti-ful, if slightly chipped, gold china cup. I sat studying the some-how familiar painting that hung on the wall, a sprawling oil of an overweight naked woman lying on a couch. Her body was wide open except for her legs, which were pressed tightly together.

"It's a Lucian Freud," Lily said. "Worth about a hundred col-lege educations. He's an old family friend."

"I can't get over this place," I said. "It's so fancy, but it's also so —"

"Informal?" Lily filled in.

"Yes," I said. "Exactly."

"I know: I've never understood why my mother likes the Foxes so much. They're total opposites. Here, they have ab-solutely zero pretensions about homemaking, whereas my mom would sooner admit to having spent her Christmas in rehab than to not knowing how to load the dishwasher."

"I can't wait to meet them," I said, taking a long sip of milky tea.

"If I were you," Lily said, "I wouldn't get too swept away yet. I think you'll find that chaos has certain drawbacks."

"Whatever you say," I said. Bridge House was heaven, and I never wanted to leave. To think that twenty-four hours ago, I'd been munching on a pillow and crying over my no-show boyfriend in depressing Berlin, and now here I was, with my best friend in a fabulous mansion in verdant, dreamy London.

After tea, Lily took me for a quick stroll around the Foxes' neighborhood, Little Venice. The main drag of the area — or the High Street, as Lily called it — abounded with cute little organic fruit shops and pubs with ridiculous names, like The Toad and Harp and The Lacy Trotwood. Everyone we passed looked put together and suave, or maybe it was their accents. Lily stopped into a little bodega and bought a tiny plastic container of milk. "It's the only thing they care about in that house," she said, "milk for the tea; Scotch and red wine for everything else."

When we returned from our tour, a tall, angular woman was sitting cross-legged in the downstairs kitchen, yapping into her cell phone: Philippa, or Pippa, Fox, the matron of the house. In her flowing blue silk dress and with riotous primary-colored makeup smeared over her face, she bore a curious resemblance to a peacock. Upon seeing us, she snapped shut the phone without a word of explanation to the party on the other end. "Well, hello, my little darlings!" she cried out, rushing over to plant a kiss on my cheek. "I'm *so* pleased you've come back, as I was just in the process of commandeering your future. That was Charlie Lappin who just rang. He's moved your job interview to tomorrow at twelve o'clock. You haven't any other plans, have you?"

"Me?" I squeaked out. "For the job interview?" Behind me, Lily laughed quietly. "No, my schedule's pretty open. Thank you *so* much for all your help. And I'm Mimi, by the way."

"Oh, darling, but of course I know that!" she said without offering her own name. She noisily threw open a kitchen cabinet. "You must think I'm a *complete* boor — it's been such madness these past couple of days and I'm absolutely shattered. We had no fewer than *three* cocktail parties to attend yesterday, and that's *after* hosting a Saturday lunch at the house. Then, this morning — typical Imogen — she got caught pinching old-lady night creams from the chemist's on Notting Hill Gate, and I had to extricate her from this dreadful security guard. Poor darling, he made her sit in this horrid little dungeon in the back of the shop, and even confiscated her mobile!"

She shuddered as she pulled out two bottles from the cabinet. "Now, Mimi, what's your pleasure, Cabernet or Merlot?" When, dazed, I randomly pointed to the one on the left, my hostess issued a little gasp of approval, crying, "A Merlot girl, lovely — I see we'll get along just *splendidly!*"

We spent the remainder of the afternoon sipping wine and nibbling enormous almond-filled olives. I couldn't get over Pippa. If Lily hadn't told me she was a big shot at the British Broadcasting Corporation, I never would've taken Pippa for a power player. She seemed too scattered, hyper, and fun. She dominated the conversation with a variety of topics, from her passion for gardening to her son Adrian's rodent fetish. No matter how minor the point she was making, Pippa spoke with emphasis and abandon. "They're awful!" she said of her son's mouse collection. "Just beastly, with their glowing red eyes and those appalling little tails. When I found one in the larder, I made him get rid of the whole lot."

"The larder?" I whispered to Lily. I wished that I had a notebook to record all the unfamiliar vocabulary Pippa was slinging about.

"The pantry," Lily translated. "Or cupboard. You'll meet Adrian soon. He's usually locked inside his room playing on his computer."

"Thank Christ he left the house and went to the cinema today," Pippa said. "He's by himself, I reckon. He's off to Australia for a marine biology summer program next week, and not a moment too soon. Though I *do* hope he doesn't limit his interactions to urchins and other slimy creatures." Pippa ran her long fingers through her hair, showcasing her impressive collection of distressed gold rings with colorful inlaid gems. Her phone started ringing. "For the love of Christ, will it ever stop? I wish mobiles had never been invented!"

Though Pippa's phone rang every few minutes, she greeted every caller with the same off-scale enthusiasm — "Hall-ooo!" — leaping up to pace the kitchen for the duration of the conversation. Then, after hanging up and sitting back down, she'd summarize the entire call for us, often reenacting whole passages of dialogue. She relayed, among other things, her neighbor Claire's "row" with her "positively gormless" nanny; her sister Tilda's deliberations about an antique credenza on the King's Road; even her daughter Imogen's request to dine at a friend's house. "Oh, and talking of which, who here is a bit peckish?" Pippa asked suddenly. "I'm absolutely *ravenous* myself."

"Don't worry about Mimi," said Lily. "She's *always* ravenous. Like a wild animal, you'll see."

"Lily!"

"Oh, don't worry, darling," Pippa told me. "We adore all animals — except, I suppose, rodents scurrying about my kitchen!" She tapped her fingers on the top of the table. "I could do with a takeaway curry from round the corner — is that all right?" We nodded, and Pippa speed-dialed a number on her cell phone and said, "Me again, darling. We'll have the usual — and please do hurry up about it!"

When she got off the phone, Pippa looked at me and it seemed to suddenly dawn on her that a houseguest had just flown in from another country. "Now, has Lily shown you around?" I nodded. "Good, good. Well, that's about it, then. Just make yourself comfortable. Towels, food, telly, and the like, it's all yours. Just make certain never to leave the doors open — our cat Lulu is under house arrest. You can leave laundry in the basket in the upstairs loo, and, oh! Please don't hesitate to use the phone. I'm sure your parents are eager to hear from you."

"I'm sure they are, thank you so much." I smiled angelically.

About twenty minutes later the food arrived, and while Pippa was transferring it all to serving dishes, the Messieurs Foxes ambled into the kitchen. The dad, Robin Fox, was tall and rangy, with a long, handsome face, a full head of salt-and-pepper hair, and an upper-crust air of distraction. He was confident and extroverted and utterly unlike his son, Adrian, who trudged into the kitchen with his shoulders slumped and his oily black hair hanging over his eyes. He had on ripped-up sneakers and a dirty T-shirt.

"Welcome to our home," Mr. Fox said, walking over to the cabinet to remove a stack of plates. "I do hope you're not too terribly disappointed by it."

Disappointed? Was he crazy? I never wanted to leave this house, ever, not even to go to a restaurant. "Are you kidding?" I gushed. "I *love* it. I had no idea what to expect, and it's totally perfect, all of it."

Lily pulled me aside and whispered, "Don't worry — he's always kidding, or 'ironic' or whatever. Just laugh politely at everything he says," she advised, "and you'll be fine."

"Please," he said, "do call me Robin, if that's all right by you."

"Sure," I said, "thanks."

Pippa lurched forward to refill my wineglass. "Here, let me get that."

Once we'd served ourselves and gathered around the kitchen island, Robin took a bite of samosa and, with the same abstract expression, began to recount an incident at his club that afternoon. Apparently, following a game of squash, he'd emerged from the locker room and landed in the midst of a chase scene. A woman had sneaked from the lounge to the "geography library," which is only open to men, he said. "Total bloody anarchy. They bolted all the doors and wouldn't let anyone out until they'd apprehended the madwoman."

"A bit sozzled, was she?" Adrian wanted to know.

"No, just completely off her trolley," Robin said placidly. "That, or tremendously keen on geography."

As dinner went on, I reveled in the Foxes' sophisticated verbal jousting, which sounded scripted but was clearly improvised as they went along. Having spent a year in the society of Dad, Quinn, and sometimes Sam and Fenella, I thought I'd grown accustomed to an offbeat domestic scene, but Barrow Street now seemed completely conventional in comparison to Bridge House.

"Now what's this about your seeking gainful employment here?" Robin asked me as he ladled another pool of dal onto his plate. "Has anyone spoken to Charlie yet?"

"I did, earlier this afternoon," Pippa said. "They're meeting tomorrow. It's going to be splendid."

"Charlie's splendid, most splendid indeed," Robin said. "Mimi, I hope you're prepared to encounter one of the most trenchant intellects in British journalism."

Despite his playful tone, Robin's words filled me with anxiety. I'd never been to a job interview before, unless you counted my first meeting with Debbie at the Teichen Institute. I could barely understand British English, let alone charm a complete stranger in it. What if Charlie dismissed me as a yokel? If I botched the interview, could I still stay on the fourth floor for the summer?

"Oh, pray don't terrify her, darling," Pippa said. "Mimi, ignore him. Charlie is certainly one of the top editors in London, but he's also one of our dearest friends and, come to that, a jolly good chap. Besides, Lily related your thrilling coup at the school paper last term. Be sure to tell Charlie. He *adores* controversy."

After the table was cleared and the Foxes had had their coffee, Lily showed me to the computer room upstairs and then said good night. I suspected there might be some interesting messages waiting in my inbox, and I was disastrously correct.

From: "Rogmahal"
To: "Mimicita86"
Date: July 1, 7:56 a.m.
Subject: Hello?

Mims, your mom seems to be under the impression you're hiding from her. Go home and have a hot chocolate. Love, Dad

From: "Rogmahal"
To: "Mimicita86"
Date: July 1, 9:43 a.m.
Subject: Hello? Part 2

Mimi, still haven't heard from you. Where are you?

From: "Rogmahal"
To: "Mimicita86"
Date: July 1, 11:32 a.m.
Subject: Hello? Part 3

This isn't funny. Game over. Go back to Mom, and I
mean N-O-W.
Love and consequences, Dad

Holy flying iguanas. I had to remedy this situation, and ASAP.

From: "Boris_Potasnik"
To: "Mimicita86"
Date: July 1, 5:59 p.m.
Subject: Where R U?

Mims, haven't heard from you. Did you get my last message?
Misses, B.

Hold that thought. There was one more.

To: "Boris_Potasnik"
From: "Mimicita86"
Date: July 1, 10:43 p.m.
Subject: Fngjfhyertrysjgsvffff!!!

That's the noise I make when I'm REALLY frustrated. What a total
disaster! The ONE day in my life I don't check e-mail every five
seconds, I miss a completely important message. Not that I could've
made it to Frankfurt in time (yeah, right, try running that one by my
mom), but at least I wouldn't have spent the saddest afternoon ever
in the arrivals hall of the Berlin airport. And I was so, so excited to
see you, Boris. I can't believe that's it — that we won't cross paths

again all summer. . . . But before I get too gloomy, some questions. How are you and where are you and how was flying with your despotic father? Is the food in first class as tasty as it looks?

I have a bit of news myself, btw. While you were sleeping off your jet lag, I sort of ran away to London. I know — crazy, right? Lily is staying here with this awesome family, who've taken me in and even lined up a summer internship for me. I've got a lot of smoothing over to do with my own family, but now I have time to figure stuff out. No regrets — I totally love it here already. I miss my White Russian prince. Really. Is there any chance your dad has some business to do in London? It would be SO fun to see you in the best city ever (so far). For now, though, I'd better get to bed. Mega day tomorrow plus have some major parental strategizing to mull over. Wish me luck.

Xoxoxoxoxoxo Mimi

I walked slowly up to the fourth floor. Lily, who had an early class the next day, had already gone to sleep, so I had nothing to distract me from the urgent awful phone call I had to make. My mom was going to kill me, no doubt about it. So, with a heavy heart and trembling fingers, I picked up the phone and dialed my mother's number in Berlin. I was scared shitless, but what else could I do? I'd left the country without her permission; surely even my unobservant mom recognized the gravity of *that*.

She answered with a new greeting: *"Ja?"* Her voice didn't sound too devastated by my pre-dawn departure.

"Mom?" I said timidly. "It's me." I waited a beat, preparing myself for nuclear meltdown: threats, accusations, mentions of the police, the embassy, military school, juvenile-detention centers, installation back in the Meyerson-Cullen abode.

But instead, Mom let out a cry of excitement. "Ariel? That you?"

Unbelievable. Was she joking? "No, Mom, it's Mimi."

"Oh. Mimi." A curdling effect. "What a — surprise. Your sister and I were just debating your whereabouts, and we got cut off."

"Well, I'll let you get right back to her," I said in a rush. "I just wanted to tell you I'm alive and in one piece, and that's pretty much it. OK?"

"I figured," Mom said, her voice cold and even contemptuous. "Looking out for yourself has never been your problem, has it? It's the other people that trip you up." She paused for a measured intake of breath. "Your note was cute; you've got a real flair for the dramatic. But the runaway charade's over, Mimi. Get in a cab and come home now. There are less drastic ways to avoid a silly little babysitting job."

"But I can't. I —"

"I'd disagree with you there, Mimi. You'll be happy to hear I talked to Debbie, who's very hurt but willing to reconsider. As for you and Maurice and myself, we all have some serious emotional ear wax to remove, but I trust we can unblock our communication channels."

"Mom, I don't think you understand. I'm not in Berlin anymore. I'm not even in Germany." I looked up at the ceiling and took in a deep breath. "I'm in London, actually."

"London?" Mom burst out laughing, but without warmth. "In that overpriced, underrated hellhole? You wouldn't last an hour there — you couldn't afford it."

"I've lasted all day, thank you very much." I didn't add: And I plan on lasting a few more. "I just wanted you to know I was safe. That's all." I took the phone away from my ear and mumbled into the mouthpiece that I'd call her again. And then, before she could respond, I hung up.

Safe under the covers, I thought back over the phone call. It hadn't gone exactly according to plan. I'd intended to tell Mom about London and my job opportunity here; I was even going to give her the Foxes' phone number in case of emergency. But, for reasons I'm unable to explain, I couldn't. And I didn't.

A Sunny Day in London Town

I WOKE UP AT DAWN the next morning, and for some time just lay in bed relishing my new and insanely awesome surroundings. Life could be truly mind-blowing, I thought as I gazed at the oil painting that hung above the bedroom door, a portrait of a much-powdered, rosy-cheeked woman with a constrained smile and a bonnet tied over her curly blond hair. As it climbed higher in the sky, the sun traced stripes across the frayed Oriental rug on the floor, and I couldn't get over the feeling that I'd stepped inside some ten-inch-thick nineteenth-century novel.

Soon the Fox household came to life beneath me, and the higher notes of a British news program wafted up from Pippa and Robin's bedroom one floor down. I stood up and extravagantly stretched out my arms, pausing to savor my utter happiness. Nothing, but nothing, could cast a pall on my first morning in London — or, nothing except the memory of my inconclusive conversation with Mom the night before. Much as I hated to admit it, I knew I had one more phone call to make before setting off on my new life.

Since it was about lunchtime in New York, I picked up the phone and — after screwing up the international dialing prefixes only a few times — succeeded in getting through to Barrow Street. My dad answered on the seventh ring, out of breath.

"Daddy, are you *ever* going to install that phone in your dark-room like you're always saying?"

"Mimi?!" he cried in what sounded like delight. "Is that you?"

Within seconds, however, his voice became hard and stern. "You have no idea how hard I've been trying to track you down. Did you get any of my e-mails? Before you say anything, Miriam," he said — and I should add that he *never* calls me Miriam — "you should know that I had a very upsetting chat with your mother yesterday."

"Yeah, well, join the club," I said, but my sarcasm went unappreciated.

"Please, for the love of God, tell me she's mistaken. You didn't run *away*, did you? I told her it couldn't be true, that our daughter is *far* too mature for such selfish behavior."

I backed up and sat back down on the twin bed. "But Dad, I didn't run away, I just — I was left with no choice —"

"No choice?" he barked. I hadn't heard him this angry since I was eleven, when I'd faked a fever to avoid going to my grand-mother's birthday party and then been caught salsa dancing in my room. "We made a deal last summer, you and your mother and I, and right now you're in flagrant violation of that agreement, so I suggest you put your cleverness to use and get back to your mother's house as quickly as you left it. If you don't have cab fare, don't worry about it — I'm sure your Mom will cover the charges."

"But Daddy!" At this point I burst into tears. My father was the one person who I could always count on to defend me, and now he was yelling at me even louder than Mom had. "I tried reasoning with her," I blubbered, "I swear I did. I tried again and again, but it's like she's incapable of listening to me anymore — like she's gone off into her own warped world and left me completely behind. You cannot even *begin* to imagine how lonely I was over there. I *had* to escape. I wasn't trying to go somewhere better — I just couldn't stand another minute of it."

I went on to recap my weeks as a prisoner, detailing the twins' fresh-air aversion and Maurice's Alzheimer's obsession. "And every time I complained, Mom said I was spoiled, but I'm not, Dad — you *know* I'm not! I just wanted to be treated like a human being, but apparently that was too much for her. What'd I do to make Mom hate me so much, Dad, can you tell me that?"

And then I dropped the bombshell. I told him I was in London. But by this point, I was crying too hard for him to yell at me. Dad remained silent for several seconds as I wept into the phone, then said somberly, with a prolonged sigh, "Mimi, you know your mother loves you. You're sure one piece of work, aren't you? You and your mother both. She said something about London on the phone last night, but I thought she was kidding. Did you really leave Berlin?"

I confirmed this, and after another pause, Dad said, "All right. How about this: you stay put for now, and I'll try to see if I can broker some truce with your mom."

"You'd do that?"

"Now, don't get too excited. I'm just saying I'll talk to her. But what she says goes. If she wants you back there, you're going back."

"OK, but please will you tell her I'm safe and in good hands? The family I'm staying with is legit, and I have this amazing job

111

at a political magazine, where I'll get to use my brain, and it's such a great oppor —"

"I'll do what I can," Dad assured me. "But if she agrees to this, you're going to have to make up your time with your mother. We're talking *all* school vacations — and that includes three-day weekends — in Houston until you two are best friends again."

"How about until we can stand each other again?"

"That'd be a start."

I trusted my father, and I had a hunch my spectacular summer was safe. If Dad was on my side, Mom would be forced to relent. She was the one who had ended their marriage and thrown our family into complete disarray, and somewhere in her lunatic head she must know that.

Sometimes Dad outdid himself. By the time we hung up, after I'd told him all about Lily and London and the Foxes' madcap mansion, he'd actually volunteered to make an emergency deposit to my checking account. "Lily should be your friend, not your banker," he said. "But this is strictly survival money," he reminded me. "Food and toothpaste and nothing else."

"I know, I know. And don't worry, Daddy — I'm completely set up in this place."

"Well, Lily's very kind to take you in like this, but the next time you feel like seeking refuge in a foreign country, I suggest you try the Republic of Georgia. It's a hell of a lot more affordable and you have some devoted friends there as well."

"What, are the Judys on location or something?"

"Bingo," he said, laughing for the first time since he'd gotten on the phone.

In the shower, I belted out the only verse I knew of Dolly Parton's "Dreams Do Come True." The Foxes' plumbing was not, I should point out, a miracle of modern engineering. The water trickled out like lava, and without warning the temperature veered from freezing to boiling, but I didn't mind; nothing could shatter my blissful spirits. I shaved my legs quickly and jumped out onto the bathmat.

Shivering, I walked back into my bedroom wrapped in a tiny blue towel that was shredded and pocked with holes. "Yeah, the linen selection around here isn't so extensive," Lily said, giggling when she saw me. She was lounging on my bed, looking pretty awesome in a luxurious Liberty-print bathrobe. "So what are you planning to wear for your big meeting later?"

I gave her a funny look: Lily was the last of my friends I expected to ask such a question. Furthermore, I hadn't given a thought to appropriate office attire yet, and I admitted as much to Lily. "I have *no* idea," I said. "My clothes are only slightly nicer than the Foxes' towels." Repulsively enough, I still hadn't bothered to wash most of the crumpled-up clothes that had been flung into my suitcase on the last night of school. After all, in Berlin, there'd been no point. What was I going to do, dress to the nines for Joshua and Nathaniel Meyerson-Cullen? *Danke,* but *nein danke.*

"I only bring it up," Lily said, "because some of my friends from acting school dragged me to Oxford Street yesterday, and I bought you a little prezzie. Actually, I bought it for me, but I'm a total battleship in it. The sizes here are seriously warped. I thought a ten would be comfy, but it looks like I'd spray-painted it on. I was going to exchange it until you called. Here, try it," she said, tossing me a bright yellow bag that said SELFRIDGES in big black letters. "I think it'll fit you perfectly, so Merry Christmas."

Though I'm considerably taller, Lily has broader shoulders, and with my undeveloped upper body, I'm usually one size smaller than she is. I thanked her effusively and then pulled from the bag a frilly, delicate garment that resembled nothing in Lily's wardrobe: navy blue crushed silk with cap sleeves and a thin belt made of pale pink ribbon. I told Lily how much I loved it. "But I couldn't possibly accept this from you," I said. Not even Pia could afford such a nice dress — except maybe with the old five-finger discount. "What if I tuck in the tags and wore it just this once, and then maybe over the weekend we could go return it — or is that way too sketchy for you?"

Lily cracked up at my suggestion. "That'd go down great at your interview, wearing a dress with the labels sticking out. Mimi, it's yours. It was, like, eighty percent off, or else I wouldn't have bought it."

I'm usually pretty easy to convince about such matters, so with no further objections, I popped into my closet to try it on. When I emerged to look in the door mirror, I grinned. Lily, as usual, was absolutely correct: I did look rather excellent. The dress clung close to my hips but not too close, and while the neckline plunged slightly low for an office atmosphere, the hem landed modestly below the knee. To my sincere astonishment, I looked much less like a giraffe than usual — maybe even half-way attractive.

"But wait — what about hose?" I asked. Unlike most of my

clothes, this dress wouldn't pair well with sneakers or cowboy boots, and the caramel-colored vintage ballet flats I'd brought required some sheer pantyhose to complete the professional look. Lily, unfortunately, couldn't help me on that front, so we went next door to Imogen's room.

"Imo?" Lily called out, rapping on the door. When nobody answered for a third time, she pushed open the door to a room she'd neglected on yesterday's tour. As we stepped inside, I was powerfully reminded of a Moroccan opium den, not that I'd ever set foot in one, with layers of candles and floor cushions and scarves strewn on every available surface. Imogen must be a real girl's girl, to judge by the vanity laden with pots of creams and lipsticks and tubes of benzoyl peroxide, and handbags and beaded necklaces spilling onto the floor, and even a stack of wedding magazines pushed halfway under the vanity.

"Must've been a late dinner," Lily said, gesturing at the made bed. Like every piece of furniture in the room, it produced a dramatic effect, with a gauzy canopy and golden satin duvet. Next to it, a tile-inlaid nightstand featured no fewer than four framed pictures of a beautiful, if acne-stricken, green-eyed girl posing with the same buzz-cutted boy. Lily pulled open a bureau drawer and motioned for me to sift through its contents with her. "Imogen won't care," she assured me. "No one in this house has *any* boundaries. Besides, she's so spoiled she probably doesn't even realize she owns half this stuff."

The fabulousness of Imogen's wardrobe soon eclipsed my misgivings. Unfortunately, 1920s boudoir-style fishnets aren't exactly the ideal accessory for a job interview. "Maybe I should just buy some hose," I said after a few minutes of fruitless searching. "Surely something will be open — it's almost nine, isn't it?"

"Dunno, sounds risky. Let's go see what Pippa has."

"Conducting a panty raid on my hostess on my first morning in her house? I don't think so."

"Don't be silly," Lily said. "You'd be doing her a favor. What if you showed up looking like a slob at her friend's office? It'd be embarrassing."

I conceded the point and we headed downstairs.

"Besides," she went on, "the Foxes have left already. Their cars arrive every morning at six-thirty to take them to the Harbour Club."

"For what, sailing?"

"No." Lily grinned. "It's this fancy-schmancy health club in Notting Hill. Most of its members are so high-profile that they keep this little basket of headscarves at the front door so that people can conceal their faces before stepping onto the street. Robin reads the papers over breakfast there, and Pippa and her personal trainer work out alongside the rest of the top fifties."

"The top fifties?"

"It's this list they just published of the top fifty female earners in London. Pippa is somewhere in the midtwenties, right after the woman who started the make-your-own soap franchise."

"Right, how could I not have guessed," I said, experiencing a moment of Baldwin déjà vu. Once again, I was the only person whose parents weren't regularly mentioned in newspapers and society broadsheets.

Lily and I had just walked into the Foxes' surprisingly bland bedroom. The walls were pale yellow; the bedding white and standard-issue. There were no photographs or paintings or figurines, none of the doodads that littered the rest of the house, just a hardcover book on each bedside table: *True Republicanism* on one and a Graham Greene story collection on the other. It was a sad room somehow, not the fun mess I would have expected.

"Now stop looking so paranoid," Lily said once inside Pippa's walk-in closet. "This is the *mi casa es su casa*-est of *casas*." She opened a couple of drawers before finding Pippa's hosiery stash. We considered four options and settled on a nude-toned sandal-toed pair. I was putting back the rejects when I noticed a tennis bracelet and piece of paper at the bottom of the drawer, a receipt from the Savoy Hotel indicating that Philippa Sanders had ordered a five-hundred-pound bottle of claret to Room 412.

"What the — ?" I passed the receipt to Lily. "Who's Philippa Sanders — is that her maiden name?"

Lily examined the piece of paper, her lip curling up as she read it. "Those foxy, foxy Foxes," she said with a shrug. "I wouldn't put anything past them."

Back upstairs, we finished getting dressed together. It was the kind of girly fun I always wished my sister and I could share. As it was, Ariel offered me cash rewards to rethink whatever "weird" or "heinous" outfit I'd chosen. Lily stepped into a pair of black clam diggers and put on a white T-shirt, inside out and backwards.

"Wow, looking good," I said approvingly.

Lily reddened on cue. "Oh, shut up, will you?"

Outside, the morning was exquisite: the air warm but not

sticky, the sky a brilliant Tiffany blue. We walked a few blocks along Regent's Canal and exchanged smiles with an elderly man who was sponging down the side of his houseboat. When we reached the Warwick Avenue Tube station, Lily gave me a brief rundown on Underground lines and transfers and Oyster cards, but I didn't understand a word of it, so she took me to a newsagent inside the station and bought me a cute laminated map. "You're sure you don't want me to ride with you part of the way?" she asked.

"I'll be fine, I promise. You have monologues to memorize, and I should *really* brush up on current affairs before the Charles Lappin cross-examination."

"As long as he's a friend of the Foxes, you're fine," Lily told me. "Trust me — this is a town that runs on family connections."

"Yes, but it's not *my* family," I pointed out.

She cocked her head to the side. "It is now."

Once Lily had left, I returned my attention to the newsstand. Dad believed the best way to get to know a place is to read all of the newspapers from start to finish, but this comprehensive approach was not an option here. There were about thirty-five newspapers, and with my attention span I'd need a week to read them all.

After some deliberation, I decided to go for a diversity of viewpoints and settled on the two papers that looked most unalike: the staid, traditional *Daily Telegraph* and the comparatively crude *News of the World* tabloid. The train came quickly, and I got into a narrow, cramped car.

The low ceiling's arch was severe, forcing all of us commuters not standing directly in the train's center to hunch over. When a seat freed up at Marylebone station, I pushed forward to claim a square cushion upholstered in a loud purple and blue pattern. Once comfortably seated, I pulled out the newspapers. I examined the serious *Telegraph* first, but I didn't have much luck with an article headlined "Burrell to Take Lib Dems Forward," and I gave up completely midway through a boring feature on women and calcium supplements. I then proceeded to the juicier, brain-rotting *News of the World,* which actually turned out to be pretty interesting. One story was about a reality show contestant who had just left his girlfriend, Camilla, for his housemate Camille. A chocolate and bacon diet promised to burn away "half a stone" in a week. And in an eye-catching story headlined "Up in Smoke!" a child services office failed to notice that single mothers "on the dole" were spending their government checks for milk and diapers on cigarettes. The two-page photo spread accompanying the article showed a grid of pictures of haggard-looking women with cigarettes dangling out of their mouths. Though at first I thought the story was silly, by the time I'd reached the end of the violently outraged text, I was so absorbed that I almost missed my stop.

Among the Astronauts

COMPARED WITH NEW YORK, LONDON WAS HUGE — not so much in population as in sheer acreage. My hair must have grown a quarter of an inch in the time it took my first train to reach Waterloo station that morning, and that wasn't even close to my final destination. At Waterloo I transferred to the Docklands Light Railway, a train that ferried me to the *Muckracker* offices at Canary Wharf.

Lily, who had been coming to London all her life, had described Canary Wharf and the surrounding Docklands as one of the liveliest parts of London, but as I shuffled onto a concourse of moving sidewalks and chain stores, I couldn't help but question her enthusiastic claim. Lively? Lunar was more like it. To me, Canary Wharf suggested a strip mall development on the moon. It consisted of a labyrinth of brand-new skyscrapers, all clean and glossy and intimidatingly vertical. Because all the buildings looked so similar, it took me a good ten minutes to find the address Pippa had given me.

When at last I got to the building, I walked into a lobby filled with immense paintings of lipstick tubes. At the security desk, I had to write my name on a clipboard and show my driver's license to the guard. "From Texas, are you?" he asked, continuing to study it for some time before handing it back. "You a mate of the Bushes, are you?"

There was something hostile in his tone, so I tried to sound winsome as I said, "Nope, can't say that I am. They're not even really *from* Texas, you know."

"Oh, I beg your pardon, miss, I suppose they must hail from the *other* Texas? Right, then. Now, what brings you across the pond this morning?"

"I have a business meeting with Charlie Lappin," I said primly. "At the *Muckraker*."

"Right, bear with me one moment," he said, typing something into his computer. "Don't have any muckrakers to speak of, but I have found your Mr. Lappin." He punched a few more keys and printed out a visitor's pass. "Here we are now — cheerio and best of luck to you. Let's 'ope you don't muck it up like those Bushes."

I stuck the pass on my dress and followed the guard's directions to the elevator. As I rode up to the twenty-eighth floor, I became uneasy. I hadn't understood most of what that guard had said down there; I just vaguely sensed that he was making fun of me. Again I wished I'd prepared for this interview a little more. Instead of poring over the exposé of pedophiles employed by the London Zoo, I should've familiarized myself with some *real* news stories, or at least figured out the basic platforms of the U.K.'s major political parties. Once on Charlie Lappin's floor, I took a seat in a low white leather chair as instructed by the receptionist, who promptly returned to filing her nails. In a last-ditch attempt at cramming, I removed the *Daily Telegraph* from my shoulder bag, but instead of perusing the Home Front pages as planned, I found myself studying the curious décor of Charlie Lappin's waiting room.

I'm not sure what I expected, really, of a political journal's reception area — maybe a row of international flags, like at the UN, or television monitors playing African news conferences? All I knew was that nothing about the lime green waiting room suggested a heavy-duty political think tank. The walls were covered with eight-by-ten headshots of remarkably bedraggled people with pasty skin and pronounced undereye circles. Despite the bright messages scrawled in Sharpie across these pictures — "Lots of love from Roz xxx" and "Cad Charlie, with all due admiration" — most of the people in them looked sickly or perhaps even beat up. They were all political prisoners, I thought, and the *Muckraker* must be involved in some noble human rights campaign.

After several minutes, the office door opened and a young man flounced past me on his way to the elevator bank. He was tall and adorable, with black rectangular glasses, straight brown hair that flopped haphazardly over his face, and the poreless skin of an infant. I wondered if he, like so many guys I find attractive, was gay. He was, after all, wearing a checkered shirt, bright red chinos, and shiny Oxford shoes — an outfit too flamboyant even for Quinn. He'd just vanished behind a set of double doors when the intercom buzzed and the secretary, who was now massaging a green cream into her cuticles, nodded to indicate that Charlie Lappin was ready for me.

With some trepidation I approached the editor in chief's door and was about to knock when a florid little man sprang out in a shamrock green suit and cartoonish red bow tie. Now, if I'd seen him on the street, I would never in a million years have pinned Charlie Lappin as, in Robin Fox's phrase, "one of the most trenchant intellects in British journalism." Charlie spoke hurriedly and seemed to have trouble looking me in the eye, targeting my forehead instead. "Sit down, sit down, very good, do make yourself comfortable. Now let's see here — tell us your name again?"

I did so, and he repeated it several times to himself. "Mimi Schulman, lovely, lovely. Now, Pippa Fox rang me about you yesterday afternoon, and as you must already know, one *never* refuses a protégée of Pippa Fox. How is dear Pippa, incidentally? Don't see as much of her as I'd like. I pop round for weekend lunches on occasion, but usually I'm too bloody busy. I must say, I've always wondered what it must be like, living in that outrageous house of theirs — absolute bedlam, is it?"

"Well, I only got there yesterday, so I couldn't say for sure," I said. "But so far, it seems like I lucked out."

"Quite, quite," Charlie murmured happily. "Do you know, extraordinary as it may sound to you now, when I first met Pippa, in the late 1960s, she was a hippie who summered in a commune in Dorset? She spent the rest of the time trawling the King's Road and making an absolute spectacle of herself at the Chelsea Drugstore. It's quite difficult to imagine today, isn't it?"

"Wow, it sure is," I said, though, remembering my host mother's peacock muumuu and scattered conversation the day before, it wasn't really. Besides, even *my* anal-retentive mother had a brief career as a flower child, and in nostalgic moods still breaks out the Joni Mitchell CDs every now and again.

"But go on now, Pippa tells me you're from Texas — tell us all about it. I've always gotten on quite well with Texans, I must say. As barmy as it sounds, I think a certain kinship exists between Texans and Brits, or certainly among our kind of people, if you know what I mean. We have something of the same . . . earthiness, I believe it is. And d'you know what, I read somewhere quite recently that Texas and England are exactly the same size. Fascinating, I found that, don't you?"

"Yeah," I said uncertainly, when it became clear that Charlie was awaiting a response. I didn't want to offend, but I was pretty sure he had his data jumbled. "I think Texas might be a little bigger than Britain, actually — I know for a fact that it's bigger than France."

"Ah, bugger France!" Charlie interjected with sudden anger.

"Yeah, France is completely overrated," I said quickly. "I've only been here twenty-four hours, but already I know I'm in the best country in the world."

At this Charlie laughed. "Ah, you Yanks and your hyperbole — not to worry, I'm enchanted, do go on. I'd be fascinated to hear about a stranger's impression of Merrie Olde."

"Let's see," I said. "Well, I love the bright red mailboxes, and the way people call strangers 'love.' I also really like the outrageous newspapers you have here. And speaking of which," I said casually, "what do you think is going to happen to the Lib-Dems under the new leadership?"

"New leadership?" Charlie blinked at me, momentarily confused. "As if I give a toss! Now listen to me," he went on. "I think we'd best resolve this geographical debate straightaway; it's preying on me." He convulsed forward and pressed a button on his phone. "Anthony," he said when a man's voice came onto the speaker. "Be a good chap, won't you, and find out the respective geographical areas of Texas and the U.K. for me, all right? And chop-chop, I've quite a bit of money riding on this one."

Charlie, winking at me, pressed some more buttons and this time a female voice answered. "Becky, darling, could you nip in here for just a minute? Bring in the paperwork necessary to add this fetching young American to our payroll records." Then to me he said, "I'm afraid it's not much, just the piddling stipend we give all interns — scarcely enough for a Travelcard. Still, you'll find, in this business, that the fringe benefits can be most profitable indeed. Free haircuts and handbags and whatnot — you can dine on champagne and canapés all summer if you so fancy, though I imagine you'll want to keep an eye on your girlish figure."

What was this place? Everything Charlie said made my brain spin. Free handbags? Canapés and champagne? The Foxes had told me I'd be working at the *Muckraker,* a political commentary journal. On the other hand — I realized with a jolt — had they really? Come to think of it, at dinner the night before, Pippa had said nothing at all specific about the kind of magazine her old friend Charlie ran. Lily had mentioned the *Muckraker* in an e-mail to me in Berlin, but it now seemed entirely possible that the Foxes had decided on another plan of action and forgotten to inform me.

"Can I ask a question?" I said in a small voice. "When you say parties, do you mean political parties? Or, like, fundraisers?"

"That's quite generous of you, though I suppose you could see them that way, if you've a very loose definition of *political*," Charlie said. "You must be thinking of our 'Worst-Dressed MPs' spread in the last issue — we only do one of those a year. In general, we try to avoid that sort of subject. Look, if the prime minister was having it off with a nanny, we'd cover the story. Our readers can't get enough shots of the princes' girlfriends shopping in Sloane Street. But that about covers it."

He was still speaking when a petite blonde clicked into the room. With her long Pinocchio nose and inch-thick mask of makeup, she reminded me of an airline stewardess from my early youth — more polished than naturally blessed. "Becky darling," Charlie said, "I'd like you to meet our newest research assistant straight from the Lone Star State, Mimi Schulman. Mimi, this is Rebecca Bridgewater, my other right hand. Becky here will sort you out with an ID card and national insurance number and all that rot."

"Halloo," the woman said through a frozen smile, sounding none too thrilled about this task. "And you'll be with us just for the summer, will you?"

"Correct," I said. "I have to go back to New York in August."

"I see," she said impassively. Though her expression was inscrutable, I could tell she hadn't taken a wild liking to me. "Well, and have you any particular skills we should know about?"

"Oh, yes, do tell us," her scatterbrained boss threw in.

"Sure," I said. And so, with Rebecca watching me blankly while Charlie urged me on with a series of exclamations — "Oh, fantastic!" and "You didn't *really*?" — I gave a long-winded account of the whole Serge Ziff exposé.

"Right. So the school didn't get the money from him after all?" Rebecca asked when I'd finished.

"Well, no. He's been awaiting trial, actually."

"A shame, that," she remarked. I couldn't tell if she was talking about Serge's predicament or Baldwin going unfunded.

"Mimi came to us with glowing recommendations," Charlie broke in. "She was sent to us by Lady Phillipa Fox, whom I believe you've met."

Rebecca visibly perked up. "But you don't mean Lady Fox of the Beeb?"

From one evening at the Foxes', I'd learned that the Beeb meant the BBC, so it was with studied calm that I said, "That's right. The one and only."

"How fantastic," Rebecca said. "We're quite lucky to have her sending young talent our way, then."

Her enthusiasm for all things related to Pippa — or, I should say, Lady Fox — was interrupted by a knock on the door. Charlie called out, *"Entrez!"* and in walked the creatively dressed dreamboat who'd caught my attention in the reception area. Up close, I could see that behind his black glasses were big googly brown eyes.

Charlie introduced him to me as Anthony Palfrey. "Anthony came down from Cambridge last month," Charlie said. "He turned down an internship in the medieval wing of the British Museum to chase down third-rate celebrities for us, so you see, we're quite an estimable organization."

"He may be clever," Rebecca said, playfully wagging a finger at the recent arrival, "but I wouldn't trust him as far as he can see without his specs. You can safely assume that everything he tells you is complete rubbish."

Anthony seemed uncomfortable with Rebecca's banter and quickly turned to Charlie and, with a little military salute, said, "Right. Sir, I have the information you requested, which is as follows: Britain measures approximately 90,000 square miles to Texas's 269,000 square miles. That would be a difference of, let's see, roughly three hundred percent."

"Blast," said Charlie. "I suppose I misheard, then. But what about France, what are those dimensions?"

"Don't know, sir," Anthony said in the same playful pseudo-military manner. "Didn't specify France, sir." Then, when neither of his superiors was looking, he flashed me a secret smile, as if to convey that we were the two sane people in the room. "Shall I orientate our young recruit then?" he asked Charlie.

"You could do, yes, that'd be most helpful indeed," the editor said to his young employee. "Photocopy all relevant paperwork and pass it along to Rebecca when you're done." He turned to me. "We'll have you sorted in no time."

I followed Anthony past the reception area and elevator bank, into a large room with cubicles cramped like chicken coops. Several stringy-haired girls in garish Mardi Gras outfits stared as Anthony and I passed them on our way to the Xerox machine.

"Don't mind old Becky," my new friend whispered along the

way. "She's a bit competitive, that's all. Dislikes all females under the age of seventy-five, I reckon."

I looked around the office. "That would mean she doesn't like anybody here."

"Indeed not. It's not all bad. She saves a bundle on Christmas cards every year," Anthony responded. "But don't lose sleep over it; she's harmless. Just a little sad."

"Your passport, mademoiselle?" he said when we got to the copy machine. I gave it to him, and he wasted no time in opening it to the photo page. He grinned at the stupid picture of me as an orthodontically challenged thirteen-year-old. God, I couldn't wait for that stupid thing to expire.

When the copy came out of the machine, he brought it close to his nose and sniffed long and hard, the way I'd seen Sam's pretentious parents do with their wineglasses. "Lovely smell, don't you think?" he asked, tipping the warm paper to my face.

"Mmm, yes," I said, suddenly lightheaded. The scent brought back happy memories of afternoons in Dad's darkroom when I'd listen to Dusty Springfield while Quinn hung freshly developed photographs with clothespins.

Anthony took a big step toward me and stretched forward to reach the cabinet above my head. "Sorry about this," he said politely, rising on his tiptoes and angling a few inches nearer. He was so close I could smell him, a blend of soap and cologne and maybe liquor. "Should be right up here," he went on, fumbling around the shelf.

I felt slightly seasick throughout this encounter. Was he

pressing up against me on purpose? But then why would he, and furthermore why did I care? Why did his proximity fill me with such a nauseating blend of delight and mortification?

"Here we are now," he said after what felt like an eternity, coming down with a manila folder in his hand.

Anthony had me wait in the reception area while he delivered my papers to Rebecca. In an effort to regain my composure, I eavesdropped on the receptionist's deft handling of phone calls. "Sorry, love, I'm afraid we don't give out e-mail addresses." Click. "You're welcome to send a letter to the editor. No response guaranteed." Click. "If you don't know the pronunciation of her name, I don't see much point in connecting you, love." Click.

What did it take, I wondered, to get a phone call put through — a secret password, a compliment on her manicure? She brightened only when a chubby, dark-haired man in army fatigues came through the door. "Ian, I was hoping you'd be in today!" the receptionist cried, ignoring the ringing telephone. She drew a banknote from her purse and handed it to the man. "I just popped round to the bank," she said. "So do give that to Colleen, won't you? Now I'm paid up on the cupid cardigan. I still owe her for the one I bought for my nephew, with the piglets. She'll remember."

"No doubt she will at that," replied the man, zipping the cash inside one of his many vest pockets.

I was hoping for more clues into this mysterious transaction when Charlie Lappin flung open his office door to admit the man.

A few minutes later Anthony returned, heaving a big stack of magazines, which he proceeded to drop onto my lap. The topmost issue — with a neon orange headline demanding "What

Happened to Joz's Curves?" — slid onto the floor, and I picked it up with a trembling hand. I guess it was settled: there would be no political journal in my future.

"Steady now," Anthony said, laughing. "Don't worry — it's easy-peasy. I'm sure all of this twaddle is the same as yours, tomato tom-*ah*-to and the like. Just cast your eyes over a few issues and familiarize yourself with stars' tragic childhoods, find out who's shagging who. We'll liaise tomorrow morning at half eleven."

I stared. Did half eleven mean eleven-thirty or ten-thirty, and how could I ask without sounding stupid?

"On second thought," Anthony said, "let's make it noon. The Henley Awards are tonight, and I might be on the tiles till quite late."

I smiled at my new friend and told him noon. It was a time I understood, and now I had one fewer question for Lily.

Baby Greens and Grown-Up Snogs

Outside the *a-ha!* offices, the sun fell soft on my bare arms. I called Dad collect from a pay phone for an update and he told me that while Mom was still furious, she no longer expected me to turn up. "You two have some real repairing to do," Dad told me. "And it's your responsibility to patch things up. I can only apply so many Band-Aids; I'm backing off."

"I completely understand," I said quietly. I knew he was right — she *was* my mom — but for the moment, I was just happy to be free of the Meyerson-Cullen terrors.

After promising Dad that I'd phone Mom once a week from London, I went strolling aimlessly around the maze of skyscrapers, past several characterless Italian cafés similar to those in Manhattan's financial district. A kebab shop reminded me of Sam, and I wished I could conjure him — make that the *old* him — for a lunch date. When, after a few minutes, I spotted the familiar Starbucks logo, I couldn't resist and went right inside. Yes, that's right — the very first eating establishment I patronized in the United Kingdom was a Starbucks. Familiar old Starbucks, with its plush velveteen chairs and four-sided shelves of thermoses and Billie Holiday CDs. Pathetic, but still. It appealed to me right then, not least because this branch looked so much like the one my dad and I sometimes visited on Sixth Avenue.

Once at the front of the line — possibly to go out on a cultural limb, or possibly because the name reminded me of Dad's and my Tuesday-night pancake dinners on Barrow Street — I ordered the one unfamiliar item on the menu, a flapjack, which turned out to be a cold mound of oats and butter, like a wet, dense granola bar. I'd polished off the unexpectedly delicious treat before even taking my seat at a table next to an older man whose shirt was buttoned wrong. He slurped down a coffee drink as he read, to my horror, a pornographic newspaper. Unapologetically, and in the bright light of day, he examined a huge color photograph of two topless girls in suspenders. Then, without a glimmer of embarrassment, the man — who was wearing a wedding band and a tag that identified him as Fergus, an employee of Waitrose supermarket — idly flipped a few pages to an article on rugby.

Confused, I squinted to read the title at the top of the page: *London Morning News*. So that was it, then — a newspaper with nudity. No doubt about it, this country was weird, and by no means as uniformly high-class as a lifetime of PBS miniseries had conditioned me to expect.

With this in mind, I turned to the stacks of the magazine that now employed me. The headline splashed in hot pink across the cover of the February 9 edition promised an exclusive peek at JULES AND FRANKIE'S SECRET SNOGFEST and featured a blurry image of two silhouettes smooshed together in the back seat of a black cab. In the upper corner of the page was a headshot of a perky blonde in a low-cut equestrian costume and the quotation "How I Escaped from Rehab — Again!"

Subsequent issues of *A-ha!* contained much the same type of stories: people "snogging" who weren't supposed to be; broken wedding engagements; eating disorder denials by stars of both genders; and "Ten Steps to a Hot Bod" as relayed by a number of "Britain's hottest sex symbols." A few headlines recurred in issue after issue:

COULD JEMINA BE PREGGERS?

HONEYMOON IN CORSICA: DEVON AND DAVINA HEAT UP
   THE ISLES

JOOLS'S BATTLE OF THE BULGE — WILL SHE EVER LOSE
   THAT CRUCIAL HALF A STONE?

PRESTON + SPARKS = FINAL SPLIT?

As I read, I mentally sketched rough portraits of what seemed to be the most famous celebrities, stuff like *Belinda Lloyd (girl band? model?) holidays with ex-hubby Damian (recovering smack addict, entrepreneur) + son Diamond. Reunion imminent? History of depression, shoe-shopping addiction? Possibly heading up organization for orphans in Laos.* Then there was *Thom Thorpe (TV presenter?). Bald, many earrings & girlfriends. Poss gay sex scandal?? Loves chocolate-orange biscuits.*

After two hours of studying the magazine, I still had no idea what any of these celebrities did, or why they were famous. I had, at best, identified several characteristics common to all the so-called A-listers whose photographs filled issue after issue of *A-ha!:* (1) They tended to be less attractive than U.S. celebrities, with personal trainers, Botox, smoothie diets, and so forth much less in effect; (2) None of them was even slightly famous in America; (3) None of them seemed to mind.

By the time I returned to Bloomfield Road, around five, my head ached with all the trivia I'd crammed into it. Bridge House was empty when I got there; only the Foxes' one-eyed cat, a gray longhair named Lulu, greeted me at the door. She rubbed against my ankles and circled my legs twice before allowing me to pass into the front room. Ever since their next-door neighbors' psychotic pit bull had mauled Lulu a few years earlier — the cause of her missing eye — the Foxes had obsessively patrolled their beloved cat's movements. I'd already been told twelve times never, ever to allow Lulu to escape outdoors. At the bottom of the stairs, I reached down to rub Lulu between her ears, thinking as I did so how perfect this summer would be if Simon, my cat in Houston, were chilling at the Foxes' with me. Lulu was a nice girl and all, but she was too skittish for my taste — and far, far less handsome than my orange Texas tomcat.

After rinsing Pippa's stockings in the sink of the fourth-floor bathroom that Lily and I shared, I headed down to the TV room and parked myself in front of a marathon of *Only Fools and Horses,* a dated BBC sitcom about old English guys who sit around the same pub all day and discuss nothing in particular — sort of like *Cheers* with lower production values. All and all, a relaxing antidote to my stressful day in Docklands.

When I opened my eyes I don't know how many minutes

later, Lily was standing above me. "*There* you are," she said. "I should've known you'd be sleeping through a fascinating documentary on Palestinian athletes."

I blinked at the television screen, which showed a man pole-vaulting over an orange tree. "Oh, Lils," I said, suppressing a yawn, "I've had *such* a tiring day."

"Well, guess what — it ain't over yet! You have exactly three minutes to get ready for dinner if we're going to take the Tube. We're meeting Imogen and her friends at a pub in Queen's Park."

"Tonight? Can't we just stay in and order Indian food again?"

"C'mon, Mimi, you're going to regret not taking advantage of your visit. There'll be plenty of time next year to play hermit. I'll be sure to assign you lots of articles if that's what you want."

I offered various objections — I was wiped out, I hadn't changed from my interview dress yet — but Lily soon convinced me to slide back into my flats sans pantyhose. I hadn't consumed anything but that flapjack since breakfast, and I was also curious about the Foxes' eighteen-year-old daughter, Imogen.

Queen's Park was just three stations up the Bakerloo line from Little Venice, and I was surprised by how quickly we reached the appointed meeting place. Fifteen minutes after rising off the couch, I was sitting next to Lily on an improbably high barstool inside The Dove on Salusbury Road. "But I thought we were going to a pub," I said to Lily.

"And so we did," she replied. "But this, Mimi, is a *gastro*pub — meaning most of the waiters have had at least minimal dental work, and you probably won't get food poisoning from the chips."

"That sounds encouraging, I guess," I said, although I was

a tad disappointed not to be at an authentically down-and-out pub like the one I'd seen on television that afternoon. Instead of having peeling grandmotherly wallpaper, plaid carpeting, and hunchbacked regulars, The Dove was sleek and spare, with communal tables and blackboards on the wall posting that night's dinner specials, dishes like "farm-fed chicken" and "salad of baby greens."

I was still scoping my unexpectedly swish surroundings when a pair of girls strutted through the frosted-glass front door. Pink-cheeked and pudgy, they carried themselves with supreme confidence. I recognized the darker-haired of the girls from the photographs plastered all over the kitchen at 54 Bloomfield Road as Imogen Fox, my pseudosister for the summer. Her skin was splattered with small red dots, but her features were flawless.

"Hello, darling!" she said when she came up to Lily. "So sorry if we're a bit late. I was on the phone with Mum and you know how she tends to rabbit on and on."

"Not at all, not at all," Lily replied. "We just got here a second ago."

Imogen hadn't skimped on the foundation or eyeliner, but the excess agreed with her outrageous outfit: a ruffled halter top with a bustle-like contraption and a waist separated several inches from skintight black pants possibly of suede. Her companion had dyed blond hair but was wearing a simpler ensemble of white jeans and a lime green sequined tank top.

"Imogen tells me you only just arrived here," Imogen's friend said to me as the waiter showed us to our table. "How are you finding it?"

"It's wonderful," I said eagerly — too eagerly. "I love it! By the way," I said, extending my hand, "I'm Mimi. Thanks so much for coming out with us tonight — this place is awesome!" I could hear how shrill and American I sounded.

"Lovely to meet you," the girl said, without giving me her name in response. She took her seat at the picnic table and smiled at me pleasantly.

"And you're . . . ?" I had to prod. "I didn't catch your name."

"Oh, sorry. Tunisia. Tooney for short."

In normal circumstances, I might've laughed out loud at this name. In fact, Boris and I used to make fun of his nouveau riche uncle for naming his twin sons Paris and London. In his presence, we called each other by ridiculous geographical pet names, like Zagreb and, my personal favorite, Tigris-Euphrates. But Boris seemed very far away from The Dove that evening, and as I shook Tooney's tiny manicured hand, I found myself saying, with complete sincerity, "Wow — what a *beautiful* name."

"Bollocks," she said brightly. "I wish my mum could've chosen something normal, like China or India, but she's completely bonkers. She's called Mary Clarke, and when she met my dad, she absolutely couldn't wait to change her surname to Varnoozis."

"Yes," said Imogen, who like Tunisia felt no need to introduce herself, "and now her two children are called Tunisia and Mirabeau Varnoozis — isn't that mad?"

"That's really —" I started to say, but the two newcomers were entirely wrapped up in their own conversation.

"Now it's come full circle," Tunisia said. "Beau — that's what we call my brother — married a Sue Smith, and my boyfriend is Bob Watkins."

Imogen clutched her temples. "Bloody hell, can we not talk about Bob for a change? He's dead boring. Obsessed by rugby, of all things! Absolutely *not* marriage material, IMHO."

IMHO? Imogen Must Have Olives? I shot Lily a confused look.

"Well, in *my* humble opinion," she said, translating for me, "*no*body is marriage material before age fifty."

But Tunisia was too busy glaring at Imogen to catch Lily's insight. "Oh, *do* stop banging on about it, won't you?" she cried. "I don't give a toss about marriage material. At least Bob doesn't spend his weekends butchering foxes in the countryside!"

"Alistair never makes any of the shots — he does it for the exercise and you know it!" Imogen huffed. "Incidentally, since when did you care so much about animals? Last time I checked, *I* was the vegetarian and you were the veal fanatic."

"You can stop trying to wind me up; you won't succeed. I'd *never* touch veal! It's barbaric."

"Rubbish — what about last week at the Wellington Rooms, after Claire's leaving do?"

"Yes, well, I split it with Bryony," Tunisia admitted. "And she'd ordered it before I got there."

At this point in the argument, our waiter came up to take our order. With a sharp look at her friend, Imogen ordered the organic portobello sandwich and mashed potatoes. "Oh, and a half-pint of lager, if you don't mind," she added.

"By the way, what's the drinking age here?" I asked Lily under my breath. The Foxes' laid-back attitude toward drinks with dinner seemed to extend beyond the boundaries of Bridge House.

Lily shrugged and put a finger to her lips. "Don't let anyone hear you ask that," she whispered back, "or you'll be accused of being 'American,' which is almost as bad as 'suburban.'" In an even quieter tone, she said, "It's eighteen, but don't worry — I don't think 'card' is even a verb here."

"Cool," I said, and ordered not a half but a whole pint with my meal, as casually as I could manage. I didn't want anyone to see how grown-up and sophisticated I felt.

Once the waiter left, I sat back and listened as Imogen and Tooney talked, seeming to forget they were sharing a table with two other people. They weren't rude exactly, just a little self-absorbed. As Imogen talked, I couldn't help but think how like her mother she was. Like Pippa, she was charismatic and uninhibited and somewhat schizoid as she skirted from topic to topic, and I could tell that she, too, found life rather easy.

It was only after the food arrived on basic white plates that Imogen addressed me directly for the first time. "I'm so sorry," she said abruptly, without even a glance at the oversize mushroom sandwich in front of her. "You must think we're such twats for nattering on like that. Do tell us a bit about yourself before Tooney and I go off again."

"Hmm, let's see," I said, flattered by her sudden attention. "Well, I used to live in Texas, and then last year I moved to New —"

"Yes, but in London," Imogen interrupted. "What do you

plan on doing here? Mum tells me you met with Uncle Charlie this morning?"

"I did," I said, assuming she was referring to my new boss. I briefly told everyone about my job interview and subsequent homework assignment. "I'm not sure what I'll be doing there, but I have a *very* cute office trainer." I blushed, remembering Anthony and the Xerox machine incident.

"Oh, brilliant," Tunisia said. "A bit of slap and tickle always livens up the workplace, I find. And I am *such* a fan of that magazine. If you dig up any dirt on Cressida, you must promise to fill us in."

"I will, definitely," I said, pleased that I actually knew who she was talking about. Cressida — no last name — was a gigantic-breasted starlet who had met her sitcom-actor husband on a reality show in the South Pacific and had recently published a "tell-all memoir" about the behind-the-scenes rivalries on *Stranded's* set. As far as I could tell, Cressida was neither an actress nor a singer, just an all-purpose A-lister with her own perfume, underwear line, and yoga video.

Before too long, Tunisia and Imogen resumed talking about themselves, while Lily and I settled back into our eavesdropping role. The lifelong best friends — they'd met in Regent's Park, where their nannies took them every morning as infants — had just graduated from the private boarding school in Kent that they'd attended since the age of nine. They were now brimming with plans for the future: Tunisia was starting at Sussex University in the fall, while Imogen was taking a "gap year," which she explained was a common thing to do. "A lot of the girls I know are going to India or Australia, but I'm dreadfully bored with travel at the moment," she said. "So I've decided to stay in London. There are a few weddings I absolutely can't skip this autumn, and perhaps I can even finish my play. I've been working on it for ages, and Dad's got this mate who's just stonking rich, and he's agreed to produce it on the West End if it's up to standard!"

"I'm impressed!" I said, and told them about the scene I had to write for my creative writing class at Baldwin. "Getting characters to sound like real people is *so* hard. And you're almost done?"

"Well, yes, in a manner of speaking," Imogen said, mindlessly playing with a pimple on her chin. "I'm finished with the outline. I haven't actually started the dialogue yet, but it's going to be completely brilliant."

"Everything Imo does is completely brilliant," Tunisia assured us.

The Curious Incident Chez Scissors Thompson

Without intending it, i drank several pints of beer at the gastropub, and the next morning I woke up feeling fuzzy in the head and bloated everywhere else. With no time to fine-tune my outfit, I threw on some navy thrift store pants and a white tank top, then wrapped an old men's dress shirt around my waist. The Katharine Hepburn look, I told myself. Or at least Katharine Hepburn playing a street person.

On the long commute out to Canary Wharf, I found myself almost looking forward to Anthony quizzing me on my vastly expanded knowledge of British celebrities. But when I reached the office, it wasn't Anthony Palfrey who was waiting for me in the reception area. It was Rebecca Bridgewater, decked out in a bandeau halter-top thingie that no woman over age eighteen should be allowed to wear.

After minimal small talk, she briskly outlined my assignment for the morning and showed me to a crowded cubicle. "These are the contact details for the cast of *Lonsdale*," she said, handing me a list of mostly unfamiliar names, each followed by five phone numbers labeled "home," "mobile," "publicist," "agent" and "PA." "You'll be polling them about their favorite ready-made meals at M and S," she said. "A few might get a bit shirty when they hear your accent, but we haven't given you any A-listers, so for the most part they'll be thrilled at the chance of a chat with the U.K.'s top celebrity magazine. Oh, and here you are: I've typed up a little script for you, so it should be fairly straightforward. Just read it verbatim and jot down the replies. Any questions?"

She didn't ask this in the most encouraging tone of voice, but I couldn't help myself. "M and S? That means . . . ?"

"Oh, but you *have* just fallen off the turnip truck, haven't you?" Rebecca said with a wry little laugh. She gave a little tug at her halter. "It's shorthand for Marks and Spencer. It's sort of an upscale Woolworth's — an all-purpose grocery store and clothing shop. Fully one-third of the women in the United Kingdom buy their knickers there, nowhere better."

Rebecca parked me inside the cubicle of a member of the advertising department named Penny, who was on an extended maternity leave. "It's your desk for the time being," Rebecca said, "but do just try to keep it tidy."

With that vaguely accusatory order, she left. I spent the next few minutes surreptitiously examining those seated around me, trying to pick out potential friends. The rows of cubicles were buzzing with people hard at work, tapping on their computers and either timidly whispering or violently shouting into the telephone. The photo editor — Decca, I learned from the masthead — was as big and loud as an elephant. "I said the pictures are on spec!" she was shouting. "Nobody pays upfront these days!"

The two middle-aged women closest to me, with their ash-colored hair and frowsy clothing, looked alike enough to be twins.

The two girls facing them seemed more promising lunchtime companions: a pixielike brunette with colorful barrettes in her hair and a pink-faced girl with glitter eye shadow who glanced up from her monitor to smile at me. Then a straight-arrow guy, or "young man" as my mom would call him, bopped over to introduce himself as Nicholas. He shook my hand and invited me to refer any office questions to him. Before I could think of any, however, his cell phone rang and he ran off.

Next I turned my attention to Penny's disorganized cubicle. Wadded-up Kleenexes and Cadbury wrappers littered the surface of the desk, and next to her telephone were two fuzzy hippopotamus figures with spring-mounted heads. I pushed the heads up and down a few times before making my first phone call.

"Hello," I said, following the tidy script Rebecca had given me: "I'm calling from *A-ha!* magazine, and for next week's issue, we're doing a special feature on celebs and food, and here's what Britain wants to know: What's your favorite Marks and Spencer Ready Meal?"

Though I thought the question sounded pretty stupid, the first star I reached, Sooty Lewison, seemed to feel otherwise. "Oh, how clever!" she cried. "Can you bear with me one instant? I'm at home now. Let's have a look-see." There were footsteps, then the sound of Sooty whispering, "It's *A-ha!*" to someone on the other end. "Hmm, let's see what we have here," she said when at last she reached the fridge. "Tagliatelle with ham and mushroom — mmm, that one's scrummy. . . . Not so keen on the chicken tikka masala — that one's been in here for *ages,* it must've gone off by now. . . . Oh, and here's liver and bacon, that one's quite nice, and the Cumberland pies as well. . . . And the smoked haddock rarebit is absolutely brilliant — yes, that's it, you'll have to put me down for the rarebit."

Sooty set the upbeat tone for the rest of that morning's interviews. Rebecca had been right: bottom-feeder celebrities truly were thrilled to hear from *A-ha!* By the end of the morning, I had a list of twelve *Lonsdale* stars' favorite Marks & Spencer Ready Meals, ranging from braised steak and something nasty-sounding called "kedgeree" to prawn biriyani with four-cheese banana fritters.

Just as I was about to call Gavin Scott-Palmer, the next actor on my list, Penny's phone beeped, and — though I knew I should've let voice mail take it — I impulsively picked it up. "Penny's desk," I said in my best official voice.

"Mimi, it's Palfrey here." Anthony's voice. Smooth, cocksure, adorable Anthony. "See you in the lobby for two?"

"For two what?"

"Two o'clock, you ninny. Or better yet, come fetch me at my desk. I'm covering an exceptionally grim event in Essex this afternoon, and you're obligated to accompany me. Consider it part of your training."

I'd met the boy yesterday, and he was already inviting me on day trips? Was this cosmic reward for suffering through Boris's detour to Frankfurt? I told him that sounded fine, provided Charlie Lappin didn't object.

"Object?" Anthony's laugh echoed across the office. "But darling, you won't be skiving — it was entirely his idea."

With no idea what he'd just said, I went back to my calls. Five successful phone interviews later, when it was almost two, I took my notes to Rebecca Bridgewater. She had me wait outside her office while she reviewed the results. "You had seventeen interviews, did you?" she asked with a trace of suspicion. "Well, I suppose that's that, then. Tomorrow we'll be starting work on a spread about bikini horror stories; I'll prepare the same sort of script for you."

After she dismissed me, I zigzagged the office for several minutes in search of Anthony's cubicle. I found him at a desk no larger than Penny's, with his head flopped over his keyboard. I hesitated an instant. "Anthony?"

Very slowly he pulled himself up and swiveled to face me. "Bloody hell, what time is it?" he asked, rubbing his eyes.

"I thought you said we were leaving at two."

"I did, but that was before you interrupted the nice little kip I was having. Christ, can you remind me why I stayed out doing vodka shots with the tech crew from *Cressington Embers*?"

I had no reply ready, so I just hovered over his cubicle as he stayed seated, yawning, stretching, and mussing his hair. This aerial position gave me plenty of opportunity to study him at close range. Today's outfit was somewhat more normal: navy corduroys, a pale pink button-down shirt, and red socks.

On the long cab ride to the train station, Anthony was busy clutching his forehead and groaning something about "the hair of the dog." He remained taciturn as we walked inside the enormous, sparkling Liverpool Street station. Still unclear on why we were going to Essex (or where, for that matter, Essex was), I waited by a pick-and-mix candy stand called Sweet Chariot while Anthony bought our tickets.

"What sort of rubbish have you got into?" he asked several minutes later of the huge bag of chocolate-covered pretzels I'd bought. "Toss them in the bin. Now. The cardinal rule of celebrity journalism," he explained, "is that one *always* arrives at these functions on an empty stomach. Filling up on freebies is ninety percent of the point."

I asked him what the other ten percent was.

"Still a great mystery. I'm hoping it will reveal itself one of these days."

It was funny how much I liked Anthony already. I usually fixate on boys I can talk circles around, like the brooding Max Roth or the enigmatic Boris. But Anthony was gossipy and almost hyperactively chatty. When he excitedly described the party we were about to attend, I could barely get a word in. Apparently, stylist to the stars Simon "Scissors" Thompson — whose flagship London salon was a tourist destination — was launching a new product line and opening a dozen new signature salons across the country. At the kickoff party for the new Essex Scissors, Anthony and I would be "profiling" the celebs in attendance. "Only the most desperate D-lister saddos will bother to show, but who knows?" Anthony said. "Perhaps they'll supply us with a few good tidbits."

"You make everyone sound so lame," I told him as we sat down in a second-class car. I was feeling a little more collected. "It *is* a party after all. Why wouldn't good people attend?"

"Love, any proper celeb with a sentient publicist is invited to hundreds of rubbish events a week. You don't trek all the way to Essex in the middle of the bloody afternoon unless you're absolutely desperate to get papped."

"Papped? And where is Essex, by the way?"

"Photographed by the paparazzi. And Essex is a dreadful middle-class suburb about three-quarters of an hour to the east of London."

"Oh, right," I said, my next question already prepared. "If it's so pathetic of the stars to go to these events, doesn't that make us pathetic for going to them, too?"

"Certainly not! We're just doing our jobs. No crime in that."

Satisfied with his briefing, Anthony rolled his sweater into a ball, stuck it behind the crook of his neck, and almost immediately fell into a deep slumber, his eyelids fluttering behind his glasses.

As the train plowed east, I gazed happily out the window at the unbroken cityscape of apartment blocks and TV antennae. I still couldn't believe I was in England, where even buying an unfamiliar flavor of potato chips or crossing a street with cars driving on the wrong side of the road made me tingle. Anthony — buoyant, eccentric, articulate Anthony — would've made me tingle even if he were from suburban Dallas. Of course, no one from suburban Dallas would have such a tingly accent.

When the train pulled into our station, Anthony pushed his glasses back in place and sprang to his feet as if he'd been awake the whole time. "Hop to it," he said smoothly. "One of our photographers, a bloke called Ian Cassidy, will be collecting us here. In case you didn't know, in the pecking order of the gossip biz, the monkeys — that's what we call the photogs — are right up there with God. They make gobs of money and spend the majority of their energy taking the piss out of lowly reporters. You'll see."

Ian Cassidy was waiting for us on the platform, and I instantly recognized him as the man who'd accepted payment for the cupid cardigan from the *A-ha!* receptionist the previous day. He was overweight and underheight and sallow, with coarse black hair and bright red ears. But though he was similar in appearance to most of the British men on the train with us, his fashion sense was entirely his own. He was decked out head to toe in camouflage, with a thick and possibly bulletproof vest with about one hundred zippers. An improbable number of press passes hung from his neck, and camera parts were strapped all over his body like armor. He looked as if he were about to go on safari.

After a cursory introduction, Ian took us to the salon a few blocks south of the station. He and Anthony made an interesting pair, I thought. Whereas Anthony was the ultimate dandy, Ian was unpretentious, almost grizzled. And Anthony was a master banterer, while Ian grunted most of his commentary. Still, the two seemed to get along pretty well. On the walk over, I trailed behind as Anthony brought Ian up to speed on the goings-on in the office.

"All the usual chaos," Anthony said. "Ogilvy's buyout went south, and all the adverts got pulled."

"Blimey!" Ian responded.

"Oh, and you'll love this: Nigel's gained two stone and is talking of converting to Hinduism."

"Yeah, yeah, he's been threatening that for ages. What else is new?" Ian sounded unimpressed. "How about Nicholas — what's happening with him?"

"There's a good one for you — he's threatening to quit if Jon doesn't get the sack."

"Always at sixes and sevens, those two."

A few minutes into this lopsided dialogue, we rounded a corner and came to the salon: a three-storied hair village with an enormous statue of scissors out front. A group of kids was testing it out to see if the hinge worked. It did.

Once inside, Ian got to work. His brow grew dark and pensive as he removed different-size lenses from his safari suit to snap pictures of the guests. Even though he was even more underdressed than I, Ian seemed comfortable in this setting, like a fish released back into the ocean. Anthony, too, appeared perfectly at ease in the sea of high-pitched laughter and overstyled personalities.

I felt exactly the opposite, like an unwieldy piece of luggage left on the baggage carousel. Anthony had instructed me to shadow him, but I was uncomfortable watching him flirt with stars old enough to be his mother. I excused myself when he told the woman who played the football player's mother on *Rosedale Crescent* that she looked "ravishing" and asked if she'd enjoyed any plastic surgery lately.

I wound up in the least populated corner of the room, over by the hair-washing stations. The food had been designed to resemble different hair types, ranging from straight lines to curlicues. I served myself a plate of spiral noodles, ladled on extra Alfredo sauce, and got to work. When I looked up midway, Anthony caught my eye. Keeping his expression serious, he put his finger behind his ear and made his glasses wiggle up and down his forehead. I scrunched my nose at him in response.

The only guest I recognized was Thom Thorpe, the "television presenter" I'd read about who was recently implicated in a gay sex scandal involving a guard at the Tate Modern. He had a buzz cut and the top of his head was bald and shiny. His complexion was unattractively pockmarked and his nose was round and wet, like a pug's. His saving grace was a pair of beautiful green eyes with the longest lashes. As a representative of *A-ha!* I knew I should accost him — "chat him up," as Anthony would say — and so, in an act of great professionalism, I left my plate on a chair and walked over to Thom.

I introduced myself as a reporter from *A-ha!* which I'd assumed would please him as much as it had the *Lonsdale* stars I'd canvassed about their favorite prepared Marks & Spencer dinners, but Thom assessed me warily before shifting away.

"Don't worry," I said, smiling gently, as I do when speaking to Boris's little brother, Constantine. "I'm just trying to collect quotes from all the famous people here."

"So sorry," Thom said curtly, "but I'm afraid I'm not really in the mood."

"Any old comment will do," I pressed on. "Like, how about

telling me about your worst haircut ever? We could run the quote along with a pict —"

"Maybe next time?"

And with that, Thom Thorpe ditched me.

At least there was still plenty of food to console me — always a balm in moments of humiliation. After reuniting with my plate, I stood in the corner watching Thom fix himself a meal of cheese curls and licorice at the buffet table. And then a crazy thing happened. In a single, balletically smooth movement, Thom set the plate on the table and swiped three pomade jars from a display case. His eyes darting around the room, he quickly transferred the loot to his jacket pocket.

He picked up his plate and started shoveling in the food. Why, I wondered, would a gainfully employed grownup, and a practically bald one at that, steal hairstyling products? Then again, Pia — whose parents would give her anything — had taught me that shoplifting isn't a need-based activity.

"Nicely done, Mimi," Anthony said, sidling up beside me and gesturing at my empty plate. "Very postwar — waste not, want not — isn't it though? I thought American birds were meant to *eat* like birds."

"I didn't have lunch," I lied. Then, to change the subject, I asked, "So, did you pick up any juicy tidbits?"

"It hasn't been half bad, actually," Anthony said. He glanced at his notepad to read some of his scribblings aloud. "Ron Rampling just got back from holiday in Croatia, where he got engaged not once but *twice*. My God, but he's *completely* mental! And oh, this one's amusing. Sasha Entbert, the sexpot from the band

Singerton, explained why she's lucky to have such small breasts — although, if I might be so indelicate as to point out, she has nothing of the sort. And the bloke from the Subatomic Machines praised Scissors Thompson's technique with the electric razor, likening him to Picasso." Anthony slipped the notepad into his pocket and then asked me, "And how are you getting on? Gathering witticisms from the pasta, are you?"

"Basically," I said, "I've just been standing here watching Thom Thorpe swipe some exclusive Scissors Thompson hair-care products."

Anthony snorted. "Baldy Thom Thorpe nicking hair products. Wouldn't that be fantastic!"

"I'm serious," I said. "Check out the left pocket of his jacket. You see the blue thing sticking out? It's a jar of pomade, and there are several more where that came from."

"You don't — why, you mean to say you're not taking the piss?" When I shook my head, he cried, "But Mimi, you're bloody brilliant! Charlie will be absolutely over the moon. We *must* find Ian."

As Anthony pushed through the crowd to locate the *A-ha!* photographer, I stood there buzzing with pleasure. So what if the Thom Thorpe pomade theft didn't exactly rank up there with my Serge Ziff scoop? I enjoyed even the minor triumphs. Thirty seconds earlier, I had been useless and conspicuous, and now, just like that, I was "bloody brilliant."

Ian loved it, too. As he refitted his camera with a ginormous telephoto lens, he was shaking with laughter. Meanwhile, poor

Thom Thorpe, who had no idea he was under surveillance, continued to inhale pasta even as Ian zoomed in on the pilfered pomade.

"She's a sharp one," Ian advised Anthony, tipping his chin my way as he screwed off the mountainous lens and returned it to one of the zippered pockets on his vest. "Watch out for her."

Slap and Tickle

When we left the salon, the sky had faded to a pale pink. "The car is this way — follow me," Ian said, walking ahead of us at a fast clip.

"You've clearly made quite the impression," Anthony confided to me. "Ian never gives lifts to us lowly hacks. He's left me stranded in the middle of the motorway at all hours of the night. It's a miracle I'm still intact."

"Stuff and nonsense!" Ian called back cheerfully. "I'm hired as a photographer, not a chauffeur."

"My dad's a photographer, too, you know," I said, though I don't think Ian heard. We'd just turned onto a busy commercial street, and I gave a little gasp at the sight of my first Marks & Spencer. I saw none of the store's famous Ready Meals in the window display, but one of the mannequins was wearing the underwear that, according to Rebecca Bridgewater, one-third of all women in the United Kingdom favored.

"I prefer the sportier styles myself," Anthony said, catching me studying the mannequin's lacy undergarments, "but to each his own, I suppose."

"Ah, here she is," Ian said, coming to a stop beside his parked vehicle, which was the transportation equivalent of his outfit: a mammoth olive green four-door pickup truck with customized tread wheels that were higher than my waist. I hadn't seen such a large car in all of Europe, or even New York. No, Ian's car belonged in a rap video, or on a South Texas highway.

After he and Anthony got in the front seat, Ian reached over to open the back door for me. "This is amazing," I said as I climbed in. "No wonder you don't let anybody inside it." I looked at the photograph hanging from the rearview mirror. It showed three young boys, a black poodle with red ribbons on her ears, and a woman in an elaborately decorated sweater.

Before we took off, Anthony and Ian phoned the office to report on our unexpected success at Scissors. "He was trying to nab off with the pomade — you'll jolly well piss yourself when you see the snaps I got," Ian bragged to someone, while Anthony gave Rebecca Bridgewater a dressed-up account of our afternoon. "Absolutely riveting stuff," he gushed, "better even than his tryst at the Tate Modern!"

The ride back was short, "much better than the way out — it was chock-a-bloc on the M25, a car park, if you want the truth," said Ian. When we entered central London, Anthony and Ian, still jubilant, seemed reluctant to bring our rollicking adventure to an end. "No victory too small for a pint," Ian declared. "Who fancies a celebratory drink?"

"It would be uncivilized to refuse," Anthony said, while I just bobbed my head in agreement, pleased to have the opportunity to hang around him a little longer.

Because we all lived in different parts of town (Ian in Peckham and Anthony in West Hampstead), Ian chose Waterloo, my transfer station just south of the Thames, as a convenient midway point. "Smashing place I know just round the corner here," he said as he parked his massive vehicle in a tour bus lot a few blocks behind the station.

After last night's outing to the gastropub with Imogen, Tunisia, and Lily, I was looking forward to finally seeing a British pub of the old school, but once again I was out of luck. The Firehouse was industrial and bare, with shelves of model fire engines and large red poles every few feet. Even so, the décor turned out not to matter, for at Anthony's suggestion, we took our beers outside and drank standing up on the sidewalk. The pavement was narrow, and sometimes we had to make room for a cluster of pedestrians or a baby carriage. In New York, drinking outside was a major no-no; here no one thought twice about it, and I enjoyed the illicit thrill of drinking on the street. Or, for that matter, drinking in public at all.

Before I'd taken two sips of my beer, my companions had polished off theirs, and Ian volunteered to fetch refills. No sooner had he left than Anthony removed a monogrammed handkerchief from his pocket and began dabbing the beer dribble off his chin. "I'm frequently abused for this affectation," he said, "but I have a sound defense: it's passed down by my grandfather."

"Did you also pick up your primary-colored-socks affectation from him?" I asked playfully. Maybe because Anthony was so verbal, he was easier to flirt with than most guys.

"No, that's my own innovation. I have him to thank for the hankies and the antique map collection — little else, I'm afraid."

"What about the rest of your family?" I asked. "What are they like?"

Over the past day, Anthony had taught me plenty about *A-ha!* and the "D-lister" set, but almost nothing about himself. I expected him, being British and all, to divert the topic, but he answered my forward question at length. He came, he told me, from a "perfectly proper" home in Richmond, a well-to-do suburb in southwest London. Like his father, grandfather, and great-grandfather before him (and probably a few more "greats" — I lost track at some point), Anthony had gone from some fancy all-boys prep school to Cambridge, where he belonged to the debate club and some eons-old secret society. "We had such larks," he said of the latter. "Every year, we had Mrs. Mulligan's Birthday and did everything in reverse order, with *digestifs* and cigars first thing in the morning and tea and toast at night."

But though he'd attended the same schools as his forebears, Anthony had pursued a different course of study. "My father's a barrister," he said, "and so are both of my brothers, and so was my grandfather, and so on through the generations. I was expected to do the same bloody boring thing myself."

"But you'd always dreamed of papping D-lister celebs?" I asked, proud at how almost local I sounded.

"Hardly! I read medieval history."

"Seriously?"

"Quite." Anthony took a big breath. "I spent an unhealthy portion of my boyhood fantasizing about King Arthur's Court. But when I came down to London, I couldn't bear the thought of working at the British Museum with all those dusty dowagers. Not in the least like Queen Guinevere — now *there's* a fit lass."

"Yeah," I said, "I see her doing bench presses at the gym all the time."

Stifling a laugh, Anthony explained that "fit" meant "attractive." "Not solely a byproduct of bodybuilding, though I quite understand your confusion. There was disappointingly little skin in medieval history, actually. We focused more on the plague, and papal usury, and famine, and torture mechanisms, and all that sort of thing."

"And you must've learned something about chivalry, too," I said, then immediately regretted my words. Was I *that* inexperienced a drinker that I became so obvious after half a pint of lager? Or was Anthony somehow, subtly and Britishly, egging me on?

Ian trundled out of the pub clutching three pint glasses. Though I hadn't finished my first beer yet, I accepted the frothing refill from him.

"Need a bit of help there?" Anthony reached for the pint I'd been holding and drained it in one gulp. "So you see," he said, proffering the empty glass, "I *do* know a bit about chivalry."

"Watch you don't get too sozzled, big Ant," Ian said sternly, just as a digitalized version of the *Beverly Hills Cop* theme erupted inside his military regalia. "Oh, blimey," he said, pulling his cell phone from one of the many Velcro straps connected to his belt. "It's me old wife. Again."

He stepped closer to the curb to take the call, leaving Anthony and me alone together again.

"So wait, you never told me if you like *A-ha!*" I said to him. "Do you prefer it to working at the British Museum or being a lawyer?"

"Need you ask?" Anthony asked lightly. "My father continues to *insist* I return to school and read law, but I greatly prefer bumbling about with Britain's finest washouts.

He broke off, a dreamy expression filling his face as he stared past my shoulder. I turned around to follow his eyes, and there, a few feet past Ian, a petite, high-breasted blonde was striding down the street in a tulip-printed sundress and vertiginously tall platform sandals.

Anthony was still staring when Ian snapped shut his phone and lumbered back over to us. "She's hearing none of it," he complained. "I took the dog out this morning and she didn't relieve herself, yeah? So then the missus comes home to find loads of piss all over the new sofa, and who's she blame? Not the bloody poodle, but yours truly, that's it. She's fit to be tied, she is. What'd she expect me to do this morning, wring out the poor sod's bladder on the greens?" Ian busied himself zipping up various compartments on his vest, shaking his head as he said, "I must apologize, but it's off to Peckham straightaway, before the missus changes the locks."

As we watched Ian dejectedly slink toward his car, I told Anthony that I should get going as well. "Oh, come on, then, we'll have one last pint for the road," he cajoled.

Though my beer was still full, Anthony dashed inside for refills. Waiting on the curb, I couldn't stop thinking about the china-doll girl he'd just ogled. Anthony couldn't possibly be interested in her *and* me. Guys transfixed on five-foot-two, ninety-pound blondes didn't tend to be all that attracted to my ungainly self.

"Why the face like a wet weekend?" Anthony asked when he returned holding our final drinks. "Don't tell me you're pining for some strapping American lad — that would be altogether *too* depressing."

"N-no," I said, too quickly. "Of course not."

"C'mon then, out with it," he pursued. "You *must* have a boyfriend."

"A boyfriend?" I repeated, taken aback by Anthony's directness. Would it put him off to learn about Boris? Or would he think I was a loser if I claimed to be single? And was I single, anyway? Officially, at least, Boris and I *were* still going out, even if we had very different ideas of what "going out" meant. Boris had yet to reply to my momentous last e-mail, about moving to London and missing him.

In the end, I told Anthony the truth: that the long-distance element had seriously complicated my relationship back home. Then, before he could think of any follow-up questions, I asked, "And you? Any Guineveres in your life?"

Did I really just say that? God, I was *such* a loser.

"Oh, here and there," Anthony said, blinking at what was left of his drink. "No, honestly, there's just one girl, Lucy. We were at Cambridge together, and have been on and off for years — you know how it goes."

"Totally," I said, bobbing my head and faking familiarity with such a setup.

"We're off at the moment," he said, "which suddenly strikes me as quite convenient."

Despite his evasive wording, Anthony's expression left little room for interpretation. He was staring straight at me as I chortled with nervous laughter, and my cheeks turned redder than the antique fire truck inside the bar.

To: "Ppazzolini", "Vrock2000", "Jessieg"
From: "Mimicita86"
Date: July 3, 9:54 p.m.
Subject: Change of Address/Altitude/Attitude

Howdy! What's new? Last I heard, Pia was caught taking
her neighbor's motorboat for a joyride and Jess finished
her interborough Romeo and Juliet story. (Bravo, btw.)
And Viv — how's Oregon?

As I think Lily already told you, I escaped Germany and
am living with her in London now, though already we
don't see each other often enough. But besides that, and
some guilt about my abandoned mother, life is lovely,
perfectly lovely. I have a new job, new slang, and even a
new crush — on my colleague Anthony (pronounced the
English way: "Ant-ony"). He's twenty and superformal in
dress and vocabulary but also wicked and hilarious and
CUTE. I wish you could see Lily here. Gone is the
tomboyish newspaper editor we all knew — she's very
worldly all of a sudden. Tres fab. Ta-ta! Or whatever.

xxxxxxxxxxMimi

To: "HWYates"
From: "Mimicita86"
Date: July 3, 11:13 p.m.
Subject: cheers!

Dear Harriet,

How are you? Remember what you said when I was
leaving your beautiful party? I hope you were serious
about my coming out to the Hamptons. It'd be nice to
hang out after my frenetic European summer. Speaking
of which, I keep meaning to fill you in on my own change
of travel plans. Berlin wasn't as much fun as the *New
York Times* Travel section would have you believe, so
thanks to Lily, I ended up coming to London, which is
confusing but wonderful. I'm learning tons — about, for
example, "smoked prawn"–flavored potato "crisps" and
the wonders of baked beans and fried mushrooms for
breakfast. And did you know that the queen is actually
only the twenty-third richest person in the country, and
"Hattie" is short for Harriet? Given your name, probably.
As for me, I'm working at this gossip magazine that's,
well, bizarre. Will send you a few issues from the office
so you can show Ed, but don't read them in public —
topless celebs show up on many a beach spread. Some
things I'll never get used to!

xo Mimi

Not Quite Bagels

W<small>E ALL HAVE OUR TRADITIONS</small>, even the most unpredictable and free-spirited among us. The Foxes' ritual was Saturday lunch, although "Saturday breakfast" seemed more accurate, since it got started long before I did. My first Saturday in London, I straggled down to the kitchen wearing only boxer shorts and one of Viv's ancient CBGB T-shirts.

I was groggy and thirsty and ill prepared for the scene awaiting me. The entire Fox clan, Imogen included, had assembled around the kitchen table amid a jumble of newspapers and saucers and vases. "Mimi!" Pippa cried when she saw me. "We didn't hear you come down!"

"I say," added Robin, "your footfall is lighter than a gazelle's! Now, can I get you a cuppa? Tea, coffee, what'll you have?"

"I'm fine, thanks," I said, too bowled over by the perfection of this family to request my usual orange juice. Even when my parents were together, we'd never had mornings like this; everyone was always too busy or too stressed. But the Foxes, even with their high-powered jobs, were straight out of a Merchant Ivory movie. A sullen Adrian sat looking uncomfortable in a button-down shirt while Imogen applied frosting to a multitiered cake. Pippa stood at the counter closest to the fridge, alternating between separating eggs into a bowl and stirring a pot of green peas. Next to her, Robin was browsing an antiques magazine with a pair of brass scissors in his hand. He compulsively clipped out any article that might prove useful for his art fund, and most tables in the vast Fox house were scattered with the fruits of Robin's research.

Everyone was perfectly dressed, too: Robin and Adrian in crisp shirts, Pippa and Imogen in cocktail dresses. Realizing how my own outfit measured up in comparison, I sputtered, "I — I'm *so* sorry to come downstairs like this!"

"Oh, tosh," said Pippa without interrupting either of her tasks. "We've seen it all, darling. The last time Imo's friends crashed out here, they tore through the house almost starkers, as if they owned only knickers."

Imogen looked up from her cake to roll her eyes. "Mum, that's an outrageous overstatement. Those were *extremely* expensive camisoles — you paid for them, so you should know."

"Mimi, care for a spot of tea?" Robin asked again, as if on autopilot.

"Do let her get changed first, darling," Pippa said. Then to me, she added, "We're having several friends over for Saturday lunch, so do hurry along and join us. And if you could, pop into the study and tell Lily we're nearly ready for her as well."

Robin made a series of clicking noises at Lulu, who had just strolled into the kitchen. God, I thought, even the Foxes' mangy cat looked elegant this Saturday morning, her missing eye like a monocle.

On my way to the fourth floor, I stopped by Pippa's office,

where Lily was seated at the computer table, doing e-mail. "You're requested downstairs at brunch, madam," I told her.

"It's Saturday *lunch*," she corrected me. "They don't do brunch around here." As she spoke, she logged off her account and turned to face me. That was when I saw that, for the first time since I'd known her, Lily Morton was wearing a skirt.

"Whoa, hot legs, what's going on here?" I cried. "Please tell me you're low on laundry — or was the real Lily abducted by aliens?"

"What*ever*," Lily said with a shrug. "I'm adapting to my new ecosphere, and so should you. Saturday lunch in the Fox household is an incredibly formal affair, so I suggest you go make yourself decent."

In the half-hour that I spent showering and changing into the dress Lily had given me on the day I arrived, the Foxes' downstairs parlor had filled with people. With Lulu stowed in the laundry room, Pippa opened the French doors to the garden, where guests were admiring Robin's new wrought-iron outdoor furniture. Imogen sat on one of the black benches beneath the clematis blossoms, laughing with the stubble-haired boy whose picture was papered all over her bedroom. When Pippa saw me standing on the terraced porch, idly surveying the scene, she rushed over with a platter of miniature vegetables. "Mimi, darling, will you be a dear and pass these around?" she asked distractedly, thrusting the platter at me. "It'll help enormously with the mingling."

I accepted the task and stepped out into the garden. Upon seeing me, Lily darted over and hissed, "Mimi, you've *got* to help! This creepy guy is practically stalking me — he won't leave me alone!"

"See what happens when you wear skirts?" I said with a smirk.

"Oh, shut up — I didn't ask for your fashion commentary. Just stick around in case he strikes again, all right?"

I was more than happy to oblige, especially since I hadn't met any of the Foxes' friends yet. Lily, who knew all of them, suggested we start by offering the miniveggies to the rather desolate-looking Julian Steadcroft. Lily told me that Mr. Steadcroft wrote historical novels set in Elizabethan England, and it struck me as an appropriate vocation, since the stooped author looked about five hundred years old. When he reached for a carrot stick, his wife, Penelope, swatted his hand away. "You've just had your dentures mended!" she reminded him. "Nothing crunchy now!"

Following this unsuccessful venture, we accosted a quivering little man in a bright rainbow ascot. Lily made the introductions: "Mimi Schulman, meet Dicky Faircrust. Mimi's my good friend from New York," she said, "and Dicky's a royal watcher."

"Oh, cool!" I said. "My mom's really into that, too — do you get a big range of bird species in central London?"

At this, Dicky's already thin lips drew into a straight line, and he cleared his throat pointedly before saying, "Ahem, no, I'm afraid you misheard. I'm not a bird watcher, I'm a *royal* watcher."

"Yeah," Lily jumped in, "meaning he studies the royal family for a living."

"Wow," I gasped, "so you actually *know* the king and queen?"

"There *is* no king, I'm afraid," Dicky drawled. "And members of the royal family never speak to the watchers. They're engaged in *far* more important matters."

Seconds later, the horrified Dicky rushed off in the direction of Robin's rosebushes. "What a freak!" I said afterward to Lily.

"Well, get used to seeing him. He's on every news show, commenting whenever a member of the royal family goes to the bathroom."

We then made our way over to Victoria Ardsdale, a sinewy thirty-something blonde who frowned suspiciously at us before plucking a miniature radish off the tray. Then, without a word of thanks, she glided over to where Robin was discoursing on different varieties of lilies. "You're welcome," I said to the space where she'd been standing.

"Oh, ignore her," Lily said. "I've known her forever, and she's never once deigned to speak to me. She's completely rude to — " Suddenly, Lily broke off and let out a little shriek. "Ack, you scared me!"

A man of indeterminate national identity had shoved between us and placed his palm on Lily's shoulder — this must be her stalker. He was in his thirties and incredibly fit, but not in the British sense of the word. He had a thin mustache that could've been drawn in eyeliner, and the top buttons of his shirt were undone to expose thick black swirls of chest hair. "Mimi," said Lily in a polite but pained voice, "this is Mario. He, ah, works for Pippa at the BBC."

"I'm down the hall, in programming as well," the man said in a possibly fake foreign accent. "I handle outreach." He rocked forward to kiss my cheeks, his lips landing repulsively close to the corners of my mouth. "I am very lucky in this job; Mrs. Fox is a *won*derful leader."

The drool had not yet dried on my cheeks when Pippa rang the bell summoning us to the table. In the procession inside, Lily and I succeeded in ditching smarmy Mario and ended up seated between a Russian couple who collected Fabergé eggs and were considering a sizable investment in the art fund that Robin managed. If they'd spoken any English, I might have inquired if they knew Boris's family back in the old country, but they didn't, so I refrained.

Robin made a big show of welcoming these guests by pouring everyone generous shots of some pricy potato vodka. Throughout the meal, he performed his one task of doling out liquor with gusto, supplying more free refills than a Mexican restaurant in Houston.

But it was Pippa who ran the party, and for the first time I saw in her the tireless, top-fifty mogul that the Rebecca Bridgewaters of the world held in such high esteem. I also understood why she and anal-retentive Margaret Morton were such close friends. Scatterbrained Pippa revealed herself to be bossy, sharp, and astonishingly efficient. She was an excellent cook, too, and served up five courses of heavy-duty dishes like lamb cutlets and creamed golden potatoes. When she wasn't rushing from the kitchen to the table, she was steering the conversation, addressing each of her guests individually, and touching on subjects that drew on everybody's expertise. At one point she even brought up Mexican food in an effort to pull me into the conversation. "The restaurants round here are getting it wrong, aren't they?" she asked. "I mean, really — chocolate fudge on a chicken cutlet? Positively foul, I tell you!"

I smiled. "That sounds like bad mole sauce. You should be able to taste the chocolate, but it shouldn't be sweet — or only a little. It should be really intense, almost sinister."

"Mmm, *sinister*." Mario said, letting the word linger in the air like strong cologne.

"I quite like the sound of that," Pippa said. "In London, even at the top Mexican restaurants, like that new place in Soho, Malo —"

"Kahlo," Mario gently corrected her. "Interesting night, wasn't that?" He was staring straight into the eyes of his hostess.

"In any event, the food was dreadful — all splodgy and greasy and absolutely impossible to stop eating!" Looking away from Mario, Pippa brought a forkful of potatoes to her mouth. "I'd say they must sprinkle it all with cocaine, but cocaine suppresses the appetite. They're doing *some*thing — *sinister* indeed, I'd say."

Everyone laughed, and so the merry meal progressed. The rest of the afternoon was a blur, what with all the Slavic spirits to taste and floral bouquets to smell and bizarro guests to observe. Even before Imogen brought out her three-tiered marzipan cake, I was completely stuffed — and I'm *never* stuffed. It was almost four when the guests finally began filing out. While Robin carried the stacks of plates into the kitchen, he congratulated his wife on another superb Saturday afternoon.

"I don't know how you manage, darling," he said, putting down a silver ladle to loop his arm around her waist. "It's equally puzzling, isn't it, how I've managed to capture the most spectacularly talented creature in Christendom for my wife."

At this, Pippa crumpled into her husband's embrace, and he kissed her tenderly on the forehead as she murmured, "All for you, darling, all for you."

Watching them, I felt a stab of sadness and envy. Had my parents *ever* been that smitten with each other, even way back in the beginning, before they had Ariel and me? Pippa and Robin were my parents' age, and they were *still* madly in love; it was insane to contemplate. Imogen could bake professionally, Adrian loaded the dishwasher without being asked, Lulu came out and purred like a pussycat from central casting — seriously, you couldn't invent a family this perfect.

From: "Vrock2000"
To: "Mimicita86"
Date: July 3, 8:15 p.m.
Subject: holy smokes

Mimi, You RAN AWAY FROM YOUR MOM? Is she going to kill you or are you going to have to kill her first? You are one brave soul. Let me know if you want to talk on the phone. Have Dad's AT&T card and he wouldn't notice if I called Jupiter. Which I might just do, btw, if I stay much longer in Oregon. The whole trip is a major letdown. . . . I'm praying the people at my record label internship will be more interesting than the kids on this tour (99% of them are from Long Island, if that means anything to you). This one girl brought 10 different designer bags — I swear to God. On a hiking trip! Not that it's all that rugged. . . . We're in this huge luxury bus that's so full of video-game gadgets and TV monitors that nobody ever looks out the window. Hmmm . . . what else? Oh, yeah, the other night, after a rest break at an IHOP, I accidentally boarded the wrong luxury bus. I fell asleep and an hour later woke up surrounded by senior citizens from Holland. It was a major ordeal to get back to the teenmobile, which had gone the opposite direction down the highway. There was one nice couple from Rotterdam who suggested I switch tours. Sort of like what you did. Man, you be crazy! E-mail me soonissima.
V.

To: "Mimicita86"
Date: July 4, 6:32 p.m.
Subject: Happy Fourth

Hey Mimi, I thought I'd be a big boy and reach out to wish you a happy Independence Day. Rumor has it you've busted free of the chains and tethers, but wait — aren't we celebrating our freedom from the *English?* Whatever. You've always done things your own way. I wish we'd said goodbye at the end of the year, but you know, life gets complicated sometimes. Or at least I do. Consider this my formal apology.

As you maybe already know, I'm at this summer program at Bennington. The courses are almost as crazy as at Baldwin — no wonder Zora Blanchard recommended it so heavily. I'm taking a class on underground Islamic art (which mostly involves reading comic books about women's secret lives) and a class on hosting your own radio show. We all get our own slots — mine's at 4 a.m. Wednesday morning and the one time the studio phone rang it was the wrong number, but I'm still enjoying it. I get to use my crazy deep voice and burn any CD I want from the killer music library. Been getting into ragtime, and they have this new wave Ethiopian jazz record I spent most of last year looking for, so I'm psyched.

The other kids are so-so. I've made friends with a girl from Tribeca named Rashida and a guy named — get this — Guy. He's from California and meditates every morning. Also, he's not into chairs — only sitting cross-legged on the floor. Rashida is a little less ridiculous, except when she talks about her "pansexuality." I think she's just trying to sound sophisticated, but I keep picturing her making out with frying pans.

I'm here till August, then back to NYC. Mom wants me to start studying for the SAT, though I can think of a few ways I'd rather spend the month (watching paint dry, for one). Send me your news, yeah? Is it true you're a cutthroat gossip columnist? Gotta love that.

Sam

At the Altar of the Soul Cathedral

THOUGH I'D NEVER MET PENNY, the woman on maternity leave whose cubicle I was borrowing, I had strong positive feelings for her. Her desk drawers were crammed with chocolate bar wrappers, card decks from Weight Watchers, and notebooks to chronicle her daily food intake. I could only assume she fell off the wagon often, because a typical entry went something like this:

> *Breakfast: 1/4 melon, tea*
> *Lunch: Mediterranean salad, 1 small yoghurt, fun-size chocolate bar (only half)*
> *Dinner: Massive brick Stilton, sautéed spinach, Cadbury Crunchee bar & other unmentionables god I loathe myself*

Penny had two distinct sets of photographs decorating her workspace. By the telephone, there was a framed shot of her sharing an oversize Polynesian drink with a man I assumed was her husband, and another of her and the same man grinning from the top level of a double-decker bus. In the second, more interesting set of pictures, Penny was posing with different *A-ha!* personalities. While with her husband Penny appeared serene and in control, her face in the celebrity snapshots was simultaneously startled and ecstatic, as if a grenade had just gone off in her ear — and she'd loved it.

Unlike Penny — and the photographers, who made too much money to complain — most *A-ha!* staffers scorned the celebrities they covered and regarded their jobs here as steppingstones to greater glories. Nicholas wanted to be a crime reporter for the *Evening Standard,* while Zoe dreamed of writing a cookery column for one of the Sunday papers. As for Anthony, well, he hadn't gotten around to mulling the future just yet. He saw this job as a placeholder, a transition between university and the great unknown commonly referred to as the rest of his life.

With the exception of Charlie Lappin and his deputy, Rebecca Bridgewater, by far the most enthusiastic person in the *A-ha!* office was Sophie, the intern from Leeds. She was short and plump, with apple-red cheeks and improbably long bangs dyed in unfortunate blond and chestnut stripes. From the little interaction we'd had, I could tell she knew more celebrity trivia than anyone else on the magazine. This made sense after Anthony shared the biographical information he had on Sophie: her father, a butcher, had taken off for Ireland when she was still a toddler, and much of her childhood was spent in front of the television while her mother held down two jobs. Little Sophie thought of television stars as a second family of sorts, and her devotion showed in her enthusiasm for *A-ha!*

I had liked her from the first morning, when she looked up from her computer to grin at me. Exactly one week later, on my second Monday at the office, she swung by my desk and invited me to coffee. "That is, if you're not too busy," she added quickly. "We can always do it another time."

"I'd love to," I said, trying not to show how flattered I was. "Just give me one sec."

"Sure, sure, you just looked so . . ." Sophie blushed.

"Frantic? I know." To put her at ease, I babbled unintelligibly while saving the e-mail I was in the middle of composing to Sam.

On our way to the elevator, Sophie inquired about what I'd been working on.

"I'm asking celebs what they're reading this summer," I told her, "but I haven't made it very far down the list. Two people named their own autobiographies, and another recommended Mother Goose. Oh, and get this — the singer from Sweetlife said she's spent a year looking for an interesting book, but hasn't found a single thing worth reading."

"But you don't mean Davina Rose?" Sophie asked, evidently perplexed. "That's odd — isn't she the one who started the literacy program?"

"Uh, is she?"

"Mmph, I believe so. There were posters of her reading and eating ice cream in bed all over my local library. And I think I saw one —"

Sophie broke off as the elevator dinged open and Rebecca Bridgewater stepped out.

"What luck," Rebecca said dryly, nodding at me. "Mimi, I was just about to go looking for you. Would you mind accompanying me to my office for a moment? I have a few bits I'd like to discuss."

With an apologetic glance to Sophie — who gaped back at me, terrified — I followed Charlie's deputy to her office, which was as messy and cluttered as Imogen Fox's room. In one corner were several rows of high-heeled shoes and a vanity cluttered with styling products, blow dryers, and makeup wands of every size. The most prominent picture on her wall was not of a suitor or star, but of four middle-aged women in sparkly sequined dresses huddled together waving champagne glasses.

Brisk and businesslike, Rebecca ushered me to her granite conference table, which was covered with proof sheets of the Thom Thorpe pomade theft. "Anthony tells me that you're responsible for this," she said in that inscrutable tone of hers.

Assuming I was in trouble, I stammered, "I . . . I was just watching him and, well, I —"

"I must say, Charlie's quite chuffed." Rebecca smiled, and the lump in my throat dissolved. "We had a bit of a chat this morning, and we've agreed to give you a bit more of an active role around here. Have you any interest in covering more events like the one in Essex?"

I thought of the stocked buffet table at Scissors and my dwindling bank account. And then there was Anthony, who never missed an event. "Well, sure, I'd *love* that."

"Excellent. You seem to have made quite a few contacts already, which should come in use. I heard you had Saturday lunch with my dear friend Vicky."

"Vicky?"

"Yes, Vicky Ardsdale — she mentioned meeting you at the Fox home?"

"Oh, *Vicky*," I said, realizing Rebecca was talking about the superbitchy blonde from Pippa and Robin's house. "You're friends with her?"

"So shall we give it a go?" Rebecca asked, pointedly ignoring my question. "Tonight there's a big restaurant opening in Leicester Square, and I've asked Anthony to take you. Do keep a bit of distance from him, though," she said. "Most celebs recognize him, but you're an unknown quantity. Let's try to keep it that way, shall we? While he conducts the interviews, see if you can't capture a more candid side of the scene. We were hoping you'd be available this evening?"

"Um, sure," I said. Lily and I had made dinner plans, but this was my job, after all. "Can't wait."

Sitting in the back seat of Ian's monster vehicle later that afternoon, I recounted my conversation with Rebecca. "She just wants me to stand around and watch what happens. Isn't that cool?"

"What sort of things?" Ian asked, glancing in the rearview mirror.

"She didn't really get into details," I admitted.

"Best of luck with that," Anthony said from the passenger seat. "And not to worry — if you don't overhear anything, we'll simply invent it."

Ian laughed. "Right. It can be the most malicious libel, but if the photograph is smashing, no one's fussed. Why I bring my slimming lens, innit?"

I relaxed in my seat, thrilled to be back in Ian's car. The high seats afforded a rare view of London — a cleaner, more colorful city than New York, with the ubiquitous gardens and bright neon concert posters set against the wan sky and old stone buildings. Londoners dressed in zany patterns and color combinations that I much preferred to the black and blue denim palette of most New Yorkers.

As we crawled forward at eleven miles an hour, Anthony briefed me on the Soul Cathedral, the joint venture of a bunch of aging rock legends — none of whom I'd ever heard of, of course. The restaurant's chief investor was Duncan Palmer, the former bassist of the Junk, a punk band whose breakout album, *Vampire Personality,* was a huge hit in the late 1970s. But they never had another single, and the group broke up a few years later. Duncan Palmer had been floundering ever since, playing at nightclub openings and art galleries and punk concierge services in boutique hotels. "Nothing he attaches himself to ever lasts," Anthony said. "I give this place a fortnight at the outside."

"Why so cynical?" I wondered aloud.

"I'm not in the least cynical — but I'm also not a complete numbskull. Duncan Palmer is a smack addict who knows buggerall about managing a restaurant. Honestly — *soul* food? How ludicrous is that!"

"Ludicrous? You can't say that! Have you ever even tasted soul food?"

"Forgive me, Mimi," Anthony said. "I'm not slagging off your nation's deep-fried culinary traditions. I just seriously doubt Duncan Palmer gives a toss about food of any sort. His waist is thinner than my arm." He pushed up his shirtsleeve and reached over the seat divider so that I could examine the appendage. His arm was pencil thin, lightly freckled, and spine-chillingly adorable.

Leicester Square was the London equivalent of Times Square — a neon mess of fast food chains, huge movie theaters, and flummoxed tourists with unfolded Underground maps. The Soul Cathedral, directly next to a twelve-screen movie theater, was easy enough to find, with spotlights above the door drawing figure eights in the gray city sky, and a red carpet unrolled into the square like a giant dragon's tongue.

Cameras flashed and onlookers gawked as overdressed guests passed through the velvet ropes. "In a bit!" Ian said, darting off to secure a spot amid the tangle of paparazzi shooting a starlet in a white minidress. By the time Anthony and I gave our names to the bouncer at the entrance, Ian had pushed his way to the front of the pack. "Miss New York, over 'ere!" he called out, snapping a picture of me. Assuming I must be famous, several other photographers followed suit.

I was grinning, my chest surging with excitement, when we got inside the restaurant, which was about a million times louder and more chaotic than Scissors Thompson's Essex salon. Sometimes my life could be pretty ridiculous. I just wished it didn't move too fast for me to take stock. The room was darker than the Mineral Gallery at the Museum of Natural History, and the crowd was a bewildering hodgepodge of aging rockers, young actresses, and self-satisfied businessmen. On the stage, an emaciated man considerably older than my father was making obscene air-guitar gestures for the cameras. "Is that who I think it is?" I screamed into Anthony's ear.

"Indeed it is," he screamed back.

"He *is* skinny, you were right," I conceded once we'd reached a quieter nook by the coat check.

"I'm always right," Anthony said, grabbing two blue cocktails off a tray. I was about to thank him when he drained both in succession. "Loosens me up for the interviews," he said.

"You should try yoga sometime," I told him.

Anthony ignored my suggestion, as he was trying to come up with the perfect question to poll the celebrities on that night. "Something interesting, but nothing too hard," he said, strobe lights playing off his face. "Last month, at a National Portrait Gallery opening, I made the mistake of asking people to name their favorite bit of British history. One scholar cited 'Independence from America.' It was positively embarrassing."

"Yikes. So you need something easier?"

"Yes, but also relevant to the event."

"How about asking about their favorite place in America?"

"No, geography's dodgy. You're giving these philistines *far* too much credit."

I saw his point. "Well, then, what about asking about soul music — like, do they prefer old school or new school? Sam Cooke or Prince?"

Anthony looked at me for an instant before slapping his palms together. "Say, that's beautiful!" he said, lurching forward to squeeze my shoulders. "I rather think I'll try that one."

I was still woozy from this unexpected intimacy when another waiter rounded the corner with more cocktails. Anthony, with a farewell wink, dashed off in pursuit of a third beverage. Left on my own, and too unsettled for sleuthing, I went over to check out the soul food spread. I'd just reached the buffet and was scooping mashed sweet potatoes onto my plate when someone tickled my waist from behind.

Assuming it was Anthony, I reached back with one arm to pat the top of his head. But instead of a soft mop, I felt a handful of coarse, almost dreadlocked hair. Spinning around, I came face-to-face with a tall, cadaverous older man with kohl-rimmed eyes. An alarmingly large amethyst amulet that could easily double as a weapon hung around his neck. Terrified, I shrieked and dropped my loaded plate. Ribs and sweet potato residue flew like fireworks in every direction. Remarkably, though, none of the revelers around me — not even those whose expensive outfits were smeared with my lost dinner — seemed to notice.

The chalk-faced man displayed crooked green teeth as he whooped, "Well done, that! Ah, how I love 'em young, I do!"

"What are you *doing?*" I cried as the man grabbed both my wrists and, over my faltering protests, delivered me onto the dance floor. Once again, no one around us seemed to find it bizarre that a sixteen-year-old girl was being forcibly tangoed by a Grade-A freak show in a leather vest and matching tight pants.

"I can tell you've a beautiful soul," he said at one point, pushing some stringy hair out of his eyes to gaze intently at me. "I reckon I could cut inside you and get a closer look."

Um, pardon — cut inside me? I had to get away from this lunatic, and fast. When, seconds later, he gripped my hand to twirl me, I made my move. I spun away from him, and I kept on backstepping, faster and faster, farther and farther away, until somehow I landed dizzy and breathless outside the door of the ladies' room.

Inside the bathroom, which turned out to be roughly the same size as the restaurant floor, I found yet another party under way. A half-dozen overdressed women around my mother's age were smoking cigarettes and striking dramatic poses on the settees and loveseats. I retreated to an empty ottoman in the corner, where, with my bag held protectively over my stomach, I breathed deeply and attempted to recover from the scarecrow freak's hijacking attempt.

At the mirrors, a woman with fuzzy dandelion hair was holding forth about her recent decision to move into her daughter's bedroom. The other women listened attentively. "Vanessa's absolutely livid," the woman was saying, "but she's got her own flat in Fulham that *I* bloody well paid for, so I simply ignore her. Other than that, it's marvelous, this separate-bedroom arrangement. I'm sleeping properly for the first time since we got married. I told Richard we should've tried this a decade ago."

"Yes, but is Richard all right with it, love?" one member of her audience asked. "If I ever proposed such an arrangement to Jonathan, he'd doubtless find somebody else to bunk with him fairly quickly."

While a few of the women gasped at this possibility, the dandelion woman just shrugged. "Oh, I suppose he whinged a bit in the beginning, but you know Richard, not cut out for a battle. Now I think he's getting on just fine — and indeed, he looks much perkier at the breakfast table these days. "

"Yes, Linda, but do watch that he doesn't get *too* perky," a woman with a heart-shaped face and long black hair warned. "I should've known what trouble I was in when Stuart started singing 'Yellow Submarine' in the shower every morning."

Just then there was a commotion outside the door, and who should barge into the bathroom but my emaciated dance partner. In the light I could see his leather pants clinging to him like Saran Wrap. Heart racing, I whipped around to face the wall; maybe he wouldn't recognize me from behind.

"Bloody hell, this is the ladies'!" one woman screamed, but the freak kept at it, the chains on his boots clinking with every step. He knocked on a stall door. "Dancing queen, you in there? I'm here for you."

When he crouched down to peer under the door of the handicapped stall, the dandelion woman named Linda shouted, "Out with you — shove off this *instant* or we'll have the police on you!" She flailed out her arm, as if threatening to beat him with her purse.

I took advantage of this opportunity to flee the scene. "Go on, love, quick," Linda urged me as I shot back into the main room. I darted through the crowd for a few feverish minutes before spotting Anthony. He was leaning against a velvet banquette, talking to yet another starlet. Why was it he never interviewed men?

"Ah! There you are, twinkle toes," he said pleasantly when I came up. "I saw you were having quite the time of it on the dance floor — well done on finding such a fetching partner."

"Funny," I said, nearly panting. I was in no mood for flirting, not with my scarecrow stalker still on the prowl. "Anthony, I need to take a break. I'm going to walk around the block."

To my surprise, without so much as a word to the starlet, Anthony said, "I'll come with you," and hustled me toward the exit. "Just as I predicted," he said on our way out, "it was a bloody awful party — I was absolutely *desperate* to leave."

Back outside in Leicester Square, he text-messaged Ian to meet us at Benjy's, a sandwich shop around the corner. Only after ducking inside this comfortingly anonymous chain did I feel safe again.

Neither of us said much as we picked at our prawn-mayo sandwiches and waited for Ian. He strolled in about ten minutes later, gloating over the photograph he'd taken of ultimate soap star hottie Tricia Evans, in a supershort dress. As soon as Ian sat down, Anthony snatched the camera and began searching for the money shot. "And where'd you slope off to?" Ian asked me. "Making friends in the kitchen, were you?"

"Close," Anthony told him. "The loo."

"You awright?" Ian cocked his head tenderly. "Those blue drinks got you a bit squiffy, did they?"

"No, I wasn't sick. I was hiding from this psychotic Alice Cooper look-alike who wanted to cut into my soul," I said. "Fun, right? I've always wanted my soul cut into."

"How apposite for a *soul* food restaurant," Anthony said, laughing.

"Come on," Ian chided Anthony. "Try to be a bit more sensitive." Then, to me, he asked, "I suppose there was no silver lining, then? Didn't manage to pick up any tidbits for Deputy Bridgewater?"

"Not really," I said. "I just sat in the bathroom listening to a group of middle-aged women discussing their sleeping arrangements."

"Go on, then," Ian prodded me gently.

As I began to relay the overheard conversation, Anthony's head jerked up from the camera. "A daughter Vanessa and a husband Richard, you say?" he asked, regarding me with great interest. "But surely you don't mean Linda Ross?"

"Uh, I don't know," I said uncomfortably. "Her name was Linda. She was nice; she saved me when that psycho guy burst in looking for me."

"Wonky Rod Stewart hairdo? Bit of a plastic surgery overload?" Ian took his camera back from Anthony and flipped through the pictures. "That's Linda, innit?" He showed me a shot of the woman from the bathroom.

I nodded again, and the men exchanged excited glances. "Why you, you're a lucky charm!" Anthony cried. He then explained the potential tabloid significance of my discovery. Linda Ross was a longtime *A-ha!* favorite, an early-eighties pop star who'd recently revived her career with a stint on the reality TV show *Idol Escape*. "Richard used to be her handyman, you see," Anthony said. "He worked on her boiler before her comeback, and now she's giving him the boot — why, but that's brilliant, isn't it?"

"N-no," I stammered, "she didn't say anything about giving him the boot. She just wanted more sleep."

"Oh, go on with you," Anthony said. "Separate beds my arse!"

"Yes, but it's so they can sleep better," I insisted. "When my family used to take trips and my sister and I had to share a hotel bed, I *never* slept."

"Sounds like prelude to Splitsville to me," Ian said. "The old missus only resorts to separate beds in extremis."

"Yes, but —" I'd liked Linda Ross, and felt indebted to her, but I didn't know how to convey this without sounding stupid or sentimental.

Across the table, Anthony was already leaving a hysterical message for Rebecca Bridgewater, repeating my report. When he got off, he looked at his phone and flicked through his text messages. "I'm afraid I must toddle off now," he said. "My flatmate's having a birthday dinner that I'm not permitted to skip."

After Anthony left, Ian offered to walk me down to the Charing Cross Tube station. "It'll save you a transfer," he told me.

Without Anthony to abuse, Ian seemed different — kind and protective, almost paternal. "This your first time in old Blighty then?" he asked on our way down the street.

I said it was, then briefly described the trip my family had taken to Rome while I was in junior high: "Every day my dad photographed us in front of a new fountain. He was so excited."

"But this round's a bit trickier, I reckon," Ian said in a serious voice. "You're on your own. Now, if you'll permit my saying, you seem like you've got your head screwed on the right way, but between you, me, and the gatepost, this city can be right difficult if you don't watch it. I'm a Londoner through and through — been here man and boy thirty-seven years now, and I *still* can't get my head round the place. Say, you got something I can write on?" he asked suddenly, stopping outside a theater. When I handed him the reporter's notebook, he wrote his number on the back with a

Sharpie he excavated from one of his pockets. "Should you ever need help, help of any kind, don't hesitate to give me a bell. I mean anything, from hanging curtains to giving the what-for to some tosser chasing you round a party. If you're ever in a pinch, Cassidy's your man."

"Thanks," I said, taking my notebook back and admiring his big blocky handwriting. We resumed walking. "And speaking of people chasing me around a party, can I ask you something? About what happened in the bathroom?"

"Fire away, love."

"Well, why do we have to print a nasty story about Linda Ross's marriage? It's not true, and she's the one who saved me from my stalker."

"*C'est la vie,* I'm afraid," Ian said levelly, stepping down from the sidewalk onto the crosswalk. "It's been like this since the beginning of time. It's human nature to need heroes, innit. The ancient Greeks had their gods, and now we've got our Linda Rosses. You see? It's continuity, like." He seemed pleased with this reasoning.

"But how can you call her a hero? We're certainly not treating her like one, anyway, dragging her name — and her marriage — through the gutter."

"Now, that there's erroneous thinking," Ian told me. "Proper heroes need their flaws like the rest of us, don't they? Look at Icarus, Napoleon, Marilyn Monroe. Their lives all went pear-shaped soon enough."

"I'm not sure I'm following," I said.

"Without us, Linda Ross and her friends would be mere mortals. We elevate them to great heights, and then we get to watch them fall back to earth. Besides," Ian went on, "it's how we arse-brained folk at *A-ha!* make our living. Quite simply, it's what we do. Look at the bright side," he said, patting my arm. "Nobody cut into your soul."

To: "Unclesam9"
From: "Mimicita86"
Date: July 8, 12:10 p.m.
Subject: Yo, stranger!

Sam,

Thank you for your e-mail. I had no idea people our age could write in full paragraphs. I'm impressed — and touched. But enough about you. How, I wonder, did you hear about *my* crazy adventure? Are you really surprised that Berlin with Mommy Dearest didn't work out? I gave it a real shot, I swear, but in the end I just couldn't stomach it. Now we're chatting on the phone for a few minutes every week and things seem to be "on the mend," as they say around here.

You, meanwhile, sound good. I think I know a girl from Houston whose older sister did the Bennington summer program, and she ended up falling in love with one of her instructors and marrying him when she graduated high school. It was disgusting!

As for me, I'm staying with Lily in this ridiculously glam house with a family to match. The one weirdo of the household, Adrian the antisocial computer/rodent addict, just left to study sea cows in Australia, so now all is total perfection. As you know, I'm Little Miss Gossip Hound, and Lily's gotten really into her life as a "thesp" (did you know she's studying acting?), so unfortunately we don't see each other much. In addition to running around overorchestrated media events and spying on "slebs" (i.e. celebs — and you'd have NO idea who any of them are), I'm trying to squeeze in more of the real London.

Last night, after a big gluttonous lunch at my host family's house, Lils brought me to this weird space in Whitechapel to see an "arresting" piece of performance art — an adaptation of *A Doll's House,* the Henrik Ibsen play about the ultimate frustrated housewife. It was unlike any theater I'd ever seen before, mostly because all the actors stayed backstage, and the only thing on the stage was an overlarge dollhouse with random objects (a lit match, a prosthetic hand, a live mouse!) shooting out of its windows. I can't say I'm dying to go back, but it was definitely an interesting experience.

xxxxxM

From: "Jessieg"
To: "Mimicita86"
Date: July 10, 11:32 a.m.
Subject: Aloha from el cubicle

Hey babes, how you holding up? Lily e-mailed me and
said you're going out with one of the Sex Pistols. I
almost believed her, until I looked him up and realized
he's dead. But now I'm wondering — what ever
happened with that Ant guy? Last I heard you were
heading to some underwear fashion show together. How
was it? And how come I never get invited to those?

NYC in the summer sucks. It's hot and sticky, my father
and his new family just announced they're moving into
an even bigger house, and all my friends are thousands
of miles away. Me, I'm at the only computer at the bank
with complete Internet access — crazy, right? All the
other computers are blocked to ensure that all anybody
does is work, work, work. I had no idea it would be so
money-obsessed and personality-free here — it's so bad
it hurts. Trevor, the hot guy who interviewed me, turned
out to be a total idiot. There isn't a single summer intern
he hasn't hit on. I guess he really takes the company's
equal opportunity policy seriously. Now the only part of
the day I like is lunch, when we can order from any
restaurant on the company's dime.

My writing class is going well. I've been working on a story about a girl whose father leaves home and starts another family, but the new family ends up being exactly the same as the one he tried to get away from. (Sound familiar?) It's still a work in progress. I'm definitely taking Kim's advanced writing next year. And you? OK, off to Xerox a receipt for some banker now. You'd think people who earn millions of dollars a year would know how to operate a photocopier, but then you'd think wrong.

Tons o' Love,
Jess

How I Grew Arctic Ferns Under My Arms

GROWTH SPURT NOTWITHSTANDING, SEVENTH GRADE was probably the smoothest year of my life. School was still easy, and every weekend I had at least three bar mitzvahs to attend. When I look back now, the year blurs into one giant procession of grinning grandmothers and chocolate fountains and taffeta dresses. Not once did I feel lonely or rejected.

My social life was similarly simplified at *A-ha!* There were always parties to cover, and most evenings found me roaming some event venue — usually a tent or a roped-off portion of a rooftop — and cramming in the hors d'oeuvres. Unfortunately, I saw very little of Lily, and was excited when she invited me to the birthday party of a theater school friend Friday evening.

That afternoon, Sophie and I were writing the text for "Stars and Their Stripes," a monthly feature devoted to celebrities exhibiting embarrassing splotches of sweat. Earlier that week, Arctic Fern deodorant — which always took out a full-page ad opposite the feature — had sent sample kits of their product to every employee at *A-ha!* Though the deodorant smelled a bit like those pine-scented air-freshener trees that hang from the rearview mirrors of New York taxis, I'm genetically programmed to accept any and all free toiletries.

Sophie and I were finishing up when Charles Lappin strolled by our worktable and glanced at our caption suggestions. *"It's getting hot in here,"* he read. *"More dots for Dotty . . . What's Cassie up to? Only Garreth nose.* Perfect." He chuckled to himself before walking off and telling us to get lost and have "cracking good" weekends.

"Can we go before Rebecca gets back?" I asked Sophie.

She gnawed her lip nervously. "She did tell us to wait for her to sign off, but I suppose Charlie *is* the boss."

"Right, so it'd almost be disobedient *not* to leave."

"You reckon?" Sophie said, and skipped off to her desk to retrieve her belongings.

A few minutes later, Sophie and I were saying goodbye in the downstairs lobby when we all but collided with Rebecca Bridgewater, who was carrying a huge shopping bag from the nearby Waitrose supermarket with several Pukka Supper for One frozen dinners poking out the top. She wanted to know who had told us we could go. "I thought we'd established that I was going to sign off on your project," she said harshly.

Sophie shuffled back toward the elevator, leaving me to explain that Charlie had given us the green light. "Oh, he did, did he?" Rebecca sniffed suspiciously. "Well then, carry on. Have a lovely weekend."

Thus released, I took the Tube to Shoreditch, where Lily and I had arranged to meet. I found her standing by a newsstand, flipping through the latest *A-ha!* I involuntarily cringed whenever I saw that week's lead headline, in huge, impossible-to-miss char-treuse letters: "LINDA GIVES RICHARD THE BOOT! An Inside Look at a Broken Marriage."

More like a repaired sleep cycle, I thought with a sigh. I tried to remind myself of what Ian said that night — *it's what we do* — but at the moment his words didn't provide much solace. "Am I late?" I asked Lily.

"You're fine," she said, putting the magazine back on the rack. "I don't know how you extricate yourself from that place at all — so many planet-realigning news stories must break every minute."

"Yeah, right," I said, and told her about the celebrity perspiration project that had consumed my day.

We walked out of the station and turned onto Brick Lane, a street I'd been meaning to visit since coming to London two weeks ago. Right away, I saw that it lived up to its fame: I felt as if I'd stepped into some parallel universe, a teeming city populated in equal parts by Bangladeshi grocers and trendy Morrissey look-alikes. The twenty-some curry houses we passed alternated with minimalist Swedish furniture boutiques and off-license convenience stores. The air smelled of Indian spices and the slightest hint of rain.

"By the way, if you're on a perspiration kick, you should like this party," Lily said. "All my friends from school are, well . . ." She paused to find the right word.

"What, stinky?"

She nodded. "You'll love them, but they're not exactly the deodorant set."

When I told her about the Arctic Fern roll-on that I was sporting, Lily laughed, and I volunteered to bring home more complimentary samples next week. "I think I'll pass," she said. And then, gesturing at the busy street we were walking down, she asked me, "So what do you think of the real London? Does it measure up to your ultralame celebrity world?"

"Of course it does! It's way better," I said lightly. "Not that I know where I am, but this neighborhood seems like the coolest I've been to yet."

"I think so, too," Lily said. "But I wasn't sure it'd measure up to your jet-set expectations."

Because she'd grown up around celebrities, Lily liked to make plain her scorn for them. I, on the other hand, had grown up around goateed psychology students and struggling photographers in Birkenstocks — could she blame me for being a little starstruck? Still, I decided not to respond as we continued down the street. The sky was blanketed with clouds and the light was silvery and translucent. We passed two men shouting at each other in the doorway of a sari store, and I wished Lily and I could stay in London forever.

We soon turned off Brick Lane and after a few more swerves ended up on a main road, outside a pub called The Old Lamb and Sack. A rusted plaque next to the door boasted that the establishment had been in continuous operation since the eighteenth century — and as we stepped inside, I wondered if it had been swept out since. A real pub at last — and how! The front room centered on a gigantic television tuned to a soccer game in Denmark. A bunch of middle-aged men with scraggly facial hair and glaring dental issues were sitting at the bar, watching the screen and issuing frightening "OOOIER!" sounds.

"These guys practically live here," Lily told me. "But don't worry. The other room is totally different. And you have to tell me what you think of Harry."

"You mean *another* Harry?" I asked. Lily smiled enigmatically.

"Will there be Indian food at this party?" I asked, trailing Lily behind the bar and into a small parlor with flocked wallpaper and a few hunting souvenirs — geese, I think — hanging precariously off the walls. Lily's friends all looked like they were a few years older than us, with outlandish hairstyles crafted with industrial-strength hair gel. I recognized several of the faces crowded around the tables from our backstage visit to *A Doll's House* the previous weekend.

"Don't you love it?" Lily effused.

"Yes, especially the geese," I said. "How about some beers?" At the bar I ordered two insanely expensive lagers, no fake ID necessary. On my way back over to Lily, nobody stepped aside for me, and I kept having to tap people on the shoulder to get by. I found myself longing for the company of Anthony and Ian — or even of the Foxes, whose careless chattiness always made me feel welcome. At The Old Lamb and Sack, not a single one of Lily's friends even smiled at me, so I half crouched in the corner, pretending to study the chemical composition of my beer.

One girl, Jules, was telling jokes at her messy flatmate's expense, while her friend Lally was arm wrestling different guys. But they were the exceptions. Almost everyone else was engaged in a heavy debate about "the craft."

"What craft?" I whispered when Lily joined me. "Are these people witches?"

"Very funny," she said. "No, it's part of the program. We're encouraged to talk about acting all the time."

Lily left me and I sat down at one of the tables, next to a guy with a shaved head who looked older than the other students in Lily's theater program. He was lecturing two enraptured girls on the merits of the "graphic imagination."

"Ninety-nine percent of the greatest thoughts don't get recorded, yeah, because they occur as images, not words," he was saying. "Make that ninety-nine-point-nine percent. Sentences, by their very being, yeah, are limited. A sentence, by definition, has *structure*."

"That's dead right, Harry," one of the girls rasped.

"Language inhibits creativity," the other put in. "Utterly *mangles* it, doesn't it?"

"We should just *be*," the first girl said. "Wordless, like cave dwellers."

Out of the corner of my eye I checked out Harry, trying to figure out what his admirers saw in him. He wasn't unhandsome exactly, just greasy and a little undernourished. The trouble arose whenever he opened his mouth to talk. "Do any of you read the *New Scientist*?" he asked. "Right, well, there was this study, yeah, positing that nonverbal animals have higher emotional connectors than humans."

"Oh, yeah, nonverbal animals," said one of the girls. "That's wicked."

"It's certainly true of my cat," the other said.

And then a third, more familiar voice asked: "Have you ever thought about doing a performance piece about this? It's *so* fascinating."

I looked up to see the person responsible for this last comment and was shocked to find Lily Morton pulling up a chair to Harry's table. So *that's* what she was doing instead of talking to me? Like the other two girls, she oohed and ahhed and batted her eyelashes when he set about comparing the "auric composition" of orange and indigo moods. I felt acutely embarrassed on Lily's behalf — what was her deal for losers named Harry? At least Harry Feder, her Baldwin crush, had a sense of humor.

"Hey, Lily," I said, "can you let me know where the bathroom is?" I was hoping she'd join me, but instead she just pointed to a black door in the distance.

I survived another hour, but by eight I was tired, hungry, and sick of being ignored. I got up to tell Lily goodbye. To my surprise, she rocketed off her upholstered armchair and cried, "What do you mean goodbye? I'm coming with you, obviously!"

Immediately, and with no evident regret, she picked up her shoulder bag and — after a quick exchange with Harry — guided me onto the street. "Mimi, thank you *so* much for coming with me," she said, her eyes bright with happiness. Then, as if to prove she hadn't noticed how neglected and uncomfortable I'd felt in there, she added, "I had *so* much fun, I'll even treat you to a minicab home!"

The minicab was a cheaper, skuzzier alternative to a proper black cab. Drivers used their own cars and were known for speeding and running red lights. I'd never ridden in one before, and I was looking forward to the long ride to Little Venice. But as soon as we got into the beat-up old sedan, Lily burbled excitedly, "Look what Harry just gave me! Two tickets to *Lambeth Nightingale,* the play he wrote and directed. They're for tomorrow night, and the cast party's afterward. You'll come with me, right?"

While I could think of few less appealing Saturday-night activities, I hated to disappoint sweet Lily. So what if she hadn't been the most attentive friend at The Old Lamb and Sack? She'd jumped the instant I expressed a desire to leave. Most people would demand that you "wait ten more minutes" and then strand you at the door for the next hour, but not Lily. As the minicab chugged down the City Road, I slid closer to give her a good long whiff of my Arctic Fern underarm.

From: "HWYates"
To: "Mimicita86"
Date: July 17, 7:06 a.m.
Subject: Bear Nest

Hi, squirt,

Thank you for the update. So FANTASTIC you're in
London and getting all this global experience under your
belt. You must be busy busy busy, but I beg you not to
miss the British Museum. My old friend Otto Jackman
curates the Assyrian wing there. He'd love you — you
must give him a call for an unforgettable private tour.

Here in NYC, love is working wonders on my
complexion. The FIANCE (!) and I have been shacking
up together in the country. After a nightmarish weekend
in the Hamptons, where I was surrounded by jerks and
BMWs and girls who made me feel like my body was
sagging to Ecuador, I confessed to him how much I
hated that whole scene. To my astonishment, he
admitted that he did, too! So he rented his house to a
screenwriter doing "research" on the Park Avenue set,
and the very next week, he BOUGHT me my very own
rustic cottage in the Catskills. It's very no-frills, our little
hideaway, and we're planning to do all the renovation
work ourselves. I love it up here — no emaciated

supermodels, just chipmunks and bears, the real deal. You must visit before school starts, with or without your White Russian escort.

Looking forward,
H

P.S. Those magazines — whoa! How about that "Whose Bum Is This?" contest? I won't say another word, but please promise you'll return to the pants-on world of high school journalism in the fall. Only say this cuz I love you, squirt.

Bridezillas in Our Midst

THE NEXT MORNING, I WAS DREAMING about walking past Big Ben to find Anthony passed out on top of the clock tower, naked but for a strategically placed issue of *A-Ha!*, when Imogen shook me awake. "Mimi! Wake up, will you?"

When I opened my eyes, she was looming over me, examining me quizzically, as if I were a UFO she'd stumbled upon in the back garden. "About time," she said. "Listen, some of us are going to Portobello, and if you'd care to join us, you'd best shake a leg. Mum just popped out to the market, so this is our only chance!"

While I would've happily attended another Saturday lunch, I was flattered by Imogen's invitation. I was eager, too, to check out the Portobello Road market she'd mentioned the other night. She and Tunisia described it as an outdoor shopping extravaganza, with vendors peddling everything from 1950s lace gloves to African fruits. "Sounds great," I said. "Is Lily coming?"

"Right here." Lily stepped out from the doorway, already showered and dressed. "Just waiting on your lazy bones."

"Meet you downstairs in five," Imogen said. "Seconds, that is."

I threw on a corduroy shirtdress and my dark red cowboy boots and hurried down to the kitchen, where Robin Fox was clipping newspaper articles. A radio debate on a proposed over-haul of Scottish agricultural subsidies droned in the background. "Where are you off to?" he asked sleepily when his daughter blazed into the room. "Lunch will begin presently — your mum has been in a tizz since well before dawn."

"Oh, but Daddy," Imogen said, turning to catch my eye, "I've fallen madly in love with a three-legged donkey and I absolutely *must* introduce him to my mates!"

"Right, then," Robin murmured, bringing his antiques sup-plement closer to his face. "There's my lass."

When we got out of the Tube station, Imogen called her friends, who told her they'd decided to hang out at a pub instead. "We'll come round in a bit," she said before clicking her phone shut. "It'd be mad not to have a look-see."

The three of us spent the next few hours wandering around the market, admiring old dishes and trying on costume jewelry. Lily bought a leather headband and Imogen a vintage poncho with rainbow-fringed embroidery. We then walked north, away from the action, to a Portuguese wine bar on Goldhurst Road, where Imogen's friends had installed themselves on benches out-side. Like Imogen, they were dressed with expensive indifference, in outrageous color combinations that would horrify my mother. Only one of the girls — the real beauty of the group — wore all black, but then she looked about a decade older and more sophis-ticated than her friends, with her diamond tennis bracelet and straight auburn hair that fell halfway down her back.

Most bars in New York seem geared exclusively to customers between the ages of twenty-one and twenty-eight, but surrounding us were barflies of every demographic: elegant ladies in pearls, old men with canes, loud young guys, and several clusters of young parents on double dates, their kids left to kick and drool in their strollers.

"Arabella," Imogen said to the gorgeous girl in all black, "budge up, will you, and make room for the Yanks?"

Once we'd squeezed onto the bench, Lily, who was already acquainted with Imogen's friends, introduced me to Hattie, Emma, Tamasin, Billie, and Arabella. Most were either on their gap years or preparing to start "uni" (a.k.a. university) in the fall. Only the girl sitting on my left, the beautiful Arabella, was pursuing an alternative avenue. Immediately upon finishing school, she'd decided to "have a go at modeling."

"She's going to be massive!" Billie said with conviction. "She's already been in loads of adverts all over the telly."

"Yes, have you seen the one for the linen sales at John Lewis?" Hattie asked. "She played the sleeping beauty under the goose-down comforter. She was brilliant — stunning, wasn't she?"

Next to me, Arabella lifted her shoulders modestly, and the conversation soon turned to the only member of the gang absent that afternoon, Tunisia, and her rugby-obsessed boyfriend, Bob. Having dined with the couple the previous night, the girls had much to discuss. "Tamasin behaved just appallingly," said Billie. "She refused to speak to him — and they were sitting next to each other!"

"Yes, well, and what do you suppose we might've chatted about?" Tamasin wanted to know. "The last rugby match he watched? Bloody hell, he is *such* hard work."

"For Tune's sake, I *do* hope she's not contemplating marrying him," Imogen said. "The idea of a wedding cake that's been done to look like a rugby ball is too horrid to contemplate."

Arabella snorted. "Imo's always going on about weddings this and weddings that," she told me. "She's positively mad for matrimony — ever since we were little girls, she loved dressing up in white sheets and playing wedding."

"Yes, and have you seen her trousseau?" Hattie asked. "It's frightening, really."

It was true that Imogen talked more about weddings than the great play she was supposed to be writing, but she clearly didn't enjoy her friends' jibes. She was scowling at the group, Lily and me included, when Arabella stood up and said, "I think I'll have another Pimm's. Anyone else fancy a top-up? You," she said, pointing at me with a beautiful girl's sense of entitlement, "come inside with me, we'll have a chat."

Pleased with the attention, I stood up and like a lap dog followed Arabella inside. While we waited at the bar, she revealed her reason for singling me out: she wanted to talk about New York, where she'd lived for a year. "I miss the energy there; it is so exciting. Everything there's just *different*."

I told her that was exactly how I felt about London, and asked her when she'd been in New York.

"Oh, dunno, maybe fifteen?"

"You lived there when you were fifteen? We must have just missed each other."

"No," Arabella said, picking up her bright red drink and plunking down money on the bar. "Sure you don't want one?"

I shook my head no and asked her again when she'd lived in New York.

"Fifteen years *ago,*" she said impatiently. "But I still remember it vividly." She moved over to a small round table and kicked out a seat for me. "It's bloody hot out. Let's cool off."

I sat down across from Arabella, basking in her beauty. She really was exquisite, with her mahogany hair and luminous complexion. For a time I contentedly answered her questions about New York, describing the all-you-can-eat sushi joints in Midtown and the free rides on the Staten Island ferry and the fancy little consignment shops on the Upper East Side. "We were on the Upper East Side," Arabella recalled, "with all the punks."

"Punks on the Upper East Side?" I repeated incredulously. "Are you sure you don't mean the East *Village?* Because the Upper East Side is about the least punk neighborhood in New York. Just ask Lily — she lives there."

"I wouldn't ask Lily the time of day, frankly," Arabella said frostily. "Sorry, I know you're good mates, but honestly, she's not to my taste. She thinks — at least it seems so to me — she thinks she's so clever."

"Lily? Thinks she's *clever?* But that's not true at all. Lily's one of the most down-to-earth people I've ever met."

"Oh, well, try talking to her about her bloody drama school sometime. Honestly, just because I decided not to get formal training, she needn't patronize me. She's always going on about bloody St. Botolph's, as if I couldn't have gone there myself if I'd wanted!"

"I'm sure she's just trying to find common ground with you," I said, but Arabella only stared at the wall.

When she got over her sulkiness, she turned to me excitedly. "Listen, Mimi," she said. "I've had the most brilliant idea! I live just up the road and I'd love to show you my portfolio."

"Your portfolio? What do you mean?"

Arabella paused. "But isn't your dad a top fashion photographer? That's what Imo told me — I thought you might have a look at some of my headshots and, you know, pass the word along if any strike your fancy."

"He's not a *fashion* photographer," I said — in vain, it turned out. My companion had already gotten up and walked to the door of the pub. I stood looking at her, self-possessed and unquestioning. At last, it all made sense. Arabella hadn't befriended me because she liked my red cowboy boots or missed New York. She'd befriended me because she thought — rather stupidly — I could advance her modeling career. The realization made me angry at, and a little sorry for, Arabella.

On the benches outside, the girls were considering what colors to dye their hair when they reached old age. "I think white is so much prettier than old-lady blond," Lily said, smiling up at me. "Don't you, Mimi?"

"Nah, I prefer bright blue," I said and gratefully sat down next to her.

"Mimi!" Arabella said. "Come along now, we haven't much time!"

"Oh, yeah, sorry." I turned to Lily. "Arabella wants me to come to her house and look at some of her modeling photographs, but I told her we have to leave for Harry's play pretty soon." I bulged out my eyes to convey my nonenthusiasm.

"Oh, you lucked out," Lily said to Arabella. "Mimi practically grew up in a darkroom. She has a well-trained eye."

"Are you *sure* there's enough time?" I asked, rolling my eyes meaningfully at my friend.

But Lily still didn't get the hint and nodded her consent. "Of course," she said — too loudly. "Just be back in an hour, OK? The play starts at seven, and it's almost five. And have fun!"

Nodding, I lingered for a second before, with a sigh of resignation, I stood and begrudgingly walked over to Arabella.

Kings and Queens

IT WASN'T MY FAULT. REALLY, IT WASN'T. I must have interrupted Arabella's portfolio tour a dozen times to remind her of my plans with Lily, but my hostess wasn't interested. "Oh, shelve it, would you," she kept saying. "We're almost to the end. Oh, here we are — this one's fab. That was real Balenciaga couture, you know. Or *some* posh designer; my memory's an absolute sieve when it comes to names. I do remember that I was too short for the skirt and I was perched on a chair. An assistant had to steady me from behind. You can almost make out his shadow."

By the time Arabella had displayed every glossy photograph ever taken of her, the sky outside had darkened. Rain misted my hair as we left her house and hurried back to Goldhurst Road. Though Arabella had insisted that she lived "just up the road," we were at least a dozen winding, identical blocks from the Portuguese bar. When at last we got there, it was almost ten to seven, and the picnic tables outside were empty.

I was too upset to speak, but Arabella didn't seem to notice. "Oh, look," she said easily after pulling her cell phone out of her black shoulder bag. "We've missed several calls."

"What?" I cried. "When?"

Arabella shrugged. "Don't know, I keep it on silent." She squinted while listening to her messages. Then, after clicking the phone shut, she told me, "Right, Lily called."

"Oh, thank God. Can I hear the message?"

"Oh, sorry, I always delete messages automatically — otherwise my voice mail's a mess. But not to worry, she just said you should meet up with her when you got it."

"Did she say where?"

Arabella screwed up her face. "Oh, bollocks. Why must I have the *worst* memory for names? She said the theater was somewhere on . . . Gold Street? Or Old Street?" Then, seeing my devastated expression, Arabella said, "I know. If it's a play, surely *TimeOut* will have a listing for it. Shall we pop round to a newsagent and investigate?"

"Yes — great idea!" I tried to high-five her, but Arabella seemed unfamiliar with this practice.

We doubled back to Ladbroke Grove and bought the magazine from a small store filled floor to ceiling with various publications. Once outside, I scanned the theater listings again and again for *Lambeth Nightingale,* but Harry's masterpiece was nowhere to be found. "Well, perhaps the production was too small to get in the listings," Arabella said, closing the magazine. "There must be hundreds of shows that nobody writes about. Besides, if it's all the way in Whitechapel, you couldn't possibly get there in time. Why don't you join me and the other girls at the pub?"

I wanted to kill Arabella, and it took every ounce of self-control not to scream. Instead I told her I should probably just head back to Bridge House. When I got there, about half an hour later, I found Pippa at the kitchen table, nursing a glass of wine and plowing through stacks of what looked like official BBC reports.

"Any chance Lily called?" I asked without much hope.

"Lily? Afraid not. Should she have done?" Pippa flipped a few pages and added, "If you fancy a glass of claret, I've just opened a bottle. I'd get up and pour you some, but I have loads of paperwork to get through and I'm absolutely knackered. Right after lunch, an old friend of mine came over in *quite* a state. She's being hounded by the tabloids suddenly and can't peel herself off the floor."

There was an inverse relation, I realized, between the attention span of most celebrity magazines and the lifespan of their repercussions. While my coworkers at *A-ha!* were in constant flux, always moving on to the next big scoop, the stories they — we — wrote stuck to their subjects like tattoos, and not the temporary birthday-party variety.

"Not that I blame her," Pippa said. "They can be barbaric, those magazines, absolutely inhumane."

"Tell me about it," I said. "I work at one of them."

"That's right, and for one of my oldest mates. You'd scarcely believe it, but before he became lord of all rubbish, Charlie used to be quite a formidable music critic — he wrote the most thoughtful, well-informed pieces. He's lucky we knew him when." Pippa smiled and returned to shuffling her papers.

Seeing she wanted to be left alone, I excused myself and went upstairs to watch TV in the den. With precious Lulu curled up at my feet, I was soon swept away by a BBC courtroom drama about a schoolteacher with an underage love interest and a shady criminal record. The plot reminded me of one of the *Law and Order* episodes that Quinn and I had watched together on Barrow Street, but these trial scenes took place in the Royal Courts, where lawyers wore woolly white wigs and addressed one another as "my esteemed colleague."

I waited for Lily until midnight, then gave up and went to bed. The next morning, I took a deep breath as I let myself into her room to excuse my disappearance. "Lily," I said, "we came back and you were gone. Arabella deleted your message so I didn't know where to go."

Lily didn't say anything. Still beneath her covers, she flipped over to face the wall.

"So did you go?"

"Mmmph."

"Should I come back later, then, let you sleep?"

"Do whatever you want," Lily said, burying her head beneath a fluffy down pillow. She was clearly finished with the conversation.

I remembered those grueling weeks last December when the contents of my diary were made public and my Baldwin friends disowned me. In comparison, missing *Lambeth Nightingale* seemed a very small transgression, but Lily was sensitive — sometimes, I thought, excessively so. Though too well raised to be openly rude to me, she was furious and I knew it. About an hour after our "conversation," she left the house, claiming she had to spend the entire day in rehearsals. The rest of that overcast Sunday dragged on interminably. To pass the time, I took a long walk along the canal, all the way to King's Cross. It took about two hours each way, but I was still home by the early afternoon, with nothing to do but worry. In my depressed state, I fell asleep early, before Lily had even come back.

On Monday I e-mailed her overwrought apologies from the office but received two-word responses along the lines of *Sure thing* and *What. Ever.* She again stayed out late at rehearsals, and the next night, when I brought a tray of milk and McVittie's digestive biscuits up to her room, she brusquely refused the treat: "Thanks, but I'm watching my weight. My show's in three weeks." She insisted she wasn't mad at me, though she sure wasn't acting unmad.

Then, on Thursday, I scored an awesome invitation to the annual "Kings and Queens" gala at the Institute of Contemporary Arts. Knowing that Lily couldn't resist an event where transvestites dressed up as their favorite members of the British royal family, I decided to invite her in person. "Royals of the living *or* dead variety," I said to tantalize her at breakfast the next morning, "which means Queen Victoria will be there and *both* Queen Elizabeths."

Her interest piqued, Lily looked up from her bowl of mushy Weetabix.

"We're talking all the King Georges and about a million Diana impersonators," I went on. "Anthony says last year they borrowed all the wax royalty from Madame Tussaud's."

"It does sound sort of funny," Lily said. "Do you think we could go together?"

I didn't understand what she was getting at. "Obviously, I'm inviting you."

"You promise you won't leave me stranded by the coat check for two hours?"

"Oh, Lily, I'm *so* —" I stopped myself. I knew how Lily operated: the less said, the better. "How's this for commitment? I'll leave work early and pick you up at school so we can walk to the ICA together."

"That works," Lily said, putting down her spoon. "The ICA is only a five-minute walk from St. Botolph's. My last class ends at seven. Can you be there by five after?"

"Not a second later. I swear on all the enchiladas in Mexico."

On the way out of the *A-ha!* office that afternoon, I declined Anthony's offer of a Tube companion. Though tempted by the prospect of goofing off in the Underground with him, I couldn't risk being dragged into a pub for some "nerve poison" (as he called his customary pre-party cocktail). I had to be on time for Lily.

The sky was a dazzling blue when I disembarked at the Covent Garden station. Having gotten there half an hour early, I walked through the adjoining shopping arcade, a slate gray structure filled with expensive soap and accessories shops. On the brick street outside, jugglers were performing for groups of tourists. I wound my way to St. Botolph's Theatre Academy, situated in a narrow Georgian house on Long Acre. I was still early, so I just sat outside on the steps, contentedly watching the passersby board the bus, their shopping bags swinging every which way. When Lily emerged from the building at five after seven, it was with a forgiving grin on her face. I smiled back and flashed her my VIP passes to the fancy transvestite shindig.

On the short walk to the party, she related her adventures

in mime class to me, and then I described in detail all the fabulous *A-ha!* colleagues she was about to meet. "Anthony might seem stuck-up at first, but give him a chance — he's just very, very British. And scary smart. And beyond adorable, too, like a grown-up schoolboy. Or almost grown-up."

"I'm telling Boris you said that."

I shrugged. "I hope you do. I last heard from him five days ago, and it was a totally impersonal description of Saint Petersburg's white nights. He copied *three* other people into the e-mail."

"That's totally low. You know who's another recycled-e-mail offender? Pia. She doesn't CC; she just copies the text of one e-mail and pastes it into separate but identical messages to ten of her nearest and dearest. She just did it with an e-mail about the Pazzolini family reunion that she sent to me *and* Jess."

"The one about the aunt who lied about needing a wheelchair?"

"You got it, too? Shame on her!"

The ICA was located at the start of the Mall, a long, tree-lined promenade, the sort of grand avenue that simply doesn't exist in the New World. Its pronunciation — the "Mell" — is also uniquely Old World. "Do you think the queen will be there?" Lily asked as we turned off majestic Trafalgar Square. She was pointing in the distance at Buckingham Palace, the queen's residence.

"If so, we'd never know. Everyone would just assume she's a drag queen."

Lily giggled. "Totally. Her first opportunity to experience life on the other side."

When we got to the ICA, the main gallery was already

packed. Above our heads was a birdcage containing pigeons with artificially hot pink feathers. A sign designated them as "Her Royal Highness's Racing Pigeons." The cross-dressing royal impersonators stood much taller than everyone else (with the exception of yours truly). Some had on white pancake makeup and stiff Renaissance collars over supershort chiffon tutus and tights, while others sported silk dresses and massive gilded handbags. Among the partygoers in regular evening attire I spotted Dicky Faircrust, the royal watcher I'd met at the Foxes'. He stood against the back wall, sipping a pink cocktail and looking appalled.

Once we'd found a comfortable spot, I stood on my tiptoes and searched for my *A-ha!* colleagues; I couldn't wait for Lily to meet them. She might not fall for Anthony, but she'd definitely appreciate Ian's outrageous safari costume. I'd scanned half the room when my eyes alighted on a familiar face, barely visible in a dark corner diagonal across the gallery. "Omigod, it's Pippa!" I cried. "What's *she* doing here?"

"Who knows?" Lily said without following my bugged-out eyes. "Crazy bohemian bash with massive press coverage — why *wouldn't* she be here? Hey, what say we go grab some grub? Screw my diet — those dumplings look totally delish."

I nodded but stood paralyzed, watching my beloved hostess Pippa confer in the shadows with Mario, her creepy BBC underling who'd taken such a liking to Lily at the Foxes' Saturday lunch. He'd found a new friend, it seemed: Pippa was laughing as Mario's hand traced slow spirals down her arm. When he leaned in and whispered into her ear, she laughed so riotously that she almost overturned her champagne flute.

Maybe this is what people do at transvestite royal balls, laugh and chatter and spill champagne, but Pippa's behavior still seemed off somehow. She was a supremely capable woman, rich and powerful, not a person who allowed things to happen to her — particularly not with a gross man with a comical pencil mustache. As I watched her tip her face upward to graze Mario's neck with her nose, I knew with a deep certainty that I'd seen something I shouldn't have seen. And, with an equal certainty, I knew I didn't want Pippa to know I'd seen it.

I went over to Lily, who was polishing off a tray of dumplings. "Let's get out of here," I hissed.

"But we just got —"

"I'm serious. I feel like I'm about to faint."

"But what about the colleagues you're always raving about? Don't I get to meet them?"

"You will, I promise. I'm just nauseated and need some air. I'll take you for ice cream."

"You do look slightly green," Lily said finally. "OK, as long as you're not, like, embarrassed of me or anything."

"Don't be ridiculous!"

On our way out of the gallery, I glanced back over my shoulder at Pippa. She was still laughing with her mouth hanging wide open, and Mario had moved his palm to the small of her back. The contents of my stomach sloshed up, and for a second there, I really did come close to fainting.

From: "Rschulman"
To: "Mimicita86"
Date: July 23, 4:32 p.m.
Subject: Check in

Dear Mimi,

Thanks for your last note. It sounds as if you're doing
well and succeeding in the work-sphere. Glad to hear it.
Likewise delighted you made it to the Tate. A-plus in
initiative, duly noted. My studies here are proceeding
quite nicely. Gregorious, the male monkey, managed to
locate a blue doughnut toy I'd hidden behind a miniature
staircase, and there's so much data to sift through now.
Maurice sends his best. He's been working on some
papers but has gotten distracted lately by his discovery
of Dahlem's Ethnographic Museum. An exhibition of
sloth heads has really captivated him, and he's there
most afternoons. I hope he can incorporate it into his
papers somehow — I want him to get the most out of
our stay here.
The M-Cs are coming over for dinner tonight. I'll tell them
you say hello, no ifs ands or buts.

Love, Mom

P.S. You haven't mentioned your summer reading. Am
curious to hear what's on your nightstand. Let me know if
you need any more recommendations.

On the Master's Couch

In the week following the cross-dressing royals party, I began to have great difficulty looking Pippa in the eye. To steer clear of my surrogate mother, I avoided the kitchen and started spending more time in my fourth-floor bedroom, reading the Martin Amis novels Anthony had recommended or listening to BBC dramas on a battery-operated radio I'd taken from the closet in the bathroom down the hall.

As my relationship with Pippa disintegrated, my relationship with my biological mother was slowly improving. Diplomatic Dad had been doing his utmost to smooth over the fallout of my abrupt departure from Berlin, and whenever we talked, he'd relay some kind message from my mom: that she missed me, that she realized she'd made some mistakes. Though I'm sure he grossly exaggerated every sentiment, his stint as a goodwill ambassador was working wonders. Still, even after several brief e-mails and Sunday-night phone conversations, I was a little surprised when Mom called Penny's extension at *A-ha!* early on Thursday morning.

It was our first direct contact since the night I'd arrived in London, but Mom saw no need for preliminary chitchat. "I'm through with the Meyerson-Cullens," she hissed as soon as I picked up. "Americans at their most offensive."

"What?! I thought they were your favorite compatriots."

"So did I," Mom said, "at least until we had them over the other night. I tell you, Mimi, they simply couldn't have been ruder. First, Debbie had the gall to call five minutes before they were expected for dinner to ask if it was OK if they didn't bring wine since they weren't planning on drinking any. I told her of *course* she didn't have to bring wine and can you believe it — she took my words at face value! Then, the second they got there, she changed her mind and asked if I couldn't give her a 'sprinkle' of Chardonnay. Not only that, but Alan decided it'd be hilarious to slap Maurice on the shoulder every time the subject of his chronic back pain came up."

"Which was often, I'll bet," I said.

"It's been obvious from the get-go that Alan has real jealousy issues with Maurice, but that doesn't excuse his callous behavior, it really doesn't."

I started laughing, picturing this dinner table scene, when Mom, with no preamble, announced that she was planning a weekend trip to London. And not at some indeterminate time later in the summer, but in approximately twenty-four hours. "Sorry to spring it on you like this, but you know how impulsive your old mom can be. I miss old London town, and I really had a hankering for some mother-daughter bonding," she said, going on to explain that she could write off the trip by attending a psychology lecture Saturday morning at the University College of London. "It's on externalized family systems — you're welcome to come."

Quick and efficient, without gauging my reaction, Mom gave me the address of her hotel. "It's called the Great Briton. It might look a tad shabby from the outside, but you can't beat the location, and they have a great all-inclusive deal. You in, Cinnamon?"

Still reeling from the shock, I quietly accepted. A weekend away from the Foxes might be a welcome change. The Lily situation was still a little shaky after the ICA event. Bizarrely, she'd convinced herself that I didn't consider her cool enough to meet my *A-ha!* friends. Though I repeatedly dismissed this charge as insane, I still couldn't answer her honestly when she asked me, "So why *did* we leave, then?"

As it turned out, "a tad shabby" was a very generous description of my mother's hotel. The Great Briton occupied a creaky row house that had seen its last paint job in the early 1970s. The lobby was as narrow as a gangway, crowded with life-size white marble figurines of Great Britons ranging from Winston Churchill to David Beckham. The receptionist, an older woman with a foot-high red beehive, seemed harassed by the necessity of putting down her copy of the *Sun* to help me locate my mother on the guest register. "Schulman, is it? Let's have a look. Here we are now, that's C-2." She dialed Mom's room and frowned. "Line's engaged. We'll have another go in five minutes' time."

"Can I just go and knock on her door? She's expecting me; I'm her daughter."

"Not possible, I'm afraid. We have tightened security." She suggested I sit down, motioning to a beat-up armchair underneath a hulking bust of Charles Darwin. The seat's broken springs hurt my butt, and I waited for the receptionist to begin heavy-breathing into the *Sun* crossword before sneaking down the hall to the guest rooms.

"It's raining daughters!" Mom cried when she threw open the door to her room and hugged me. Much to my shock, she was wearing khaki pants and a white silk shirt with no words on it. She looked almost, well, *normal*. "I was just talking to Ariel," she said. "She and Decibel are having a fabulous time signing musicians in Ibiza, and she's fallen in love with sardines!"

"Yuck," I said, dropping my duffel bag to the floor. "Well, at least she's eating *some*thing."

Mom, whose attention span hadn't increased in my absence, shook out her hair and asked, "So what do you think of the new 'do? Not too much of a statement, is it? I let Dagmar take me to his salon."

I looked at her hair, seeking out wild new streaks or curly extensions, but it seemed to be the exact same monkish bowl cut she'd had since my infancy. "It looks so much fresher," I lied. "Nice job."

"No, really?" She squirmed happily. "As for you, Miss Moonbeam, aren't you looking terrific! Even in drizzly London, your freckles haven't gone into hiding!"

I chose to ignore this dubious compliment, and Mom went on. "Now, I don't know about you, but I'm famished. I have a voucher for the Café Great Briton, or would you prefer to venture outside?"

I picked the latter option, and we walked over to Goodge Street, which changed names about five times before running into Edgware Road. On the hourlong walk, I was impressed by how well Mom seemed to know central London. She took me to the exact same Lebanese restaurant she remembered from the fellowship year that she spent in London in the early 1970s, right after finishing college. "Oh, isn't this exciting!" she squealed as we stepped inside.

Every table inside the brightly lit restaurant had a little plastic sign with a number on it, presumably to help the waiters keep their orders straight. That night the precaution seemed unnecessary, given that the only other diners were a table of guys in Manchester United shirts. Mom handled the ordering, and over delicious hummus and lamb kebabs, she astonished me by asking me questions about my life in London. Could I handle the third-rate plumbing? Had I been to Windsor Castle? Did I love crumpets as much as she did and did I want to stay here forever?

Weirder still, she wasn't just asking questions — she seemed genuinely interested in my answers. I responded with growing disbelief; curiosity about other people wasn't usually my mom's specialty. "You feeling OK, Mom?" I asked at one point.

"I'm great, thanks. Make that 'tip-top,'" she added in a hammy English accent. "Why?"

"You seem a little, I don't know, un-you."

"*Un*-me. It's more like I'm more me than I've been in a long time," Mom said, then with no transition started telling me about her cranky ninety-year-old tutor at King's College from way back when. "He didn't believe in giving women work of any substance, so I became excellent at making tea — always pour the milk in *after* the hot water. I didn't mind; I loved it here. We almost moved here when you were little, you know. If I hadn't gotten that offer from Rice, you might have had one of those tip-top accents yourself."

"That's news to me," I said, genuinely surprised by this information. "But I don't get it. When I first told you I was staying in London, you said it was overpriced and underrated."

"Did I?" Mom smiled dimly. "Well, maybe I was jealous — wished I could've done the same thing myself." She sighed and clasped her hands together. "It looks like that'll never happen now. Sometimes, Mimi, what seem like the tiniest little life choices can determine a lot more than you could ever predict." To my quizzical glance, she said, "You'll see what I mean more when you get older." She sighed again, twirling a triangle of pita bread in the yogurt dip.

Then, perhaps to explain her increasingly strange behavior, Mom suddenly announced that she was "bushed" and needed to "hit the sack" right away. We took a cab back to the Great Briton to find our room dark as a bat cave. I tucked myself into my cot and immediately passed out. I slept through the night, and even through Mom's lecture the next morning.

Over a late breakfast in the repulsive Café Great Briton, Mom — who had again dressed with remarkable care in a navy pantsuit — suggested we make a pilgrimage to Sigmund Freud's house in Hampstead. She'd visited it a million times already, but according to her, "That place never loses its magic. Besides," she went on bouncily, "no daughter of mine is permitted to spend a summer in London without paying a visit to the master!"

"You sound like a religious freak," I observed through a mouthful of syrupy baked beans.

"Works for me! Means I haven't lost my fire."

After a quick aerobic stroll around Russell Square, we took a cab north to Hampstead. Like me on my first morning in town, Mom couldn't help commenting on the price of the trip, but when we got out on the shady residential street where Freud spent the last two years of his life, she recovered her good spirits.

Perhaps because I'd expected to waddle behind Mom while she gasped at boring documents behind glass, I was pleasantly surprised by the museum. Freud, it turned out, didn't collect just lunatics but antiques and African sculptures as well. Mantelpieces and tables supported vases and sphinxes, a mummy covering festooned a wall, and an arresting statue of Athena stood sentinel on his desk. But what most thrilled Mom was Freud's couch. "Just look at it!" she cried. "All the revelations that took place here!"

A tour group of senior citizens scuttled cautiously around the raving American, but Mom gave no indication of noticing. "They have the same pillows and everything! Do you realize what a huge deal this is?" she asked me.

I assured her that I did, adding that the couch looked very comfortable.

"Try telling your dad that," she said with a laugh. "He'd kill me for repeating this, but if you think Maurice is bad, you should've heard your dad gripe after every visit to Dr. Rudemeyer. Throughout the whole session, he couldn't stop bitching and moaning about how uncomfortable —" She stopped short, realizing she'd said too much.

"What are you talking about, Mom?" I asked slowly. "Who's Dr. Rudemeyer?"

"We're done here, aren't we?" she said, with a reverent glance at Freud's couch. "Maybe we should go sit down somewhere and talk."

A few minutes later, at a dessert bar on High Street, she handed over some information straight from the you-wish-you-didn't-know-this file. It seemed that, for a couple of years before their separation, she and Dad had confided their problems to a marital counselor every week.

"But Dad hates shrinks," I pointed out. "And anyway, you didn't have any problems before you left him."

"If you could only hear yourself, Mimi," Mom said. "Do you really think that washes? I'm sorry we never sat down for a real family chat about this before, but our decision to separate was by no means out of the blue. We'd been having problems for some time."

I felt weighted down with sadness, and slightly betrayed, too — but not by the woman sitting across from me. Why had Dad never mentioned Dr. Rudemeyer to me? Two years they'd gone to a counselor together? I sort of preferred thinking my parents' marriage had been perfect until Mom's sudden midlife crisis.

Knowing I'd heard enough, she signaled for the waiter and ordered me something called a sticky toffee pudding. "I don't care what they say about British cuisine," she said, "sticky toffee's just *divine*."

And it was. When the dessert came, I focused all my energies on inhaling it. Mom sat back and watched me eat, without once asking to borrow my spoon.

From: "Ppazzolini"
To: "Mimicita86"
Date: July 25, 3:12 p.m.
Subject: Ciao, bambina

Mimi,

Whassssssssssup? I'm hurt that you jet over to see Lily, and you haven't even mentioned coming to Italia. It's hot here — not the weather, but everything else. Actually, I haven't seen much daylight in a little while. Nona's dad is out here for the Lake Como film festival, and she and I have been living inside movie theaters and at afterparties. Nona's dad is staying with Tom Ramsey, who just bought a villa out here to store his Oscars and rotating cast of lady friends. Nona was hoping to stay there, too, but Tom has an 18-and-older rule, so she's camping out on a Pazzolini bunk bed.

I think I saw your favorite Baldwin alum, Nikola Ziff, sitting by her lonesome at the festival's Cinema Paradiso café. I fear this means she's pursuing an acting career instead of college — big shocker there, huh? If I run into her again, I'll be sure to tell her you send your regards. Or . . . maybe not.

Miss you, my bellissima,
Xoxoxo Pia

Home to Roost

AFTER MY WEEKEND WITH MOM, I hoped to forget about the ICA party, but I found myself unable to erase from my mind the image of Mario tracing Pippa's back and had some difficulty settling back into the rhythms of life in Little Venice. I felt obscurely guilty around the Foxes' — as if knowing Pippa's secret somehow implicated me in it. For the first few days following Mom's visit, I kept busy at events every evening, remaining at Anthony's side until late at night. In the mornings, I lay in bed reading until Pippa and Robin left the house.

But that Wednesday, just as I was scooting out the door, Robin Fox — who for reasons unknown had skipped his ritual of reading at the Harbour Club that day — called out after me. I doubled back to the drawing room, where he sat surrounded by the usual shreds of clipped-out newspapers. "Spot of trouble," he said. "One of our dinner guests this evening has just split from her husband, so he's quite understandably canceled on us, and she hasn't yet decided if she can bear to come on her own. I've already asked Lily, and I'm hoping you too can help us fill out the table. Helene Lassin and Nigel Bosworth from the Royal Opera House will be here. Do tell us we can depend on you to join us?"

I accepted the invitation with a forced smile and made a mental note to look up Helene Lassin and Nigel Bosworth when I got to work.

"Right, cheerio!" Robin said as I backed out the door. "See you for eight, then!"

After work Anthony and I went to a bar inside our building complex. Employees from neighboring skyscrapers were clumped together in wolflike packs of ten or more. We found a spot on the radiator, which was cool from disuse. "Come on," Anthony said, pulling a fifty-pence coin out of his pocket. "Are you resistant even to bribes?"

He was trying to cajole me into accompanying him to the opening of a Harley-Davidson franchise on Park Lane later that night, but I was staunch in my refusals. "You don't know *how* much I wish I could come," I said, stealing a hungry glance at his liquid brown eyes. "But the Foxes are having a dinner party and I promised I'd attend."

"Jacquetta will be there," Anthony said with a suggestive lift of his right eyebrow. "Could be our big break."

Jacquetta Schloss was London's pop star of the summer. It was impossible to walk through a clothing store or sit in a pub for longer than ten minutes without hearing her single "This Is a (Love) Holdup," a catchy ditty in which Jacquetta sings about cornering the object of her affections and making him confront her feelings. Because the magazine with the dishiest story on Jacquetta Schloss was a guaranteed sellout, Charlie Lappin and his competitors were frantically scrambling to tarnish the singer's reputation in print.

"Jacquetta and I were at Cambridge together," Anthony told

me. "Or we were for a term, before she dropped out to become a pop idol. If I introduce you as my clueless American cousin, she'll doubtless keep you entertained." Scooting off the radiator, he tipped his chin at my basically untouched half-pint of Guinness (which was, I discovered too late, way too strong for me). "You'll have another of the same, will you?" he asked me.

"Sorry, but I should be heading out pretty soon."

"Oh, pray don't be boring, Schulman. One more, that's all I ask of you."

"You know I can't drink very much before a dinner party at the Foxes'," I told him. "I've hardly seen them all week, and I need to stay on their good side. I don't exactly have too many other places to live for that price."

"Oh, bollocks. You can always stay in my flat and cook and clean for your keep. You'd look smashing in a French maid's uniform."

Smiling, I stood up to leave, but Anthony was insistent. "Right, Schulman, here's my final offer. I order myself one more drink and a pack of crisps for you. You keep me company while I kill my liver, then we leave when I finish my drink or in ten minutes, whichever comes first."

Without waiting for a response, Anthony shot over to the bar. When he returned, he was humming "This Is a (Love) Holdup" and sipping a Scotch. True to his word, he finished his drink in eight minutes and walked with me to the Canary Wharf station.

Back at Bridge House ten minutes before eight, I found Pippa and Lily in the kitchen, furiously scooping store-bought containers of tiramasalata and olives into ceramic bowls. "If you ever tell your mother this is how we do things round here," Pippa told Lily, "I'll be devastated."

"Oh, please," Lily said to Pippa. "This is a hundred times more home-cooked than anything Mom has ever made. Off camera, that is. Besides, you save your fire for Saturday lunch — everyone knows that."

"Looks amazing — especially those." I said, indicating a plate of minitoasts topped with smoked salmon and crème fraîche.

Minutes later the doorbell sounded, announcing the arrival of Helene Lassin, the first-chair flautist in the Royal Opera House, and her very, very elderly husband, Nigel, the company's former conductor. He was so elderly, in fact, that for the hors d'oeuvres part of the evening, which we spent munching on proscuitto-wrapped asparagus and sipping champagne in the upstairs parlor, I mistook him for her father or even grandfather. He was completely bald, stooped over, and had a clear plastic tube running from his nose to the inside of his shirt.

"Can you *imagine* marrying such a hideous old git?" Imogen whispered to Lily and me. Across the coffee table from us, Helene was delicately wiping spittle from Nigel's chin. "Even if he *is* a world-famous conductor — or was twelve centuries ago — I can't get my head around it. It's enough to put one off marriage altogether."

Coming from Imogen, Bridge House's resident matrimony fanatic, this was a pretty intense criticism, and Lily covered her mouth to muffle her laughter.

While waiting for the final guest, Pippa's maritally troubled childhood friend, we made polite conversation for what felt like hours but was probably more like fifteen minutes. After Robin reported that Adrian was enjoying himself on the Indian Ocean, we discussed Helene's latest gig. She'd recently returned from Berlin, where the Royal Opera had performed Mozart's *Così fan tutti*. "It's always Berlin, isn't it?" Helene reflected in a bored voice.

"Do you know what, Mimi was just there," Robin said.

"Were you?" Helene asked without interest. "And how did you find it?"

"Um . . . exciting, I guess," I said, knowing Helene wouldn't be interested in my induction into the white slave trade.

"Exciting, you say?" Helene frowned. "I always find it a bit melancholy — rather depressing actually. Nigel can never stay awake there for more than ten minutes at a stretch."

At the sound of his name, Nigel let off a king snore and his body convulsed spasmodically. His eyes popping open, he said, "Yes, yes, there we are now. Moving on to supper, are we?"

Pippa rose and, after glancing out the window, nodded. "Yes, I suppose we might as well do. When I spoke to Linda this afternoon, she seemed quite keen on coming, but then she's in such a state I imagine it slipped her mind altogether, poor dear."

Slowly, for Nigel, we headed downstairs into the Foxes' spectacular dining room, with its deep burgundy walls and the disconcerting Stanley Spencer nude positioned just above the serving sideboard.

Pippa was serving the carrot and coriander soup when the doorbell rang. "Oh, that'll be Linda, lovely," she said, dropping the ladle. "Imogen, will you finish with the soup while I get the door?"

It's funny how you rarely have any idea when disaster is about to strike. I was just sitting at the table, slightly bored but content, waiting for some random upper-class English lady to join us and spend the night sniffling or drinking too much wine. But after briefly murmuring in the hallway, Pippa walked into the dining room followed by none other than Linda Ross, the dandelion-haired woman who had relayed her marital sleeping arrangements in the Soul Cathedral ladies' room — the woman whose private confession I'd exposed to the entire United Kingdom.

I almost gasped. Oh, God, I thought, heart thumping loudly against my chest — *this* was the friend whose husband had just moved out? The one Pippa had spent the better part of a Saturday talking off the cliff?

I felt terrible. Dizzy, ashamed, and most of all terrified that Linda would recognize me, the agent of her undoing. The accusations and curses were already unspooling in my mind like a scene from daytime television. I wanted to get up and run.

But when Pippa made the introductions, Linda — her hair wilted, her face pinched with fatigue — only gave me an impassive smile. Even so, the night was young and my future still in jeopardy. I shifted lower into my seat and stared at my endive salad to avoid meeting her eyes.

While Linda, paying no attention to the other guests, updated Pippa on her miserable existence, Helene once again steered the general conversation to classical music, a subject I know embarrassingly little about. I made no contributions until Nigel, who turned out to have an incredible memory for dialogue that took place while he slept, asked me how I'd found the concert halls in Berlin.

When I admitted that I hadn't actually entered any Berlin concert halls, Nigel looked a bit confused. "Right, yes, I see, how very fascinating indeed," he murmured, watery red eyes narrowing. Then, almost accusingly, he asked me, "So what *do* you do, then, to pass the time?"

With a furtive glance at Linda Ross, I answered quietly, almost in a whisper: "I'm working for a magazine — or really just interning there, for the summer only."

But low volume was not the best tactic with Nigel, who like many ninety-year-olds had only half a working ear. "WHAT'S THAT YOU SAY? A *MAGAZINE?*" he bellowed so loudly that even Linda Ross looked up, startled.

Perhaps because I'd turned bright red, the former pop singer squinted at me with new interest. "I say, have we met before?" she asked. "You look oddly familiar to me."

Here we go, I thought, praying, Powers That Be: Please help me. Please, please, do *not* let Linda Ross connect the dots and realize that the person across from her brought about the collapse of her marriage. Everyone sat there, gazing at me expectantly, and with absolutely no cool whatsoever I clenched the tablecloth.

And then, to my surprise, Lily spoke. "Everyone thinks Mimi looks familiar," she said. "This actress who's the spitting image of Mimi has had bit parts in practically every film in the last decade, and people are always confusing them."

This was completely untrue, and though I couldn't guess

why Lily had chosen this opportunity to practice techniques from her improvisation class, I didn't care. I wanted to jump up and hug her.

Linda was still looking at me, only half convinced. "How odd. I'm certain it's *you* I've seen, but perhaps my excellent memory has gone to seed along with the rest of my life."

Before she could pursue this line of thought, the kitchen timer buzzed and Pippa jumped up. Linda, rising to help her friend, forgot me. By the time the two women returned to serve the main course of pheasant and roast potatoes, Robin and Helene were comparing notes on an exhibition they'd both seen at the National Portrait Gallery, and the crisis seemed to have passed.

Miraculously, I got through the never-ending meal intact, but I was way too skittish and jumpy to enjoy myself. In my room afterward, I lay in bed, exhausted from the effort of avoiding eye contact with Linda Ross all evening. For distraction, I'd brought up the latest *Tatler,* already mangled by Robin, who'd clipped photographs from a story entitled "The New Power Yachts" and another on eighteen-year-olds who get Botox. The real meat of the publication, however, was intact: the dozen-some pages of party pictures in the back of the magazine, in which all the featured women were labeled like "Lady Kenneth Kilburn" or "Mrs. Wendell Ulster." (The Judys would not approve, and neither did I.) I was skimming the pictures, thinking maybe I'd pick out some faces from an *A-ha!* event, when I saw the "White Nights Gala" collage, commemorating the Saint Petersburg Ballet's performance on London's South Bank.

At the very center of the spread was a familiar captain of industry: Boris's dad — tall, athletic, and psychotic Alexei Potasnik. He stood surrounded by beautiful ballerinas with tight glossy buns and flying-saucer eyes. How strange, I thought, that his dad had come to London and Boris hadn't mentioned it to me. Not that Alexei and I were such close buddies, but even so, surely Boris could've accompanied his father on the trip? Or, worse, what if Boris *had* come to London and not told me? But why would he do that? As I studied the pictures, searching for Boris's shock of white hair, I reasoned that I was probably still in Berlin, or even in New York, when this photograph was taken. I was just being paranoid and illogical, that was all. The Linda Ross near-miss had taken a real toll on me, so, tossing the magazine aside, I flicked off the light and inched under the protective warmth of the duvet.

To: "Unclesam9"
From: "Mimicita86"
Date: July 28, 10:54 p.m.
Subject: something wrong in the atmosphere?

Good morning, Vermont! I got that CD you burned me of
your radio show. Thank you very much, very much
indeed (imagine the last bit said quickly, almost inaudibly,
and you'll practically be in England). You picked some
great songs, esp. the Chinese version of "Heart of
Glass." Impressive taste as always! Seems like you're
having a pretty good time up there. . . . As for me, well,
London continues to treat me right, I guess. Going to all
these decadent parties — I'm getting spoiled and don't
know if I'll be able to handle another Baldwin dance. No
complaints about the rooftop book parties or soul food
restaurant openings, but life on the home front is getting
sort of complicated. I swear, my host family is beginning
to make the Mom-Maurice-Dad triangle seem almost
functional. I'm beginning to miss the good old days, back
when you and I would spend the day finger painting. Ah,
sweet oblivion. Do they sell it on the Internet?

More soon,
Mimi

P.S. Any chance you've heard from your Russian friend,
or is he lost in space for good?

The Other Side of Father Christmas

IT'S ALWAYS CHRISTMAS IN ENGLAND. Even in the middle of July, Britons discuss the holiday as if it's just days off. Red and green tinsel clings like ivy to pub walls and television advertisements bill everything from new air fresheners to puddings as "Christmassy." A month into my stay in London, I'd lost count of the number of times people tried to revive flagging conversations by asking, "So, made any plans for Christmas?"

It didn't seem all that bizarre, then, that my coworkers at *A-ha!* were so thrilled about the magazine's annual Christmas in July party; they needed little encouragement to get into that jingle-bell spirit. A single office-wide e-mail announcing a celebration for the "friends of *A-ha!*" transformed a staff of hard-working gossip reporters into giddy kindergartners. Sophie was in charge of the office advent calender; the twins were baking mince pies; and Zoe had special-ordered an elf costume.

I alone failed to catch the holiday bug, and I don't think it was because I'm half-Jewish and unaccustomed to splashy Christmas celebrations. Since the night Linda Ross had come to the Foxes' dinner party, I saw the darker side of my job more clearly, and I didn't like it. At first I'd considered *A-ha!* a harmless, amusing gossip rag with little or no connection to the real world. I'd never suspected a misleading scoop could derail a marriage, but Linda's undereye circles had suggested otherwise.

I found it hard, then, to get too enthusiastic about Thursday night's "pseudoholiday do" (as Anthony called it) at the Porthole, a slick hotel bar in St. Martin's Lane, only a few blocks from Lily's school in Covent Garden. She, alas, would be in rehearsals that night and unable to be my date.

The *A-ha!* staff would make up only a small portion of the attendees; the magazine's marketing team had spent two months securing RSVPs from celebrities of every stripe. "It'll be completely over the top," Ian said when he popped by my desk. "Wilder than the BAMYs. Oh, and hold up a minute," he said as if suddenly remembering something. He searched his vest pockets at length before pulling out a sparkly snowman brooch. "Remember you said you had nothing festive to wear? There you are now, courtesy of the missus." He watched with satisfaction as I fastened the brooch to my shirt, then said, "Now you're Christmassy. Lovely-jubbly."

Later that afternoon, when Charlie Lappin summoned me to his office, I realized that my feelings for the editor in chief had changed since my encounter with Linda Ross. If Charlie was friends with Pippa, and Pippa was friends with Linda Ross, then surely Charlie and Linda were friends as well? And if they were, wasn't it doubly cruel of Charlie to betray the poor woman?

"Oh, hallo there," said Rebecca when I came in with a mild and, I hoped, unreadable expression on my face. "We're just getting the next few issues sorted and wanted to fill you in."

"We're doing a celebrity weight-gain special next month," Charlie said. "Should be a slap-up issue, with loads of salad dodgers' jiggles and cellulite, a wrap-up of the top diet pills, and a sidebar on chubby chasers."

I no longer tried to translate a word of what he said and asked only, "But didn't we just do a weight-loss issue shaming overzealous dieters? Won't readers think that's hypocritical?" I forced a chuckle to balance out the criticism.

Charlie shook his head. "That was donkeys' years ago — who can remember a full fortnight back?"

"In any event, we've plenty to work on in the interim," Rebecca said gravely. "Most crucially, our coverage of the BAMYs next week. Surely you're aware of how huge the BAMYs are?" When I didn't answer, she went on, "They're our Grammys, only bigger, since almost nobody bothers about the other awards shows. Most of our staffers will be doing the same old routine — waiting until the celebs are well in their cups to chat them up."

Charlie broke in here: "But since you, Mimi, possess such an exciting raw talent, we've conceived a task commensurate with your skills. So, do you think you'll be up to shadowing Jacquetta Schloss? All our stories are about how brilliant and nice she is. Tit boring, if you ask me, particularly when *Sizzle* just ran a smashing exposé on —"

"I saw it," I told him. Who in the office hadn't read our rival publication's damning report on Jacquetta stealing the cricket-player boyfriend of "supermodel" (unknown outside the U.K.) Jemina Cochrane?

"We need something even more massive," Rebecca said. "Can you manage?"

"Of course!" I said, surprised by the enthusiasm in my voice. Five minutes ago, I'd been ready to quit this whole job — but that was before Charlie Lappin had singled me out for my "exciting raw talent." The only catch that occurred to me then had nothing to do with morality: "But I don't have a ball gown."

"We're not *that* daft," Charlie said. "Nobody's expecting you to be traveling with your trousseau. Becky here has rooms full of clothes given to her gratis by loads of fab designers. She's run up and down the scale, and been every size this side of Winston Churchill." He turned to chuckle at his deputy, whose face had gone as red as a strawberry. "Becky, you'll lend her something suitable, won't you, love?"

Rebecca, looking as if she'd swallowed a slug, nodded weakly.

After work, Anthony, Decca, Sophie, Nicholas, and I squeezed into a taxi to the Porthole. Sophie spent much of the cab ride rhapsodizing about her favorite holiday of the year: ". . . All the rellies from Henley come up, and we just stuff our faces with choccy oranges . . . and on Boxing Day Mum makes her roast venison . . ."

"Aren't you the lucky one," said Decca. "We go to Clapham Common and watch my dad in the carol singing. Then Uncle George starts singing along and Aunt Fiona tells him he sounds like a chipmunk and they have it out with each other in front of all the little children. It's more excruciating every year."

Anthony sat next to me, his elbow jutting into my rib cage — by accident or design, I couldn't make out. At one point, he pulled a full-face lamb mask over his skull and declared, "It's diabolically hot in here!" Almost immediately, he peeled the mask off again and pushed it on top of his head.

"A lamb?" Sophie sounded appalled. "I don't see what you're playing at. What does a lamb have to do with Christmas?"

"You've seen the nativity scene," Anthony answered. "I'm the sheep." He leaned into my ear and proceeded to *bah*.

Outside the hotel, we stepped out of the cab into a blinding flash of light. "That one was for the wife," Ian called out to me. "She's keen to see how the snowman worked out." With that he trotted off, promising he'd find us later.

I was expecting Anthony to abandon me once we were inside as per custom, but that night he was in an uncharacteristically attentive mood. "What'll you have," he asked, "mulled wine or a bit of nog?" I chose the former — I hated eggnog, even as an ice cream flavor — and sat down next to him on a brown leather sofa that ran perpendicular to the bar.

Next to us on the couch, Zoe, who was usually too busy breaking celebrity news to look up from her computer, had kicked up her legs and was singing along to "White Christmas" with Sophie. Anthony and I remained seated after the two of them left for the bathroom. He did get up frequently, but only to fetch more drinks — mostly, as usual, for himself. By the time I'd finished my first cup, he was already on his fourth, and I once again reflected with amazement that Anthony, at twenty, was still below the legal drinking age in America. He already seemed to have decades of practice under his belt.

"What, you've never seen an open bar before?" I teased.

"Whoever mixed this batch did a crap job," he said, frowning at his nearly finished eggnog. "I think they forgot to add the alcohol."

It was odd how attention-deficit-disorder Anthony stayed so focused all evening — and even odder that *I* was his focus. Only once did I catch him checking out another girl, and that was Vanessa Daniels, a former Miss London who now did weather on one of the breakfast TV shows.

We giggled together as we watched Rebecca Bridgewater being courted by Terry O'Connor, a hirsute radio DJ who, as Anthony explained, had split from his wife — "his childhood sweetheart, mind you" — after she caught him sending erotic text messages to their twenty-one-year-old nanny. "There was a big to-do in the press, typically," Anthony told me, "and he was so gutted he publicly vowed never to look at another woman again."

Terry was now swaying his hips and lifting Rebecca's hand high in the air, trying to cajole her into dancing with him. Decca was pushing Rebecca toward her suitor, encouraging her to "Go on, go on."

To the techno version of "Winter Wonderland" blaring overhead, Rebecca started wagging her hips, joining Terry in a racy variation on the salsa. "I can't watch this," Anthony said, shielding his eyes as he tugged me to my feet.

"What's going on?" I asked.

He made no answer as he piloted me down a corridor and toward a dark phone booth. Before I could get my bearings, Anthony drew me into the booth and used his foot to pull the door closed. The back of his hand brushed my arm, and my stomach went completely squishy. "Is this where you bring your sources for tips?" I asked in a pathetic attempt to sound adult and collected.

Still without answering, Anthony leaned against the door and pulled me close. He administered a sloppy kiss to my cheek, then readjusted his mask, which was sliding up his head. His breath smelled of nutmeg as he moved his lips to my eyelid, then my forehead, then my other lid, and my other cheek, all with the methodical motions of a clock. Finally he placed his mouth on my lips and, after such delicate preparation, rammed his tongue right down my throat. His movements were rapid and confident, his tongue spinning like a helicopter blade inside my mouth. As I struggled to keep up, I found it difficult to lose myself in the moment: the mingled taste of eggnog and alcohol was too overpowering.

Then, just as abruptly as he had begun, Anthony scooted back an inch and yanked the lamb mask back down over his face. "Right, then," he said through the mouth slit. "Shall we return to the festivities?"

Dizzily, I followed him back to the main room. I still couldn't figure out if I'd enjoyed the experience. Maybe I'd need another test drive to decide.

Hide-and-Go-Stalk

I SPLURGED ON A BLACK CAB HOME, my first since the trip from Stansted. It must have rained while Anthony and I were in the phone booth, for outside the slick streets reflected streetlights in blurry orbs. My head felt just as blurry as I tried to unscramble the events of the last few hours, but it was too much for me, and the three boys I had ever kissed (Sam, Boris, now Anthony) smeared together into a weird hallucination on the ride through London.

Blomfield Road was gorgeous in the foggy evening. The vines and droopy flowers that clung to the sides of the big white houses glistened with dew. I let myself inside, but instead of going straight upstairs I ambled to the back of the kitchen and unlatched the broad French doors that led into the garden. Robin Fox, an avid gardener, had after long deliberation positioned his new wrought-iron bench directly next to the jasmine blossoms. I took a seat there and breathed in the fruits of his hard work, thinking how remarkable it was that any corner of such a loud city could smell so sweet.

I leaned back into the cold metal of the bench and closed my eyes, thinking about my fifteen minutes in the phone booth with Anthony and wondering if he'd been drunker than usual. I had trouble conjuring his face without elements of Sam and Boris grafting themselves onto it: Sam's reddish brown eyebrows, arched in ironic disapproval; Boris's electroshocked hair, poking skyward.

And sitting there, I felt a flaring up of anger at Boris. If he'd been a less incompetent long-distance boyfriend, I'd never have followed Anthony into that phone booth. But I had, and though I wasn't sure if I'd had any fun in there, I certainly didn't regret the experience. No, instead I felt proud, vindicated almost, after a summer of Boris's slights. Anthony was hot, possibly the hottest male who had ever paid attention to me. He was also witty, clever, and a far more experienced kisser than Boris and Sam combined. And, of course, he had the best accent ever.

Suddenly, there was a shriek from the kitchen. "Lulu! My God, Lulu darling!"

I opened my eyes to see Pippa standing at the threshold of the door I had left open, and, just like that, I understood. Oh God. How many times had I been told? In the Foxes' household, there was only one rule: Never, ever, ever let poor maimed Lulu out of the house.

Pippa's eyes, hot with rage, lighted on me. "*What* are you doing out there?" she yelled, charging into the peaceful garden. "And where's my Lulu? Pray tell me you've locked her inside the laundry room. Where is she? Tell me you know where my Lulu has gone off to!"

"I . . . I . . ." But ultimately, there was nothing to say: I knew how much the Foxes loved their Lulu. "I'll go get her," I declared, despite having no idea where she was.

I spent the better part of the next two hours crawling around the neighborhood, clicking my tongue and calling out "Luuuuuuluu — *Luuuuu*luu" over and over again. Through gardens, behind garbage cans, under cars, you name it: I looked there. The night was growing thicker and darker, but I couldn't give up, not if it meant facing Pippa without Lulu in my arms. Then, just when my despair was becoming unbearable, I spotted a familiar four-legged creature poking around a rosebush. My chest flooded with happiness as the slim gray cat arched her back and meowed at my approach.

"Lulu," I whispered, moving slowly to avoid scaring her. "C'mon, Lulu, that's *such* a good little girl, c'mon, girl, let's go on back home."

After considering the matter, the cat meowed again and trotted toward me. I scooped her up with trembling arms and thanked my lucky snowman brooch. "Hey, little girl," I cooed softly, and planted a kiss on her gray nose.

Except that her nose wasn't gray. It was white. Lulu was completely gray, down to her whiskers and toe hair: this cat, on closer inspection, had not just a white nose, but white paws and a triangular patch of white on her chest. And not one but two sparkling green eyes. This cat, in other words, was not Lulu. I released the wriggling animal from my arms and returned to Bridge House in defeat. There was no point. I'd searched everywhere; Lulu had vanished.

When at last I entered the kitchen, I gasped to see Pippa sitting at the island with Lulu curled up in her lap. "Oh, hullo,"

Pippa said mildly. "I found her immediately after you left. She'd fallen asleep behind the curtains, you see — she does that sometimes, the naughty little puss."

Inside me, relief and outrage swelled up, competing for dominance. Why hadn't Pippa come to tell me? Had she any idea what I'd gone through these past two hours?

But Pippa didn't seem too preoccupied by my state of mind. She was focused on Lulu, rubbing the cat between the ears and playfully admonishing her. "You're a naughty little pussy, aren't you?" she kept saying. "Naughty little pussy!

"Oh, and Mimi." Pippa looked up and met my eyes with a level, ice-cold gaze. "I've just had quite a fascinating phone call from my friend Linda Ross — our guest at dinner the other night, surely you recall? It seems she finally remembered where she'd seen you before. It was in the loo of a restaurant, wasn't it? Just a few days before your employer published that damning report on her marriage."

Pippa's voice was flat, her face expressionless. I made a gargling sound of protest, then stuttered out, "It wasn't my idea at all. I didn't know she was your friend and I didn't want to run the story. Nobody would listen to me, I swear!"

Pippa, evidently, didn't want to listen to me, either. "I must say, well done, Mimi. You've surpassed even dear Charlie, and he's always been a bit of a bastard. At least he has the good sense to know the difference between public and private, I'll say that for him. What were you thinking, *eavesdropping* in the loo? Really, I mean, that's a bit too vulgar, even for *A-ha!* I rang up

Charlie just now, and he'd no idea how you'd obtained your little revelation.

"Charlie would never do anything so indecorous. Of all the times Charlie's been over here, he's never once printed a single snippet of our conversation, not unless he's been specifically asked to. He'd never behave so . . . indiscreetly. But you — you . . . I'm sorry, but it's just not on, Mimi, not on at all." Lips trembling with rage, Pippa shook her head, and without another word, stood up and took the cat upstairs to bed.

For several minutes afterward, I remained frozen in place at the kitchen island, paralyzed by the horror of my actions, all the horrible consequences I'd never fully confronted. It didn't seem appropriate to follow Pippa up to her room and remind her of all the secrets I *hadn't* spilled, namely her affair with Mario. I found myself wishing I were still toiling away at the Meyerson-Cullens. Suddenly a summer of workbook exercises and gluten-free snacks didn't seem so awful.

Early the next morning, as bright yellow sunshine fell in patches across the floor of my bedroom, I momentarily wondered if the previous night hadn't been some overly complicated dream, a regrettable product of my hyperactive imagination. First Anthony. And Lulu. And Pippa. And God — Linda Ross.

Then I saw the little white rectangle of paper slipped beneath my door. With a feeling of premonition, I jumped out of bed and picked up the letter. I admired the heavy pulp paper. This was no Rite Aid envelope. It was the stuff of aristocratic correspondences. I flipped it over, half expecting to find the royal watermark on the other side. Then, finally, I forced myself to open it, and to read the following message:

30 vii
Mimi,
I apologise for the inconvenience I'm about to impose on you, but after the ghastly occurrences of last night, I cannot simply carry on as if nothing has happened. I'm afraid I must request that you find alternate lodging for the remainder of your stay in London. I expect this news won't come as a complete surprise to you — indeed, it might even be welcome. We've made ourselves scarce for the day so you can gather up your belongings and make arrangements for your departure in privacy. If you are unable to stay with a friend, I'd be happy to recommend a reasonably priced hotel.
With my most sincere regrets, and all best wishes for future endeavours,
Philippa Fox

Loose Ends

My eyes welled as I read, and reread, Pippa's letter. Against my better judgment, I stuck my head out in the hallway and called out Lily's name, but there was no answer. I slammed shut my bedroom door — what was until recently my bedroom door, that is — and lowered myself onto the bed.

What was I supposed to do? I had no money for a hotel, and I didn't have any English friends, not real ones. Then again . . . I shot up, recalling what Anthony had said the night of his Harley-Davidson event, when we'd joked about my living with him and being his French maid. So what if his intentions toward me weren't entirely fraternal? Mine weren't either, and round-the-clock sexual tension sure beat homelessness. I grabbed the phone and dialed his mobile number.

"Palfrey here," he said in his well-bred voice, sounding surprisingly smooth for somebody who'd consumed such quantities of eggnog the previous night. When I'd left the party, he'd been persuading Decca to affix a branch of mistletoe to her backside.

"Anthony!" I cried, and immediately launched into a garbled account of my crisis, minus the Linda Ross detail. "A cat! It's so petty, really, the whole thing, but what else can I do? I can't leave; my plane ticket isn't until August twenty-second, and, well . . ."

"Beastly, that!" Anthony cried after I'd finished. "I do say, the Foxes sound positively spastic. So what's next for you?" he went on lightly. "Surely you could pay a fee and change your ticket, assuming the airline isn't too extortionate."

My heart thudded. Anthony knew exactly what I was asking of him, and he was choosing to ignore it. "I guess I'll find a place to rent or something," I said softly, feeling foolish for having called him in the first place. "But, um, can you tell Charlie and Rebecca that I probably won't be in today? And please don't explain why — just say I'll be back by Monday."

"Not a problem at all, love. And best of luck to you — I've no doubt you'll sort it out." Then, with a cheerful "toodle-pip," Anthony hung up on me.

I was too staggered by Anthony's dismissal to move. Then another idea came to me, and I started to dial Sophie's number, but midway through remembered she was from Leeds and staying on her great-aunt's sofabed for the summer. Admittedly, I had hit a low point, but I'm too tall to sleep in anyone's bathtub.

Just as I dissolved into tears, Lily charged into the room. "C'mon, no need for that," she said gently, rushing over to me.

"What are *you* doing here? Don't you have class?"

"Not till noon," she said. "And even if I did, did you *really* think I'd make you go through this on your own? I was in Pippa's office, killing time till you woke up."

"I'm so glad you're here." I sniffled. "I didn't do anything, nothing on purpose."

"I'm sure you didn't," Lily said. "I'm sure this'll blow over eventually, but maybe you should still do as Pippa says and vamoose."

Once I'd blown my nose a few hundred times and told Lily the whole story, I started to feel different, more optimistic, about the whole situation. Rather than suggesting I sleep in a cardboard box on Oxford Street for the rest of the summer, Lily actually volunteered to put me up in a hotel for the next week.

"No, I couldn't," I said. "That's crazy, and I've imposed on you enough already."

"Well, then, what?" Lily asked. "Is there anyone else you could stay with? Someone from work, maybe?"

"I hear there's a spare bedroom at Linda Ross's," I said with a snort. And right then something struck me. I jumped up and grabbed my little steno notebook off the floor. Ian Cassidy's number was scrawled on the back of the hard cardboard cover. He'd given it to me with specific instructions: "If you're ever in a pinch, Cassidy's your man." If this didn't qualify as a pinch, I don't know what did.

The second Ian picked up the phone with a steely "Yeah?" I knew everything would be resolved somehow. As calmly as I could, I relayed my fall from grace, with Lily sitting beside me, nodding encouragingly.

"Right." Ian began humming, as he did when calculating something important, like which route to take or which lens to use. "Try this one on for size. You camp out at Camp Cassidy. We'll come collect you straightaway."

"Don't be ridiculous, Ian!" I cried. He had a poodle the size of a horse, a notoriously high-maintenance wife, and, at last count, three kids. "I wasn't asking you to put me up, I swear. And it's Friday — don't you have to work today?"

"Now you listen, I wouldn't've offered if I weren't being dead straight with you. One of the chief advantages of working at night is the flexible mornings," Ian said, "and Colleen works from the Peckham homestead. Now come again, where do these Fox toffs live?" Ian sounded ready for a barroom brawl, and how I loved him for it.

"There's good news and there's good news," I told Lily after hanging up the phone. "Ian's going to come and rescue me, and you're finally going to meet my favorite person from work."

"If I'd known this was what it would take," Lily said with a mischievous grin, "I'd have gotten you kicked out weeks ago."

An hour later, when the car pulled up out front, Lily and I had already stuffed my clothes into my bags. My size ten and a half red cowboy boots — my all-time favorites — wouldn't fit, so I stuck them upside down in a shopping bag and then followed Lily down the stairs to the front door, without even stopping for an appreciative last glance at the Foxes' Chippendale armoires or giant candelabras or Lucian Freud paintings. I was feeling strangely uplifted, ready to leave it all behind, when I heard Lulu mewling from behind the laundry room door.

"I'll thank you for this one day, kitty," I told the cat before closing the door to Bridge House for the last time. Beyond the gate, Ian and a plump woman were clambering out of a large car — not Ian's industrial truck, but a maroon minivan that looked most un-safari-like. I couldn't help but smile.

"There she is, poor love," the woman said, toddling forward to engulf me in a motherly embrace. "I'm Colleen Cassidy."

Colleen was a big-shouldered, solid woman who was even shorter than her husband. She had puffy brown hair and was wearing a lavender sweatshirt with a bunny rabbit printed on the front and a furry tail printed on the back. Come to think of it, she herself looked not unlike the Easter Bunny, with her cotton-ball cheeks and pointy chin. As she hugged me again, I struggled to identify the harpy who was always chewing Ian out on the phone — that is, until she gave her husband a little shove with her elbow and snapped, "Ian, don't just stand round like a tit. Help the dear with her bags!"

"Awright." A humbled Ian took my suitcase and hoisted it into the back of the van. "You can sit in front with me. You're in the rear, dear," he told his wife.

I introduced Lily to the Cassidys, then hugged my friend goodbye. With one last murmured thank-you, I slowly climbed into the front seat of the Cassidys' car. As we pulled away from the curb, I looked out the window to see Lily, then the rows of grand homes, recede into the distance. It was like watching the final credits in a movie.

"You all right?" Colleen asked me from the back seat.

"Completely," I assured her. "I can't thank you enough for coming to my rescue."

"Think nothing of it, love. Now there, do you fancy a nose-bag now, or shall we just carry on straight to Peckham? I'm sure we can scrape something together. There's bacon and cheddar and last night we had some lovely pasta."

"You know," I said, "for the first time in my life, I don't think I'm hungry."

Ian snorted. "Famous last words," he told his wife. "This girl's got quite an extraordinary appetite. Which is funny, innit, 'cause when I first met her, I thought she was one of those anemic lasses."

"*Buli*mic," Colleen corrected him. "Anemics are the pasty ones, isn't that right?"

"Well, I'm neither," I said. "Just insatiable."

"I know the feeling," said Colleen amicably. "I've been known to put away a whole box of Quality Street chocolates in a single go. I get sick the day after our anniversary every year."

The traffic stalled at the periphery of Regent's Park. It was a glorious summer day, with a cloudless bluish gray sky. The park's trees were thick with leaves, and groups of respectable old ladies strolled in identical sensible black shoes. Colleen was telling me about their sons, Hugh, Robby, and Roddy. Hugh had just turned six; Robby and Roddy, the twins, were eight. Another set of eight-year-old twins? A bit rich, as Ian might say.

"They're quite good lads, really," Colleen told me. "Don't set things on fire, don't give me any cheek."

"Take after their mum they do," Ian said. He was fiddling with the radio dial and after a few false stops settled on an inane talk show on BBC 4. A group of men were joking around about the afterlife — or, more specifically, whether they'd prefer to turn into earthworms or mosquitoes when they die. "Blimey, what a question!" Ian cried indignantly. "Mosquitoes have a crap life span — only about three weeks, innit? That's scarcely time enough to reach Manchester."

Colleen was of another opinion. "So you'd rather live underground, would you? No, thank you — I'll take a mosquito's life any day, even if I end up squished between Roddy's fingers."

From my seat up front, I had an impressive view of London in all its mind-boggling immensity, and I leaned forward to take in the panorama of old buildings, brightly colored storefronts, and endless majestic monuments that whished by outside my window. The stately Strand, the gentle arches of Southwark Bridge, the hungry crowds jostling their way through Borough Market, then into quieter residential sections of South London, with modest semidetached houses and well-maintained commons.

"Now keep your eyes peeled," Ian said as we turned down a street of empty car lots and a dilapidated mosque — scenery Sam would no doubt love. "You're about to get a taste of Peckham. Hold on to your seat."

I'd always assumed Ian lived in the neighborhood equivalent of himself: working-class, old fashioned, and one hundred percent English. But in London, I was beginning to learn, there was no such thing. Peckham was a wild jumble of languages and colors and smells, a place where betting parlors and traditional English sandwich shops alternated with produce stands carrying hairy root vegetables and cell phone stores specializing in "mobile phone unlocking." A sign in one off-license said MONEY FOR GHANA, and another down the block advertised MONEY FOR SUDAN.

Ian downshifted on Alpha Street, parking the car in front of a white terraced house that was a twentieth the size of the Foxes'. "Here we are then," he said, gesturing at the bright façade. The trash cans waiting to be collected out front had cat images spray-painted on them, and a bird feeder dangled from the tree in the front yard.

"You have bird feeders!" I squealed as I got out of the car. "I've always wanted a bird feeder. Do you get a lot of birds?"

"Hooligans, chiefly," Ian said. "Of the *Homo sapiens* variety. We had to plug up the seed dispenser."

"It's terrible, really," Colleen jumped in, "just dreadful — I keep telling Ian we'd best move out to Ealing, or another part of town more suited for children, but we do have our roots here."

"Here's where we met, back when we were still teething," Ian said. "She was my first sweetie."

"Peckham was completely different back then," Colleen told me. "Flowerpots on every doorstep, and you knew everybody, you know? Nowadays we've got race riots and —"

"There are no race *riots,*" Ian said. "Just a bit of friction now and again."

"And then these awful yobs from down the road were coming round in the middle of the night and leaving us little surprises," Colleen went on. "Once they put in loo paper and another time it was chocolate birds, which is quite sick if you think about it — birds for the birds to eat! That's like cannibalism, innit? It's not as if we couldn't afford to move, mind you," she told me. "It's just Ian's a stubborn bugger, and he's happy as Larry having the odd pint with his old school chums. And I suppose it's rather convenient, with my mum down the road . . ."

In front of us, Ian was unlocking the door. "Oh, for fuck's sake," he grumbled as a squawking noise issued from inside. "She let the canary out again, did she? Bloody hell."

Colleen looked at her husband sharply. "You're free to hire a proper child minder while you're gallivanting around London all night and day. Otherwise, Mum can bring whomever she likes round the house, so you be civil, or you'll get an earful later."

"Yes, but why can't she keep the bloody thing in a cage?" Ian muttered. But another sharp glance from Colleen did the trick and he nodded, chastised. "You're right, love. I don't know how we'd manage without your mum."

A small kid, presumably Hugh, rushed out to greet us. "We're playing lethal ninja terminator," he told his mother, then ran back inside, screaming the whole way.

Ian led us into the house, where a scene from a wildlife program on the Discovery Channel played at fast-forward. A tiny woman lay stiffly on the living room couch with closed eyes, sleeping through a radio program I recognized to be *The Archers,* a long-running soap opera about a farming community. Above her, a canary swooped in frantic circles while a trio of chubby miniature Ians whirred back and forth, thwacking each other with plastic machine guns. A black curly-haired poodle of brontosaurus proportions shambled over and energetically sniffed my inner thighs. "That's Sylvia," Ian told me. "Behave, Sylv!" he snapped at the dog on his way back out.

"Get back into the death chamber, go on then!" one of the twins shouted to his younger brother, packing him into the coat closet.

"Hugh, out here!" roared Colleen behind me. "Don't wind me up now!"

Once the boys had lined up before her, their mother addressed them. "Mimi here will be staying with us for a spell," she said sternly. "If you're not perfect little angels with her, they'll be no video games for a fortnight, you hear? Mimi, I'd like you to meet the sprogs: Roddy, Robby, and Hugh."

Ian returned heaving my suitcase and simultaneously muttering into his cell phone. "Mm-hmm, Rachel from *Lonsdale* and her new squeeze?" he said to whoever was on the other end. "The café at Harvey Nicks? Right, then." After hanging up, Ian looked at us with sparkling eyes. "I'm off, then — back in a bit!" He nodded at me, kissed his wife on the cheek, and ran out the door.

"His tipsters, I reckon," Colleen said, moving an ottoman aside to make room for my bags.

In the kitchen, she made me a pot of strong tea and a cheddar-mayo sandwich. The kitchen table was overrun with photography equipment, scattered lens caps and film rolls that reminded me of Barrow Street. Amid Ian's clutter were invoices and catalogs from Loose Ends, Colleen's employer. When she asked me if I'd heard of the company, I had to shake my head no.

"I'm quite fond of Loose Ends," she said. "But then I would be, wouldn't I? I've a bit of a knack. Last year, I was the number four seller in the Greater London area, and Ian and I got a free weekend holiday at this lovely B&B in the Cotswolds."

For the rest of the afternoon, Colleen, an expert hostess, went out of her way to make me feel at home in Peckham. She gave me keys and a stack of matching towels and washcloths, and instead of just telling me where the nearest railway station was, she walked me there and back so I could repeat the journey on my own. When he returned early that evening, Ian invited me to join him for trivia night at his local pub, but I decided to stick around for Colleen's Loose Ends party. The boys took their gravity-defying bouncing upstairs while a dozen or so women, including Colleen's mom, Jackie, and her free-flying canary, Diana, crowded into the living room to drink Blue Nun wine and examine the new "aquatic undertones" sweater collection Colleen was selling. When she'd finished her presentation, I impulsively ordered a blue cardigan with starfish, waves, and porpoises for my mother. A devoted Freudian, she was partial to clothing with symbolic content.

After the guests left, Jackie put down the glass of sherry she'd been nursing all night and went upstairs to check up on the kids. Colleen and I remained in the living room to tidy up. "Oh, Sharon must've left this behind," Colleen said, plucking a pink sweatshirt out from underneath a couch cushion. "Try it on, will you?" She threw the garment at me and waited for me to put in on before walking me over to the full-length mirror.

"Nice with your eyes," she said from my side. "I say you keep it."

Looking in the mirror, I saw the sweatshirt was emblazoned with foil hearts. It then struck me that Colleen's face resembled a heart, with her pointy chin and sandbag cheeks. "You like it?" she asked me, and stood there looking slightly nervous as she waited for my verdict.

"Like it?" I asked her reflection. "It's perfect."

To: "Rogmahal"
From: "Mimicita86"
Date: August 1, 7:43 p.m.
Subject: Luv-Jub

Dad,

I hope you haven't been worrying about me — and
please, for the love of burritos, don't start worrying now
just because I put the word "worrying" in the first line of
this e-mail. I promise everything's fine, but maybe you
should sit down before reading on, OK?

So here's the deal: the Foxes sort of evicted me. I'll tell
you the whole story in person or on the phone or
whatever — I don't really feel like going into it now,
frankly. Just know that I didn't do anything too
objectionable, at least not on purpose. Also, before you
freak out, let me assure you that I've found a new and
improved host family: the Cassidys. (I'm writing from
their house and I'll put their number at the bottom of the
letter.) Ian Cassidy is a friend from work and, as he
himself would say, you two would get along "like a house
on fire." He's a photographer at the magazine and his
family is wonderful. They live WAY south of the river in
Peckham, which is officially part of London but can only
be reached by an extraspecial aboveground train that
connects to the Underground. I'm sleeping comfortably

on the downstairs sofa (though I do get woken pretty early by the Cassidy "sprogs" and Sylvia the ginormous poodle). I wish you could meet everyone here, I really do. Don't really know what my plans are, but I'll call you ASAP, OK? Or better yet, you call me!

Lovely-jubbly (that's an English expression for who-knows-what?),
Mimi

From: "Unclesam9"
To: "Mimicita86"
Date: August 4, 12:14 p.m.
Subject: re: Life Sucks

Mimikins,

I'm so sorry to hear about your recent catastrophe. Your
crapola luck doesn't seem fair, does it? The new family
sounds great, but you still must be pretty freaked out.
You want me to call you? Let me know when and where
and I totally will.

Things are cool with me, more or less. Back from the
Birkenstock state. Spent the weekend, against my will, at
the bat mitzvah of the daughter of my mom's most
tedious friend (which, as you know, is saying a lot). The
service was nine hundred hours long and beyond
boring — even my dad, King of Dullsville himself, was
nodding off. The party was out of control in a completely
different way. It seems little Jocelyn dreams of becoming
a movie star (fat chance of that, trust me), so the
whole deal was Hollywood-themed, with trunks of
movie star costumes and old-fashioned photo booths.
Because I had nothing better to do, I chose the
Humphrey Bogart duds and my parents opted for
Richard Burton and Elizabeth Taylor in Cleopatra —

funny, right? I uploaded the pics and am attaching for your amusement.

As for B-Dog, I don't have a clue. I haven't heard from him all summer. Sorry I can't be more helpful.

OK, gotta go if I'm going to make this mountain biking workshop on the Hudson River, but I'm dead serious about what I said: Let me know if you need anything.

Sam your man

Buttercup Belle

By the end of my first weekend south of the river, I was an old Peckham hand. The neighborhood's layout was easier to grasp than other parts of London, and my new neighbors were chatty and warm — particularly Tom and Lester, the two old men who seemed to be permanently glued to the bench outside The Rose & Crown pub.

Though the sugar-addicted Cassidy spawn woke me insanely early every morning, I still felt happy and energized. My "pep" even drew comment from Colleen's mother, Jackie, who was usually too absorbed in the goings-on in Ambridge, the fictitious village where *The Archers* was set, to notice much else.

I slept fitfully Sunday night, probably because I dreaded crossing paths with Anthony at *A-ha!* the next day. But at the office Monday morning, he was as playful as ever, as if my phone call Friday morning had never happened. He made silly faces at me whenever he passed my cubicle and I was on the phone, and made me shriek when he sneaked up behind me to press an ice-cold water bottle against my neck. By the end of the day, I'd concluded he didn't think anything strange had passed between us, and I'd completely forgiven him his inhospitality. What had I been thinking, making such a suggestion in the first place? I'd been so forward, so American. Ian, when he'd heard the story over the weekend, had laughed and said, "The boy fancies you, clear as a bell. Wants to maintain an air of mystery, that's all."

For the rest of the week, everyone at *A-ha!* worked feverishly on preparations for the BAMYs issue. Some reporters had been assigned to find out what the stars would be wearing in order to put together a "Dress Like a Diva" spread. Nicholas was working on a feature about the judging committee, and had been granted access to all their meetings. Anthony agreed to help me with my big assignment — the Jacquetta Schloss scoop I had been ordered to obtain — and volunteered to introduce me to his former classmate at the ceremony. Knowing how much Charlie and Rebecca were counting on the story, I accepted the offer gratefully.

Friday morning, I arrived at Canary Wharf to find the *A-ha!* offices practically empty. Charlie Lappin had given his staff the day off, for primping purposes. I'd shown up only to pick up the dress Rebecca had left for me. Though I'd given her all my measurements, I had serious misgivings about the deputy editor's taste, given her preference for skimpy getups that were age-inappropriate even for me. And if, as I suspected, Rebecca wasn't wild about me, she might choose to take out her aggression in the form of a hideous costume.

But when I unzipped the garment bag Rebecca had draped over Penny's chair, I pulled out a magnificent gown straight out of an old Marilyn Monroe movie. It was butter-colored satin, with a low-cut back and a series of fabric flaps that tied in back. Wow. Maybe Rebecca didn't have it in for me after all. There had to be a catch — maybe she'd intentionally chosen a dress that was too small for me.

The surrounding cubicles were empty, so I crouched down to find out. I had just tugged the dress over my hips — success! — when the voice of Charlie Lappin crowed "Hell-o-o-o-o!" over the cubicle wall. Thanking God I'd left my wrap dress on underneath, I shot up and greeted my boss with crimson cheeks.

"Practicing for tonight?" Charlie said, chuckling. "You look perfectly splendid, but if you don't mind my saying, I'd lose the extra layer if I were you. I believe the point is to see some skin."

As I stood there feeling compromised in my unzipped, double-dressed state, Charlie launched into a description of the BBC documentary he'd watched at the gym that morning. "Brilliant bloke," he said of the Spanish chef profiled on the show. "He used to be a surgeon and now he uses his medical instruments in the kitchen. He doesn't make a single dish without the help of a syringe. Must be loads easier to operate when your patient's already dead — no cries of protest, ha! Anyway, do tell Pippa how much I enjoyed it."

I nodded slowly, deciding to save the story about my being evicted for another occasion. Once Charlie had spun back toward his office, I checked my e-mail, reviewing the digital pictures various loved ones had sent me over the summer: Pia looking ridiculously glamorous reading an Italian edition of *The Valley of the Dolls* on a teak deck chair; Viv barely able to wrap her tiny arms around an immense tub of popcorn; Quinn and Dad sitting on our stoop on Barrow Street, raising their Snapple bottles to the camera. And last but not least, my pal Sam winking from beneath his fedora and twirling an unlit cigar between index and middle finger. Not for the first time, I looked closely at this picture, fascinated. Was it the stark lighting, or the dashing costume, or the effect of his new mountain biking habit, that made my gangly carrot-top friend look so different? He seemed older, more confident — almost, dare I say it, attractive.

I shook my head rapidly and switched off the computer. There was no time for such speculations, not with just eight hours left to figure out how to tie the dress's baffling network of flaps.

Battleship Down

THE BAMYS TRADITIONALLY TOOK PLACE in the Royal Albert Hall, a Victorian building so baroque and fabulous that Alfred Hitchcock featured it in not one but two movies. But at last year's ceremony, the drummer from Eternal Radish clogged the pipe organ with chewing gum, and the BAMYs had not been invited to return. The less impressive site of this year's event was the Royal Horticultural Halls, a convention center rented mostly for gardening shows and charity jumble sales.

When Ian and I first got there, it was still light outside, and uncomfortably hot, but the nominees and their entourages were dressed to the nines in Swarovski-encrusted tuxedoes and breathtaking couture gowns. I silently thanked Rebecca Bridgewater for choosing such a wonderful dress, and Colleen Cassidy for braiding a silk gardenia into my hair.

Ian snapped away at the red carpet scene, and I watched the procession by his side. "Hey," I whispered at one point, directing Ian's attention to a muscular black-haired woman working her way toward the entrance. "Didn't she already go inside five minutes ago?"

"An old trick, that one is," Ian said. He drew a paper towel out of one of his many pockets and wiped it across his forehead.

"They pop out the back door, then come round and make a second entrance, just on the off chance we missed them the first time round. You know who that one is?" Ian pointed to a brunette with harsh cheekbones and liquid blue eyes.

When I told Ian I'd never seen the woman before, he nodded with satisfaction. "Expect not," he said. "She doesn't leave her flat too often these days. That's Anna Engbert, that is. She had a bit of a fling with Charlie Lappin several years back — I always pitied the poor lass after that one. He broke her heart, he did."

"No way — Charlie Lappin, a heartbreaker? I can't imagine anyone taking him serious —"

"Put yourself in the shoes of a young actress and the editor of *A-ha!* might seem a bit more appealing."

"Where is Charlie, by the way? I saw him this morning."

"You didn't hear? He's avoiding public events."

"Charlie Lappin avoiding public events? But he's the most —"

"Social bugger you've ever met? Don't I know it." Ian changed flashes. "It was some image consultant's crap idea. I give it a week."

"If that," Anthony said from behind us. He was wearing red suspenders under his tuxedo and socks to match. After complimenting me on my "smart frock," he told me he'd just seen Jacquetta Schloss inside. "Shall we?" he asked, extending his arm.

I was thrilled to be trotting up the red carpet with Anthony, but as soon as we entered the main hall, which was swarming with people, he disentangled himself from me. He parked me by a potted palm and told me to stay put. "I'll come find you the moment I see Jacquetta again," he said.

I waited there like a fool, refusing to budge from my spot in case I missed Anthony. He didn't return until the curtain was raised and the boy band Make It broke into their latest single. "I don't know where Jacquetta buggered off to," he said. "But not to worry, we've still loads of time — I'll fetch you after dinner."

And with that we separated. While Anthony had been selected to sit at the *A-ha!* table, I, like most of the lowlier staffers, had to stand upstairs in the "overflow" area. On my way there, I walked right past Sophie, not recognizing her until she called out my name. She looked gorgeous in a red off-the-shoulder dress and a simple pearl necklace. Her hair, usually multicolored, was a uniform shade of brown and set in a chignon.

"Soph!" I cried. "You look stunning!"

"Oh, shush," she said, blushing the color of her dress.

"What's your assignment tonight?" I asked. At the office, Sophie mostly wrote capsule reviews of unauthorized celebrity biographies and sidebars about beauty trends.

"You mean why was I dispatched to an event with living and breathing people?" she replied sardonically. "No doubt there were extra tickets, but to Rebecca Bridgewater's credit, she did try to make me feel important. Said I'm emergency backup, meaning if anybody catches on fire, I'll be here to collect quotes from onlookers. And you? Oh!" She ducked as a crane attached to a camera swooped perilously close to her head.

"Nice save," I said, and we started to walk upstairs. "Well, if all goes to plan, Anthony's going to introduce me to Jacquetta Schloss, and I'm supposed to trick her into making some meaningless statement that Charlie can twist into a scandalous confession."

"Charlie? Twist words?" Sophie widened her eyes in fake surprise. "Impossible!"

When we got upstairs, Sophie installed herself by the balcony to watch the ceremony, leaving me to wander on my own. While the first-class ticket holders were feasting on a four-course meal in the main auditorium, the rest of us had to make do with old-fashioned popcorn machines. Each machine popped a different flavor, and I kept busy tasting the wide selection. "This one's interesting," I said, presenting Sophie with my best find yet — chocolate. "Sweet and salty at the same time."

"Plech." Sophie spit it out into a napkin. But when she looked up at me, her eyes were wide and shining. "Mimi, isn't this just marvelous? Have you ever seen such a spectacular event?"

Looking down at the stage, which was illuminated by little arrows of blue neon, I shrugged in uncertain agreement. "Yeah, it's great," I said. It didn't feel right, telling Sophie how disappointed I was by the BAMYs. For all its spaceship sound effects and cutting-edge lighting whirligigs, the event felt a little drab, less inspiring even than last semester's dance at Baldwin.

"Ghastly of the magazine to put you up here," Anthony said, coming up behind us and sticking his hand into the bag of popcorn. "Whose idea was this, popcorn for the media circus?" he asked, and as Sophie had he spit out the bite. "You should be outraged!"

"We're fine," Sophie said politely, smoothing her hair and

smiling wide. As I watched the color rise to her cheeks again, I realized that she, too, must have a crush on Anthony, and I felt stupid for not having noticed it before.

"Sorry to intrude," he said. "Just had a Jacquetta update. She's at table eight, and I told her there's somebody I'd like her to meet. So you'll come down for dessert and we'll make a bit of magic, yeah?"

Before I could respond, he gave the gardenia in my hair a tweak and skittered off, leaving Sophie and me to exchange embarrassed looks. When the servers finally came out to clear everybody's dinner plates, I said goodbye to Sophie and headed down the stairs.

Anthony was slouched between Decca and a woman I'd never seen before. He was playing with an empty wineglass, dangling it upside down by its stem; a few red drops had rolled onto the tablecloth. At my approach, he got up somewhat unsteadily and once again told me to stay put. But this time, he acted fast. Just a few minutes later, he returned arm in arm with Jacquetta Schloss.

London's favorite pop singer was dressed like a bumblebee, in a black and yellow gown that made her look puffier than in pictures. But she was also more beautiful, with clear green eyes and dimples that cut deep into her cheeks, like fishhooks.

"Right," Anthony said, careening back into his chair and nodding up at me. "Jacqs, it's my pleasure to introduce you to Mimi Schulman. Mimi's a colleague of mine from across the pond, and she doesn't know you from a bar of soap. But she's been assigned to cover you for our BAMYs issue, so if you'd be so kind" — he paused to feed himself chocolate cake with his fingers — "as to throw the dog a bone, I'd be much indebted to you."

I felt my throat constrict and cheeks turn red. I didn't say anything. Had Anthony just called me a dog? In front of Jacquetta Schloss?

But Jacquetta simply smiled at me kindly before telling Anthony, "Careful! You're dropping chocolate crumbs everywhere." She turned to me and offered me her free hand; the other was gripping a martini glass. "It's a real pleasure to meet you, Mimi — I'd be happy to chat for a bit. Let's go back to the bar, shall we? I'm desperate for another drink."

The bartender made a big display of welcoming back his "favorite customer." With a wink, he asked if she'd be having another cosmopolitan. "And make it stiff, Frank," Jacquetta said, then twirled around on her barstool to focus on me. Though she was one of Britain's biggest superstars, the singer impressed me with a fresh, nearly self-mocking quality. She thought nothing of hiking up her pantyhose in front of me, and when she laughed, she threw back her head to reveal enormous nostrils. If she weren't famous, I thought, we could be almost friends.

"I'm famished," she said, glugging down her cocktail. "All they served at this dinner were wretched little steaks. They're so miserly at these functions."

When I told her about the old-fashioned popcorn machines, Jacquetta's eyes bulged like a pair of green Ping-Pong balls and she begged me to take her upstairs. I brought her to a back corner of the upper level, where the pickle and chocolate popcorns were side by side. "What a stupendous idea," Jacquetta said through a mouthful of pickle popcorn. "Mmph, absolutely delicious." She laughed as she wiped her forearm across her mouth. "You must think I'm *such* a pig."

"No, not at —" I was about to boast of my own impressive appetite when a tall mustached man burst through the crowd, heading straight for us. "What are you doing?" he cried to Jacquetta, snatching away her martini glass. "Not in the first three months! My God, have you gone *completely* round the twist?"

Jacquetta looked at the man, her expression horrified. Then, almost under her breath, she hissed, "Relax, would you? It's just cranberry juice."

Now it was the man's turn to look horrified. "Oh, right then," he said hurriedly, handing the drink back to Jacquetta. "Sorry about that."

"But I thought you were having a cos —" With a jolt, I cut myself off. The first three months — what did that mean? And then it clicked. Jacquetta *had* made a great show of downing her cosmos, hadn't she? When I was younger, my mom's friend Freida, who had her first baby at age forty-three, used to drink iced tea in a beer mug so people wouldn't guess she was pregnant until, as she put it later, "I'm out of the danger zone."

Was Jacquetta Schloss doing the same thing, and for the same reason? Had she arranged a show with the bartender she was so chummy with?

"Mimi," she said, "I'd like you to meet my manager, Desmond." She glared hard at the mustached, and now ashen, man. "Des,

Mimi is from *A-ha!* magazine. She's interviewing me for the next issue, trying to dig up a bit of" — she coughed — "dirt. Shouldn't be too hard now, should it?"

The man went from dun to red to purple to a strange shade of eggplant. I could nearly hear him wheeze. "Jolly good, carry on," he squeaked. "I'm a bit tired tonight, so I'll just be toddling off."

After the interruption from Desmond, Jacquetta and I tried, and failed, to revive our pleasant conversation. My accidental discovery of her secret showed on my face, and it was with a marked strain that she answered my subsequent questions about the house she'd just purchased in Islington. But it wasn't until I thanked her for her time that she widened her eyes and gazed pleadingly at me. "I beg you, do be kind to me," she said. "I can't bear to be in the tabs again, not about *this*. Not yet. I'm horribly stressed as it is; it'd be simply too much."

I told her I'd do my best, though I had no idea what I meant by that.

Back downstairs, I found a spectacleless Anthony wrapping up an interview with Dina Taz-Dellingpole, a socialite who had her own *Dress to Impress* television show. "Hey, where are your glasses?" I asked. "Can you see all right?"

"Where are your glasses? Where are your glasses? Where are your glasses?" Anthony parroted drunkenly. "She loves fussing, this one," he told Dina. "My glasses are . . . around here somewhere. But more to the point, Dina was telling me about her boyfriend's pornography addiction, so if you don't mind."

"Actually," Dina said, "I said calligraphy."

"Right." Anthony nodded and scribbled into his notebook.

"So," he asked me afterward, "learn anything juicy, did you?" We were seated next to each other at an abandoned table.

"Um . . ." I bit down on my lip and blinked hard. A vision of "Jacquetta Preggers!" headlines scrolled through my head. Here was my big chance to immortalize myself in *A-ha!* magazine history — in the history of all celebrity journalism. But for some mysterious reason I couldn't bring myself to do it, not now, with my colleague and would-be confidant so besotted and incoherent. It would be a waste of such a potentially huge moment. "She loves pickle-flavored popcorn," I told him at last.

"And?" He blinked both his eyes.

"And she just bought a house in —"

"Islington. St. Peters Street, to be precise. Bloody *every*one knows that. Is that really the lot of it? You talked to her for ages and that's all you got?" Anthony's voice was harsh, almost angry. "That's a bit weak, Schulman. Charlie will be absolutely livid. So much for being the lucky charm of the summer."

He shook his head and leaned back, balancing on the chair's two hind legs. Then he leaned back some more and the chair toppled backward, taking Anthony down with it. He groaned as his head hit the floor and his glasses shot out of his jacket pocket.

"Battleship down," cackled one onlooker.

"Looks like we'll be needing a bin," added another.

Anthony didn't look the least bit embarrassed. "Ah, my specs, lovely." He strained forward for his glasses, which had landed a few inches away, and put them crookedly back on his face.

"Anthony," I whispered, crouching down. "Please, let's get you out of here."

"I'm fine." He sprang to his feet just as a waiter passed with a tray of red wine. "Oh, cheers," he said, lurching forward for a glass.

"Jesus Christ," I said, "that's the *last* thing you need!"

But Anthony had already downed much of the wine in one gulp. "See?" he said. "I'm fine." He raised his hand as if making a toast, but his arm jerked and what little wine remained sloshed up and out of his glass. The red liquid cascaded in an arc through the air, as if in slow motion, before finally, horribly, spraying all over the front of Rebecca Bridgewater's butter yellow couture gown.

Noddy & Co.

THOUGH THE CASSIDY HOUSE HAD FOUR BEDROOMS, it still felt cramped. The boys usually congregated downstairs, waging pillow wars or boosting their sugar levels with chocolate milk and Pirate Puffs. Colleen had established a firm rule against playing video games before I woke up, a rule her sons cleverly circumvented by first waking me up, *then* turning on the video games.

"Why are you climbing over me?" I groaned early Saturday morning. I tried to sit up, but somebody's foot was pinning my shoulder down. "Do I look like a tree?"

"You're a tree and we're baby birds," Robby chirped.

"We can fly!" Roddy catapulted onto me, landing on my bladder. "Tweet!"

Unwilling to miss out on the action, Hugh swooped onto the arm of the couch and then crashed down on my ankles. Once again, I found myself outnumbered, outwitted, and outsugared. At least, I reminded myself, the Cassidy boys were normal; at least they weren't humorless mutant freaks like the Meyerson-Cullens. That said, at six in the morning, on four hours of sleep, I found it hard to make such subtle distinctions. With another groan, I pulled myself off the couch and asked Hugh if I could borrow his bed. Before I'd reached the top of the stairs, the video consoles were out of the closet and the boingy theme to Space Flight Seven was on at full blast.

When, sometime after ten, Colleen knocked on the door of Hugh's room, the day had turned bright and beautiful. A little family of sparrows buzzed past the window, and for several seconds I actually forgot the horrors of the previous night: Anthony's awful behavior, Rebecca Bridgewater's ruined dress, my unwelcome knowledge about Jacquetta Schloss.

"You awright?" Colleen asked, sitting at the edge of the bed. She was wearing a short-sleeved sweater with appliqué turtles on it — definitely a Loose Ends original. I could hear Sylvia thumping up the stairs. Within seconds, the dog had entered the room and was slobbering all over my face.

I smiled stoically and, determined not to burden Colleen with more problems, told her I was just tired. "That's a shame," she said. "We were hoping you might fancy a wee excursion this afternoon. Ian's buggered off to the office, and the lads have their hearts set on a trip to Chessington, but it's quite difficult to take them there on my own. Even with my mum coming along, I could use a bit of extra support."

Chessington, Colleen explained, was the boys' favorite amusement park, located about an hour's drive outside of London. "They go absolutely bonkers there."

Lily and I had agreed to spend the afternoon — her last chunk of spare time before her big performance the following Friday night — at the Victoria and Albert Museum, checking out the exhibition on adolescent uniforms Sam had told me he'd read about in *The New Yorker*. But I couldn't refuse Colleen in her moment of need. "Sounds like fun," I said. "Do you mind if I bring my friend Lily? Remember, you met her last weekend?"

Colleen glowed at the suggestion. "But of course you can, love. She was lovely, your friend, and the people mover's always got room for one more."

Then came the more embarrassing question. "Colleen, would you, um, mind, calling up and asking for her yourself? I kind of don't want to chat with whoever might be on the other end."

Seconds later, Colleen passed the receiver to me with a wink and Lily's voice came onto the line. "You'll probably hate to skip out on Saturday lunch," I began, "but maybe you'd like to meet up earlier than planned?"

To my surprise, Lily sounded thrilled. "Robin's making *sweetbreads,*" she whispered into the phone. "Any idea what those are?"

"Um, bread that's sweet?"

"Not even close. Hurry."

We agreed to pick her up outside the Brixton station in an hour, a slight detour on the road to Chessington. By the time Lily got into the car, Robby and Roddy were already squabbling over which ride to go on first, Sir Walter Squirtsalot or Professor Burp's Bubbleworks. I worried that the boys' energy might overwhelm my friend on the drive to suburban Surrey, but she seemed to enjoy herself. She certainly had way more fun that *I* did. I spent the whole ride blinking out the car window, mulling over the Anthony-Rebecca–Jacquetta Schloss predicament.

Because we were all too tall for the rides, Colleen, her mother, Jackie, Lily, and I just stood around watching the boys get strapped into cars and blast through third-rate approximations of pirate coves and coral reefs. Outside the spooky house, Colleen and her mom began animatedly discussing the latest episode of *The Archers,* in which the vicar gambled away church funds and the fishmonger's wife took up Jazzercise.

"I'm correct in detecting they're awesome, right?" Lily said, tilting her head at my hosts. I nodded fervently. "They're not feeding you gruel or denying you shower access or anything, are they?"

"Not even close — they're great. When I'm out late, Colleen keeps dinner hot for me, and her mother taught me how to play Sudoku a few days ago." I didn't mention that, every morning, I had to fold up the sheets and duvets and stack them neatly under the coffee table while Roddy, Robby, and Hugh pogoed hyperactively around me.

"So what's up, then?" Lily wanted to know. "You've been acting kind of draggy."

"Hard to explain," I said, "but it has nothing to do with the Cassidys." I told her about my conversation with Jacquetta Schloss the night before, Anthony's rudeness when I approached him to discuss it, and my growing doubts about the whole enterprise. "She was so *nice,* Lily," I said. "I can't explain why, but the more I think about it, the less right I feel about spilling the beans about her pregnancy — especially after the way Anthony treated me. But then, if I don't say anything, I'll be in even *more* trouble for screwing up Rebecca's dress, you know?"

"It's always total apocalypse with you, isn't it?" Lily said with a loud, open-mouthed laugh. "I wouldn't worry about the dress — there's no way she paid for it, and you said yourself she has millions of them. As for Jacquetta What's-Her-Name, well, my God, Mimi, it's just a summer internship — get a little perspective, will you? Nobody expects you to uncover all the world's secrets. Now, I hate to change the subject," Lily said suddenly, "but if I don't tell you now, I'll lose my nerve. First you have to *swear* not to tell anyone, OK? Not even the other girls."

Intrigued, I solemnly promised, and Lily went on, "So, um, you remember Harry, right?"

"Harry from Baldwin or Harry from your theater class?"

Lily blushed. "Harry from my theater class. Well, the night when you were supposed to come to *Lambeth Nightingale* with me, we kind of hung out a little, and then yesterday we met up for coffee after class and, well, we . . ." Lily, now the color of a pimple, trailed off.

"Let me guess. As we say at *A-ha!* you *snogged*?"

"Be quiet!" Lily hissed, but it was too late. Colleen and her mother had turned around to see the two of us hopping up and down excitedly.

Luckily, at the same moment, Robby, Roddy, and Hugh tumbled out the exit of the pirate cove. Hugh was wailing in terror as his older brothers swung him back and forth between them.

"He got scared, he did!" Robby cried exultantly when his mother demanded an explanation. "Scared of Captain Hook — how wet is that!"

"I am *not* wet!" Hugh protested, then resumed wailing.

"It's awright, love, it's awright." Colleen bent down to scoop up her youngest son. With Hugh slung over her shoulder, she shot a ferocious look at the twins and muttered, "You 'aven't 'eard the end of this one, lads!" And then, to Hugh: "C'mon, love, why don't we get a bit of nosh, wouldn't that be nice? Come along now, darling, you can have anything you fancy . . ."

For better or worse, the Green Goblin Food Court truly lived up to its name. Every single thing to eat there was, you guessed it, green. The boys ordered foot-high mint ice cream cones, Colleen and her mother green tea and "Shamrock pudding." Lily abstained, while I, idiotic as ever, ordered the "Gobby Pizza," an unholy mess of green dough, green cheese, and tomato sauce that was also green.

"Some pizza you got there. Looks very . . . environmental."

Ian had sauntered up in his usual army vest, but with a few weekend touches: a Paddington Bear–type sun hat on his head and a stripe of zinc oxide on his nose.

"What are you doing here?" I cried. "I thought you were at the office."

"Was. But I never miss the show on Saturdays, not if I can possibly help it." Then, after kissing his wife and warmly greeting Lily, Ian turned to me and asked, "You up for naughty?"

"Up for *what?*"

"Naughty. With the dancing."

"Sorry, what?" I asked again.

"Noddy the puppet bear!" Colleen's mom broke in impatiently. "You don't mean to say you don't have Noddy back in the States?"

And what a loss that turned out to be. Noddy the Bear, Celeste the Sea Lion, and Eugene the Eagle robots put on a show every hour at Chessington, lip-synching to taped music as they rolled across the stage. While most parents snoozed in the back,

Ian dragged us right up to the second row. Little Hugh, clearly familiar with the lineup, sang and clapped along as Priscilla the Prairie Dog came out from behind a prosthetic tree for "Twisty-Wisty Rock."

By the time we got home that night, I was too exhausted to worry much about Jacquetta. After heating a Marks & Spencer shepherd's pie for dinner, Colleen ordered the family to bed early. Once everyone had gone to sleep, I decided to call my dad, knowing he could help me make sense of life. I got out the Nigerian phone card I'd bought on the High Street in Peckham and dialed his number.

"How's our favorite cub reporter?" he asked, delighted by the sound of my voice.

"I'm OK," I said tersely.

"Well, we lowly Barrow Streeters are *very* impressed with your exploits. Quinn's been bragging to anybody who will listen, and Sam said he wishes there were Mimi stocks he could invest in."

"When did you talk to Sam?"

"Thursday night," Dad said. "I ran into him at a P.S. 1 opening for an Iranian photography show. He was with some nice girl from his summer program."

Before I could press for details, the phone beeped and a Nigerian voice announced the impending expiration of my card. I quickly said goodbye to Dad, then lay down on the couch and started thinking about Sam — a welcome relief from pondering Jacquetta Schloss and the ruined dress. Which "nice girl" had he taken to P.S. 1? Why hadn't he mentioned it to me, and why did I care?

Sunday morning, the Cassidys left early for a cousin's christening in the suburbs, and I woke up to an empty house. Sophie was at the magazine and Lily had rehearsals that day, so I had no option but to start scrubbing the wine stains off Rebecca Bridgewater's gown. I'd noticed a "Loose Ends Garment Care Tips" sheet taped to the wall in the Cassidys' laundry room. The instructions weren't very detailed, but toward the bottom of the page there was a line that said, "For really tough stains on your delicate fabrics, try vinegar!"

Vinegar? Sounded weird to me, but then, I remembered the time Mom had used toothpaste to remove a cranberry sauce stain at Thanksgiving. I guess I had a lot to learn before I'd ever be crowned Miss Housekeeping. I rooted through the cupboard until I found a slender green-glass bottle of Sicilian Balsamic Vinegar, and shook out its contents along the dress's soiled neckline. To my horror, the liquid that coursed out was tobacco-colored and loaded with sediment. Rather than removing the wine stains, the vinegar had added a whole new slew of dark brown blots, and the dress now looked like it had been worn by somebody who was eating spaghetti with her hands tied behind her back.

Frantic, I slammed open drawers and doors in the kitchen until, under the sink, I found a squirt bottle labeled MR. WINKLE'S ALL-PURPOSE STAIN REMOVER. I immediately aimed the pump at the dress's neckline and pulled the trigger three times. A gray chemical halo rose over the dress like a mushroom cloud. A harsh smell filled my nostrils as I waited for the vinegar stains to disappear. At last the vigorous fizzing sound gave way to silence, and I saw for the first time that the dress's rich fabric had dissolved to the density of a Kleenex and was now bedizened with little brown pills.

"No!" I screamed, loud enough for Sylvia to start barking violently.

I arrived to work early the next day, with huge knots in my stomach. I could hardly breathe as I sneaked into Rebecca's empty office and placed the bag containing the object formerly known as the world's most beautiful dress on her chair. I left a letter of apology on her keyboard and walked quickly to Penny's cubicle, where I spent the morning doodling pictures of Noddy the bear and praying that Rebecca Bridgewater and Charlie Lappin wouldn't come looking for me. I had no desire to discuss either the dress or Jacquetta Schloss or, for that matter, anything.

But Charlie called me in at three, or rather, his receptionist did. When I got to the editor in chief's office, Anthony was sitting on Charlie's couch between Hamish and Tessa, two feature writers. It was the first time I'd seen Anthony since the BAMYs, and he looked sober and composed in his mold green sportscoat, with his glasses back in the center of his face. "Oh, and this one's a laugh," he was saying to Rebecca. "Pam Osbeth set her ring tone to the *Welcome to the Doncasters* theme — you know, *dee, dee, do, do, dee*. Such a slap in the face to her ex —"

Charlie interrupted: "Very well, very well, but I'm not yet satisfied with the Linda Ross caption." He held up a picture of Pippa's fallen friend leaning toward a young man in a tuxedo with two empty glasses of champagne in his hand. "Look at this chap — he's barely twenty. What about 'On the Hunt for a New Toy Boy' — how does that strike you?"

"Yes, but we've loads of other pictures from the same pre-BAMYs party," Rebecca pointed out. "I'm afraid our readers will be able to tell that he's just a member of the catering staff. They've all got those penguin suits on and there seems to be at least one in every picture."

"Shhh, Becky love," Charlie said, "we both know that our readers believe precisely what we tell them."

"I suppose you're right," Rebecca conceded, and thus the evil caption was born.

I couldn't quite believe how these people operated. When I was working on my Serge Ziff profile, I dug and dug until I'd patched my limited clues together. But here in *A-ha!* land, people went about the business of reporting in an entirely different manner. They'd seize on whatever particles of information had come to them — an overheard snippet of dialogue, a meaningless photograph — and simply make up the rest. Listening to them, seeing how casually they distorted the truth, I felt short of breath.

"Mimi, thanks so much for stopping by," Charlie said, noticing me at last. "Just wanted an update."

"An update?" I swallowed.

"On Jacquetta," Rebecca said impatiently. "We need to write all the headlines before the end of the workday."

The assembled staffers looked at me expectantly — or, everyone except Anthony, who sneezed into his linen handkerchief, then resumed flipping through his spiral-bound notebook. As I stood there, something strange happened. A sense of resolve formed inside me, shooting up like a magic beanstalk. As I looked at the editors' hungry eyes, I knew I would *not* turn Jacquetta Schloss into another Linda Ross: the consequences were too great, and for what — the approval of *these* people?

"Well, actually," I said after an excruciatingly long silence, "I didn't get much. She was *extremely* careful and didn't offer anything provocative at all."

"Oh, get out with you," Charlie said. "Surely she mentioned *some* concern. Sex addiction? Prozac? A fling with a backup dancer? Anything?"

"Nope," I said. "She just told me about the colors she wants to paint the dining room in her new house. That's pretty much it."

"You can*not* be serious," said Tessa.

"But Anthony," Rebecca Bridgewater all but whimpered, "didn't you help her?"

"I tried," Anthony said, "I really did do. But I'm afraid I was absolutely hopeless at it. What else is new?"

The editors all laughed, and for the first time, Anthony Palfrey's self-deprecating charm infuriated me. He still hadn't made eye contact with me when Charlie icily thanked me for my efforts and excused me with a curt "Oh, never mind, then."

I stood outside his office for a few seconds afterward to hear what everyone was saying about me. "Seems like I wasted a perfectly good ball gown on that one," Rebecca complained.

You have no idea, I thought, as inside the office Charlie said, "How were you to know? I thought she had potential myself, but she doesn't understand a twig about personal connections. D'you know, I heard she and the Foxes had a fan*tastic* row, and now she's camping out in *Peckham!*"

"That right?" Anthony drawled. "A bit clumsy, that one is."

Perfect Plan

In that awful week after the BAMYS, two of *A-ha!*'s top competitors had cover exclusives on Jacquetta Schloss. *Sizzle* broke the story of her stealth visits to an Overeaters Anonymous meeting. *Right* had a two-page account of a screaming match between the singer and her mustached manager, Desmond, at a BAMYs afterparty. And for the coverage in *A-ha!?* A single red-carpet shot of Jacquetta and a little graphic speculating on her choice of paint color in her new house.

I was responsible for this oversight and everybody knew it. But my punishment was less dramatic than I'd expected. After the confrontation in Charlie's office, no one directly criticized me again. Instead, my colleagues just treated me as if I were invisible, and suddenly I was excluded from any and all afterwork events. Anthony steered clear of me, approaching Penny's cubicle only when he needed to borrow my stapler. Charlie Lappin, more to the point, ignored me altogether.

Rebecca had been surprisingly blasé about the wrecked dress. When I apologized to her in the hallway the day after returning the soiled garment, she'd merely shrugged and said, "Oh, well, I wouldn't be caught dead in that rag, anyway." Her comment was so offhand I wanted to scream.

I was now stuck with the most thankless job at *A-ha!*, compiling the "Say What???" page, *A-ha!*'s collection of regurgitated celebrity wit and wisdom. Every day, I had to comb dozens of newspapers for quotations that we could lift and run next to pictures of the stars. The task was beyond boring — and it never seemed to end. There was always one newspaper or gossip Web site left to read.

That Wednesday, to cheer myself up, I went to see *Sabrina*, Quinn's favorite Audrey Hepburn movie, at a repertory theater in Leicester Square. But all the scenes between Sabrina and her wonderful father left me even more homesick than before, as did the constant hubbub and chaos of the Cassidy household. Though Ian and Colleen made sure to include me in every aspect of family life, I couldn't stop worrying that I was beginning to wear out my welcome.

When I got to work on Thursday morning, gloomy as usual, I logged on to my e-mail account and opened a message marked Highest Priority from Dad. He'd forwarded his Expedia itinerary for travel — the very next day. It was a miracle! I read the message three times before understanding Dad had been assigned to take pictures of New York's mayor accepting some award from the prime minister's office, and would be landing in London the following morning. "Hope you still need a date to Lily's play," he'd typed above the itinerary. "I'm planning to sleep a few hours, but come find me at the Sanderson after work." He included the hotel's address, and a million *x*'s and *o*'s.

How weird that Dad would be staying at the Sanderson — the same swanky hotel where just last week Ian, Anthony, and I had celebrated the Egyptian Travel Council's new promotional blitz. The images of my sweet dad snoring in his hotel bed and Anthony astride a prosthetic camel were irreconcilable, but I was too ecstatic to dwell on it.

The next day, I tried to plow through my work quickly, but my mind kept straying from the celebrity interviews piled ever higher on my desk. Instead, I found myself reading more human interest articles, like "Britain's Most Dangerous Bus Shelters" or "East Anglia Mail Carrier Caught Feeding Dog Ecstasy Tablets." I was never going to finish my required reading by the end of the day.

For lunch, Sophie and I bought plastic-wrapped sandwiches and ate them by the waterfront. Sophie was acting a little strange, sweeter than usual but also slightly shifty. When I pressed her, she reluctantly admitted she'd covered a film premiere with Anthony the previous night. As she spoke, she covered her face with her hands, as if unable to bear my reaction. "You must be furious," she said through netted fingers. "I feel simply *aw*ful."

I did indeed experience a little wave of envy, but it soon passed. Putting down my mayonnaise-rich prawn cocktail sandwich, I told Sophie to look at me. "I don't mind at all," I said honestly. "I swear. Was it fun?"

Sophie couldn't prevent a great smile from spreading across her face. "I had a chat with Robbie Norfolk, and Gemma Gaines-Bristle came by, too. I know you think these people are wankers, so it's quite embarrassing to go on about it, but Mimi, I used to write Gemma Gaines-Bristle fan letters when I was a little girl —

I'd decorate them with lace and stickers. And last night I actually *met* her, and she repeated my name! It was" — her eyes fluttered shut — "extraordinary."

And right then, sitting out on East India Quay with Sophie, I felt certain that *A-ha!* would carry on fine without me. "Listen, Soph," I said, "I'm seriously happy for you. I've never *heard* of Gemma Gaines-Bristle, so the experience would've been totally lost on me. I ask just one favor from you, OK?"

Sophie nodded expectantly, still a little scared.

"Promise you'll invite me back to London to celebrate when you make editor in chief." And then I reached forward and hugged her, and the two of us burst out laughing. I added, "And when I figure out what it is I want to do, and then I do it, you'd better take the next flight to New York."

Back upstairs in Penny's cubicle, I still had plenty of interviews to read for "Say What???" but I no longer even pretended to focus on the task. After staring dumbly at an article on the musical theater adaptation of Madonna's English years, I found Rebecca in her office, reading a book called *Saying Yes to Yes: How to Stop Dating and Start Mating.* Probably best not to interrupt her, I decided. And, with no further deliberation, I left the office for what might well be the last time.

The train ride to Oxford Circus seemed to drag on for hours. I couldn't *wait* to see Dad, and when I got to the Sanderson Hotel, I bounded into the lobby like a puppy just let out of its cage. While waiting behind a Japanese businessman for use of the in-house phone, I thought about how different the Sanderson was from the Great Briton, the dump Mom had chosen for her London visit. As anybody who's stepped foot inside our cushy apartment can attest, Dad tended to live beyond his means, especially when I directly benefited from his extravagances.

I couldn't believe Dad and I were in the same building. My head was dancing with pictures of the two of us running around town as I waited for him to pick up the phone. "It's me!" I practically bellowed when he answered on the seventh ring.

Minutes later, the elevator opened on the sixth floor to my bleary-eyed father outfitted in jeans, slippers, and a hotel robe.

"Mimi!" "Dad!" we cried simultaneously, throwing our arms around each other and rocking back and forth.

While Dad showered and I checked out the Sanderson's deluxe cable options, I noticed the latest issue of *A-ha!* on the nightstand — the one with the Jacquetta Schloss nonstory in it. Though *A-ha!* was the last thing I wanted to discuss that night, I was touched that Dad had bought it. However confiding Mom had been on our weekend together, she'd expressed absolutely no interest in my internship.

"You don't look so tired," I told him when at last he emerged from the bathroom, dressed and shaved and ready to rumble.

"Well, I'm seeing my daughter for the first time in several lifetimes, so that helps," Dad said, crossing the room. He mussed my hair. "It's longer. I like it."

We spent the rest of the afternoon catching up in the Sanderson's outdoor lounge, eating chicken and sweet corn sandwiches. Dad updated me on New York life, and I learned more in that one conversation than from all of our phone calls and e-mails. He told me Quinn was getting serious about his photography, and might even land a gallery show in the fall. Dad's own career was booming as well. He'd reconnected with a woman named Victoria Eastwood, whom he and Mom used to know well. Victoria was now the photo editor of *Buzz,* a glossy culture magazine with a budget that rivaled the gross national product of most European countries. After just two assignments, Victoria had made Dad a regular contributor. "We have Vicky to thank for my plane ticket," he said. "She's been throwing more work at me than I can handle."

"Work?" I repeated. "Is that *all* she's throwing at you?"

"Must you always be such a teenage girl?" Dad shook his head, but he was grinning from ear to ear.

That afternoon, I never mentioned my parents' visits to Dr. Rudemeyer — I was too happy to being it up. But as I sat listening to Dad talk, I couldn't help wondering what other personal information he chose not to discuss with me. I had, I knew, quite a lot to learn about both of my parents. And I realized I might not always know what was best for them.

Around dusk, we took a cab over to St. Botolph's Theatre Academy in Covent Garden. Lily was starring in *Blithe Spirit,* a 1940s comedy that my seventh-grade drama teacher had taken us to see in Houston. Given all I knew about Lily's actor friends, I was expecting some arty and confusing interpretation of the play. It was a welcome surprise to see how straightforward the production was — and how excellent.

By far the most mesmerizing actor up there was none other than Lily Morton, and that's *not* my bias speaking. Seeing her on the stage, I almost wondered why she wasted her time in the *Bu-*

gle office when she could be auditioning on Broadway instead. During a scene in which Lily was prowling tigerlike around the kitchen, spooking a woman who can't see her, Dad leaned over to me to whisper: "She's got it."

When the lights came up, I saw the Foxes seated in the second row. I looked at Robin and wondered sadly if he knew the truth about his wife and Mario. I pointed my former hosts out to Dad and he offered to give Pippa a wedgie. "Though she looks like she already has one," he added. At this, I laughed so hard I almost choked. I still wasn't eager to reunite with my host family, though, so we waited in our seats for a good ten minutes before presenting Lily with the bouquet of irises Dad had made sure we bring.

"Thank you!" she said, handing the flowers to the guy at her side. Like my dad, he was tall, lanky, and pale, but unlike my dad, he wore a tight-fitting suit and tie. Doing a double take, I realized this man was a cleaned-up version of Harry, the philosopher-playwright of Lily's dreams.

"I'm amazed, Lils," I said, talking about both the play and her romantic conquest. "You make me proud."

"I do try!" Lily said, flushed and beaming. Then, turning to my father, she said, "I'm so happy you're here! There's a cast and crew party and you're more than welcome to come."

But Dad declined, citing jet lag. "These old bones don't travel like they used to. You should go, Mimi. I'll leave a key at the front desk for you."

I would hear of no such thing. Knowing Lily would understand, I explained that my dad and I had a dinner date. "We do?"

He looked pleased but still tried to protest. "You couldn't possibly be hungry *again*."

I jabbed him; Lily and Harry laughed. "Listen," she said, "we've gotta run — but thank you guys *so* much for coming. I hope you enjoyed it." We assured her that we had, enormously, and watched them hurry over to join their fellow drama students.

"So where next?" Dad asked.

"I don't know — let's play it by ear."

As we walked through Covent Garden, I considered, and quickly rejected, all the places-of-the-moment I'd visited as an *A-ha!* intern. In the end, we wandered into The Elk and Cheese, the one quiet pub within walking distance of St. Botolph's. It was refreshingly untrendy, with most of its patrons sitting alone on pincushion seats, watching a televised horse race.

"I love it," Dad said. So did I; in fact, I couldn't remember feeling this comfortable in my whirlwind month in London. "Remind me — how much longer are you here?" he asked after we placed our identical orders for roast beef and Yorkshire pudding.

"As if you weren't counting down the days!"

Dad blushed. "Well, I mean . . . I was just thinking. Two weeks isn't too long at all, is it?"

"No, not really." I bit my lip, abruptly realizing how long it would feel after Dad left. London had been amazing, but it was not my home and never would be. It was time to move on. I'd been suspecting this since the BAMYs debacle, but now, as I sat across from my father, the truth hit me with a startling clarity. "But I was actually thinking," I said after a pause, "maybe it could just be two days?"

"Two days?" Dad put down his fork and took a sip of water. He held the glass up to his face and slowly exhaled before saying, "So, um, you're thinking of going back to Berlin?"

I shook my head. "What would I do in Berlin? Mom and I are on pretty good terms right now, Dad, and I don't want to mess that up. No, I want to come back to Barrow Street — the sooner, the better."

Dad, evidently trying to strike a balance between saying what he felt and saying what he thought a good parent should say, swallowed and asked, "But what would you do until school starts? I'm teaching the intensive course at the Open School, and Quinn's my TA, so we won't be around much."

"I promise to take good care of myself," I said, thinking of everything I could do back in New York: brush up on photography techniques, or volunteer at a community newspaper, or explore outer-borough ethnic restaurants with Sam. "Oh, pretty please, Daddy?" I asked in the sugary voice that always got to him. "I'd just really like to do something that doesn't involve the cast of *Lonsdale*."

"The cast of what?"

"Exactly."

Back to the Wilderness

I GRIPPED THE LADDER HARD and pictured myself plummeting headfirst to the floor. Terror must have streaked across my face, for Ed called up reassuringly, "You're almost there — one more step and you're golden."

I squeezed my eyes shut, grabbed the rails, and climbed another rung. The day before, Ed had painted the sunroom a warm yellow, and now he needed my extra height to finish the job. "Perfect," he told me. "Now you need to open your eyes. I'm going to hand you the roller brush."

Steadier now, I took the brush and smiled down at Ed's shiny bald head.

Only a week after dinner with Dad at The Elk and Cheese pub, I was tucked away in New York's Catskill Mountains, helping Ed and Harriet prepare their country house for their September wedding. London felt very, very far away, and with my career as a troublemaker behind me, I welcomed this less scandalous chapter of my summer. Since arriving upstate, I'd refinished a dining table and three chairs and chipped away the upstairs bathroom's ugly moss-colored tiles, and that morning, when Ed was at his fly-fishing course, Harriet and I had beautified the fungus-infested garden pond.

It was funny how things worked out, I thought, angling forward to apply a final dab of yellow paint. When I'd first arranged this trip upstate, Harriet had suggested Boris join me, little suspecting I hadn't heard from my so-called boyfriend in more than a month and had no idea what our current status was. Neither of my female friends in the city could come up, since Jess was still at the investment bank and Viv at the record company. Only Sam readily accepted my invitation. After a family trip to visit his grandmother in Florida, he was all too eager to get a break from his parents.

"Tremendous," Ed said of my handiwork when I descended the ladder. "Now you only need to go around the room and do that about twenty more times."

No complaints from me. I loved working on Ed and Harriet's rural retreat, which felt less like a chore than an ambitious art project — somehow, the perfect antidote to my London adventure.

Given what I knew of Ed's finances, I'd expected a huge mansion, and when I'd first arrived I could barely conceal my surprise when Harriet took me inside a modest, almost ramshackle farmhouse — a hodgepodge of uneven ceiling beams, peeling wainscoting, furry bathroom tiles, and rickety cabinets. Ed and Harriet had a ridiculous amount of work on their hands. Or, I guess, all three of us did.

Downstairs was a large kitchen, screened-in porch, cramped living room, and their bedroom, which had cedar walls and an excellent stone fireplace. A narrow staircase led to a bathroom with faulty plumbing and two tiny bedrooms divided by an oblong hallway. The walls were thin, and conversations were easily overheard, but for Ed and Harriet, this only enhanced the place's cozy charm.

Two hours later, Ed and I surveyed the room. Outside, the clouds shifted, and afternoon sunlight filtered through the window, casting a glow on the yellow walls. I clapped, Ed whistled, and then together we called Harriet in to admire our work. "Perfecto!" she cried, inserting herself between us. "Excellent timing, too — Sam's bus gets in soon."

"How soon?" I asked.

"Now soon, so let's get moving."

I persuaded myself I didn't care that I had no time to shower or change from my disgustingly sweaty work clothes — it was only Sam, after all. Even so, as Ed's Land Rover chugged down the steep driveway, tree branches scratching against the windows, I felt jittery and couldn't stop wiping my palms on my cargo shorts. Sam and I had spoken on the phone several times since I'd returned — and for hours, too — but because he left for Florida the day I got back, we hadn't yet seen each other face-to-face. I wondered how our first meeting would pan out. Though I'd come to rely on him in e-mail and on the phone this summer, our in-person relationship might be as awkward and awful as it had been at the end of last semester.

A fifteen-minute ride down dusty roads took us to the Phoenicia bus station — or rather, to the bench outside of a fishing supply shop where buses occasionally stopped. While Harriet and Ed discussed dinner — Ed was impatient to inaugurate the Ulta-Flame 5000, a state-of-the-art barbecue he'd installed in the backyard — I ran inside the shop to use the bathroom. The toilet was sealed with red duct tape, so I contented myself with washing my hands and splashing cold water on my face.

When a bus appeared in the rearview, my stomach fluttered nervously. The vehicle came to a stop a few feet behind us and disgorged a handful of passengers. Sam was the last to emerge, and at first I was taken aback by the change in his appearance. He had a large army backpack slung over his shoulder, and looked almost preppy in chinos and a plain navy T-shirt. But, more remarkably, the boy who once lived in fear of the sun and spent his summers hiding under baseball hats had darkened to a handsome bronze, a color that complemented his freckles and reddish hair unexpectedly well. He'd also grown a few inches, and his once bony shoulders looked strong and boxy.

Ed honked three times, while Harriet turned and, as if reading my expression, commented, "Zowie, he sure looks hale and hearty, doesn't he?"

"He looks like Sam," I said impassively as my own cheeks darkened a few shades. Then, rousing myself, I jumped out of the car to greet him.

"Hey there," he said when I reached him, dropping his backpack to hug me. I could feel his nose jut into the side of my head. I drew away quickly and stammered out, "Come — c'mon out to the car. I can't *wait* for you to see Casa Ed and Harriet!"

Sam followed me to the Land Rover and tossed his backpack on the car floor. As we slid in next to each other, he said hello to our hosts in a voice that now struck me as deeper than I'd remembered. On our ride back to the cottage, I kept my eyes focused on the seat backs in front of me as Sam regaled our hosts with an account of the crazy ex-Marine who had ridden next to him from Port Authority. "He kept asking me if I'd ever considered enlisting, and told me I shouldn't, because the government would try to steal my internal organs —"

Then suddenly Sam broke off and looked out the window for the first time. "Wow," he said, "it's so — quiet here."

"Quiet?" Harriet hooted. "I love you city boys. This is the main drag. You wouldn't know quiet if it walked up to you on the street and tapped you on the nose."

By the time we got back to the house, the sky had grown dim over the mountains, and the first stars twinkled above us. While Harriet showed Sam his room and Ed fired up the grill, I set the picnic table with mismatched plates and tea lights.

Over dinner, Sam entertained Ed and Harriet with anecdotes about his summer program, while they detailed the home-improvement projects that lay ahead.

"Tomorrow's a fun day," Harriet said. "We can take Sam swimming at the sinkhole, and then there's an estate sale in Ticonderoga, so I thought we'd load up on picture frames, and some furniture if they have it. If we get some nice wood pieces, Mimi can teach you how to refinish them."

"Yeah, right," Sam said with a laugh. "Mimi Schulman refinishing furniture — in your dreams! Whenever she came to our country house when we were little, she spent all day lying in the hammock reading Betty and Veronica comics."

"Well, I haven't read anything but power drill instructions since I got off the bus," I said proudly.

"It's true," Ed said. "She's a very talented Miss Fix-It. You should see her wielding that drill."

Over dessert — store-bought carrot cake with cream cheese frosting — the four of us gossiped about the people we knew in common. "Isaac's been trying to learn how to play the piano all summer long," Sam said of Pia's math wiz boyfriend. "He wants to be more well rounded for his college applications. I guess we're all going to have to start soon. Think of the fun that awaits us next year." He rolled his eyes. "Next stop: stress city."

"Tell me about it," I groaned, though in truth I wasn't too worried about any of that just yet. For the time being, Sam's news about my dad held much more interest. The night they'd run into each other at P.S. 1, my father had stood before a painting talking to the same woman for more than an hour. "A woman who isn't Fenella von Dix?" I asked skeptically.

"Not unless Lady von D's had a lot of operations. This woman was sort of short and squat with curly blond hair. And she was seriously into your Dad, too — staring at him, as if, like, hypnotized."

"Ew, don't be gross! I'm sure you're making the whole thing up."

"Why would he be making it up?" Harriet asked. "Your dad's an extraordinary guy — why wouldn't a woman be hypnotized by him?"

"Ew," I said again, but I did see her point. Dad was pretty special, and I should probably get used to sharing him with others. For the past year, despite all my issues with Mom, I'd secretly hoped she'd reconcile with him. But I now understood that both of my parents had moved past that possibility and that resenting it was a waste of everyone's time.

When I'd called Mom the week before, the day I left London, she had told me to take care of my dad: "That's what you're there for, after all," she'd said in an unrecognizably gentle voice.

"I will," I promised her. And then, before we hung up, I told her I loved her. I hadn't said "I love you" to her in years, or not without prompting, and the sentence came out sounding funny. But Mom, uncharacteristically, made no awkward follow-up comment complimenting my emotional growth. "I love you, too," was her only reply.

That night, sitting around the picnic table, I turned to Sam and asked, "Speaking of running around P.S. 1 with an unknown female companion" — I coughed — "Dad mentioned you weren't exactly alone there yourself."

"It's true," Sam admitted, and looked at me like he was trying to figure something out. "I went with Rashida, my buddy from Bennington, but she promptly ditched me for a group of art students who invited her to play strip Scrabble."

"Strip *Scrabble?*" Harriet repeated. "God, when I was younger, we just stripped!" When Ed, next to her, cleared his throat, Harriet patted his hand consolingly and added, "Not that I remember any of those days, of course."

"Were you bummed she didn't invite you?" I asked.

"She did," Sam said, "but I wasn't into it."

"What are you, a *saint?*" This from Harriet again.

"Hardly." Sam shook his head. "I guess I'm just not as impulsive as Rashida. Following a van of rowdy sculptors to Corona,

Queens, isn't exactly my idea of a fun night on the town. Been there, done that. Know what I mean?"

We all laughed, and by the end of the meal, I no longer felt shy around Sam. After we cleared the table, Ed and Harriet settled in the living room to watch the second half of *The Sweet Smell of Success,* which was playing on the one channel to which they had reception. The movie, about a gossip columnist, didn't appeal to me for obvious reasons. Besides, it was too beautiful a night to spend watching TV. I grabbed a couple of flashlights and asked Sam if he'd like to see the lily pond Harriet and I had cleaned.

"If you're quiet," I whispered when we got there, "you can hear the geese. And there's an owl, too. Sometimes he goes crazy."

We stood stock still, the smell of Sam's Ivory soap lacing the fresh country air. "Hey, I think I heard something," he said. "Shh, don't move." He placed his hand on my back, his fingers pressing lightly against my shirt.

"Yeah," I said in a near-whisper. "I think I heard it, too."

That warm August night, Sam and I seemed to be precisely where we'd left off. Or no, that wasn't exactly right. Because where Sam and I left off was a bad place — riddled with hurt feelings and deceptions about Boris and complications with Viv. And now, here we were. He was still my oldest friend in the world, but I was only just getting to know him.